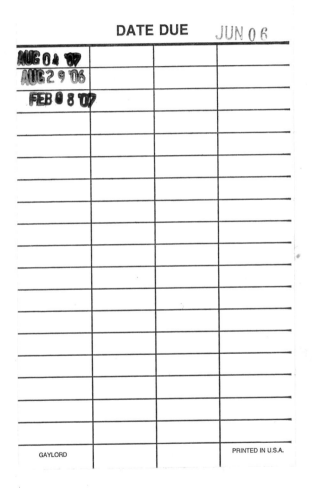

Voodoo
Heart

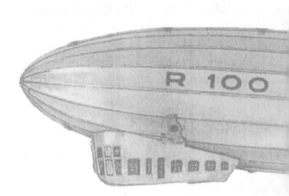

SCOTT SNYDER

Voodoo Heart

stories

THE DIAL PRESS

VOODOO HEART
A Dial Press Book / June 2006

Published by The Dial Press
A division of Random House, Inc.
New York, New York

Some of these stories appeared in slightly different form in the following
publications:
"Blue Yodel" in *Zoetrope: All-Story*, "Happy Fish, Plus Coin" in *One-Story*,
"About Face" and "The Star Attraction of 1919" in *Epoch*, "Voodoo Heart"
(excerpted) and "Wreck" in *Tin House*.

Book design by Helene Berinsky

Library of Congress Cataloging in Publication Data
Snyder, Scott.
Voodoo heart / Scott Snyder.
p. cm.
ISBN-10: 0-385-33841-4
ISBN-13: 978-0-385-33841-7
I. Title

PS3619.N95 V66 2006   2006040160
813/.6 22

Printed in the United States of America
Published simultaneously in Canada

www.dialpress.com

BVG   10 9 8 7 6 5 4 3 2 1

For Jeanie

CONTENTS

Voodoo
Heart

Blue Yodel

T HE BLIMP PASSED FIRST, SILVER WITH SIX WHITE FINS AT THE tail, like a giant bullet fired slowly through the sky. It glided far above the sugar pea field, too high to cause a stir. Its long black shadow skated over the dirt road between the rows of bright green plants, over the barn beyond, and then the blimp was gone and for a long moment all was as before. A spotted rabbit scampered out into the road, sniffed the air, then darted back into the trellised stalks just as Preston Bristol's Model T came crashing through, trailing a thick cloud of dust and chalk. The car was weather-beaten—one headlight missing, the other yellowed and cracked, the tires patched with flapping runs of tape. As it bounced along, tiny continents of rust rattled loose from the peeling hood and were whisked up and off.

Inside the car, Pres had his right foot jammed on the gas and his left foot pressed on top of his right. He squinted through the sunlit windshield at the blimp up ahead, still unable to accept it as a fixture of the sky and not something conjured up by his eye, a floater, a stain. He'd lost the blimp in a cloud formation over the Arkansas border and hadn't seen or heard mention of it in nearly a week. Now, suddenly, here it was, right in front of him, coasting along not even a quarter mile ahead. Pres could see the great aluminum blades of its propellers. He could see the windows of the blimp's cabin—the windows! He tried to find Claire behind one of them, but all the curtains were drawn shut. Pres had never been inside the blimp (this—two hundred, maybe three hundred yards behind it—was the closest he'd ever gotten), but even so he could picture its empty dining room, the booths of buttoned velvet, the golden maple dance floor across which he imagined someone, a man, swinging Claire past all those drawn curtains, pressing the stiff blond brush of his mustache into her ear. Pres glanced at the .38 lying on the passenger seat. He wondered whether anyone up there would try to stop Claire from coming home. He stuck his head out of the car window and listened for her voice.

"Claire!" he yelled at the blimp. "Claire, can you hear me?" But there was only the roar of the wind in his ears.

As the field gave way to grazing land, the front of the car nosed inside the blimp's shadow. Pres felt a gust of joy blow through him. He would catch it this time. He had it! As if in agreement, his map, weighted down in the backseat by a rock, began to beat its corners against the seat leather.

Pres had started after the blimp in late February of 1918. Now it was only the middle of spring, but the past couple of months seemed to him like a cannon through which he'd been shot from twenty-one years young straight into the sagging net of old age. His hands ached at the joints. His ankles had swelled. His back was sour from hunching over the wheel. Last week, while undressing for bed, he'd noticed a dusting of silver in his black hair. He wondered if Claire would look any different to him, if all that time up in the air had changed her somehow. As the car splashed through a series of deep-rutted puddles in the road, he imagined her emerging from the blimp a radiant version of herself, tanned as a pancake and sugared with freckles, her eyes the brilliant green of the stripe inside a marble. He wondered what he'd say to her, how it would feel to touch her. She was his fiancée and his best friend, his only friend, and yet he had no idea how he'd react when he encountered her again. Would he kiss her? Crush her against him? Maybe she would make the first move, though, he thought. Maybe she would grab him by the ears and cry into his neck and tell him exactly what had happened, why she'd left at all.

A cloud appeared ahead of the blimp, simply rolled in from nowhere. More than a cloud, it was a vast island, beginning as a thin shore of vapor and quickly thickening to tangled, cottony fields before billowing up into tall forests of green-and-black thunderheads. Sadness seized Pres so fiercely he began to shake. Not yet, he thought, his eyes fixed on the blimp, which was already nearing the first tendrils of haze. He was too close. He'd come too far to lose the blimp again. He reached for the gun on the seat beside him. In his mind, he pointed the .38 out the window and blasted six large bullet holes in the blimp's gas cells. The helium poured out with a flute-like music as the airship deflated and settled gently to the ground. But even as he aimed the gun, he knew that it was too small to do any real damage, that he himself was a tiny, harmless thing.

Pres watched as the cloud swallowed the top of the balloon, then its silvery bulk, until only the cabin was visible, sailing along beneath the cloud's underside. He watched until the blimp was gone.

For a long while after, Pres kept the car pointed down the same road. Every few moments he glanced up at the cloud cover for punctures or tears, any hole that might afford him a glimpse of the blimp. How much time passed this way he couldn't tell—an hour, two? The land shifted, became hilly and wild. When the clouds lifted, revealing nothing behind them but an empty tabletop of blue sky, Pres stopped watching the air altogether and scanned the ground for clues.

In the past he'd found things thrown down from the blimp—Claire's things. Back in Cayuga he'd discovered one of her shoes standing up in the road like a dart. When he'd pulled it from the ground he found the impression of Claire's foot still inside, a soft dent where her heel had been. He'd torn the shoe apart looking for a message from her, something written beneath the fabric, maybe carved into the heel. Outside of Pittsburgh he'd found her flowered hat floating in a pond, half pecked-apart by birds. A few times he'd come upon the smashed remains of cola bottles—Dapper Boy's Pop, Claire's favorite. The bottle tops were always sealed, the caps carefully twisted back onto the severed necks. Pres believed Claire was using them to send messages to him, that she wrote desperate notes and sealed them inside these bottles and then flung them out of the blimp, hoping they might find a soft landing. Each time he caught sight of a bottle neck he screeched to a stop and searched the area for her note. He picked through the grass, checked the bushes and trees, but the note always managed to blow away before he came looking.

Pres had met Claire in a wax museum near Buffalo. He was twenty and just orphaned with a pinch of money. She was nineteen. Her job was to stand very still among the dummies and then come to life and scare people. The first day Pres came by, the museum's manager had Claire sitting on a bench of figures sculpted to look like they were waiting for a train. She had a circular valise covered with exotic stickers by her feet and wore a hat that drooped over one eye. On one side of her a young boy in overalls sucked on his ticket; on the other a plump man frowned through a monocle at a pocket watch chained to his vest. Pres had never seen such a pretty girl. Her hair was short, shorter even than his, ending at her ear in a soft, curling point that made him think of a beckoning finger. She looked so ready to leave, too, so eager, leaning forward with her hands on the edge of the bench, her neck craned to see down the tracks. Her lips were parted a touch in the middle, as though she were kissing the station—her whole life—good-bye. When Pres leaned in close he saw her tongue inside, pink and wet in the flickering light from the lamp on the wall. He wanted to kiss her, but even more he wanted to be the one she was waiting for, to be what was coming to collect her. He tried to angle himself so that she was looking right at his face, but every time he positioned himself inside her gaze, she shifted her eyes, rolling them a bit so that she was always looking just over his head or to the side of his ear. It wasn't until she burst out laughing that Pres realized she was a real girl, playing with him.

Pres's face burned; the girl was laughing so hard she had to hold on to her hat.

"Enough already, birdie. I knew it was you," he said.

"Sure, I could tell," she said.

"I did. I saw you shaking. You make a lousy statue."

"So get out of here so I can keep on being lousy at it," she said, and then she started arranging her pose, settling back into place like a clay figure hardening under a flame.

"Fine with me. I got a real job to get to, anyway, a serious job." Pres spoke a little too loudly, as though she were already out of earshot. But he wanted to stop her from retreating. "I work at the Falls of Niagara. I'm on the new patrol. I watch for people trying to go over in barrels."

She blinked a few times and then looked at him like she'd only just noticed him standing there. "Oh, you're still here? Get going already. Someone's coming."

Pres heard the brush of shoes against carpet coming from

around the corner. "They use young guys like me to spot barrels because we got good eyes, see?" he said, and crossed his eyes at her.

"Fine, fine, you goon. Now shut it. I need to concentrate."

"If I don't warn the guy on hook before the barrel gets into the rapids, that's it. Whoever's inside is going over."

"Shh," she hissed through the corner of her mouth. "I can't stay steady with you talking. You'll get me fired!" She cocked her head to peer down the tracks again.

"I mean they're dead. Swept right—"

She grabbed his hand and pulled him down to the bit of bench between herself and the man with the pocket watch and then she was kissing him. It wasn't a good kiss; she mashed her whole face against his straight on—jammed her nose into his, her forehead into his brow. He could feel the ridge of her teeth behind her lips. But Pres liked it, the feeling of being pressed into this girl, of having collided with her. He was about to kiss her back when he became aware of someone else in the room, watching them, and he froze. He stayed with his lips pressed to hers, his wrists pulsing in her cool hands, and waited for the person to leave. It occurred to him that whoever was looking at them probably assumed that Claire was kissing him good-bye before leaving on the train, and it felt dizzyingly strange to think of someone standing there, saddened by the portrait of parting lovers who were really only kissing hello.

All that summer, on bright evenings, Pres would drive through the city to Claire's parents' home. When he reached the yard, he would slow the car to a quiet roll and open the passenger-side door and then Claire would creep from the hedge and jump in. The two of them would speed off through town with the headlights off, taking the unlit streets, some of them old gravel horse paths, until they arrived at the forest at the northern city limit. There, Pres would tuck the car behind a screen of bushes and they'd get out and follow the railroad tracks through two miles of woods to the clearing where the blimps were made.

A high gate blocked them from getting close to the facility, but through gaps in the trees they could see the fireworks of construction blazing across the hangar's translucent walls—arcs of bouncing blue sparks, loops of flame. Pres and Claire spread their blanket on the grass by the fence and watched along with the other lovers who'd come from town, visible to each other only during particularly fierce bursts of light from inside the hangar. Claire often brought snacks, while Pres offered up a jelly jar of apple wine bought from one of the men who made it in his tub at the boardinghouse near Pres's place. As they sipped and ate, the two of them whispered guesses back and forth as to who the other spectators were, who those two glowing cigarette tips belonged to, who that woman was being kissed there with her hands above her head, her fingers laced through the fence links. Pres figured that all the people at the clearing were from nearby, people they knew, but Claire liked to pretend they'd ventured there from the kinds of places she read about in travel magazines.

"I bet she's from Spain. See how her hair's pulled to the side? That's a Spanish style." Or "That man beneath the trees, he's got fat on him like a Russian. They need it because of the tundra."

She knew things about places he'd never heard of, cities with rivers for streets, countries where for part of the year the sun never dropped below the horizon, where a single day lasted for weeks.

Pres had trouble visualizing such places. He'd never ventured more than fifty miles from Niagara. His parents had died in bewilderingly quick succession, and the single greatest comfort to Pres, the sole comfort really, was knowing that the city in which he lived contained all the artifacts of their lives: their friends, their haunts. Two streets west of the house was the tannery where his father had worked. Three blocks toward the river was Harbor Lights, his grand-parents' restaurant, above which his mother had grown up. Here was the chapel where his parents had been married. There, the cemetery where they lay. The city was like a private museum that Pres could tour whenever he pleased.

Even now, nearly a year after their deaths, Pres had trouble imagining himself going much of anywhere at all. But sometime early in the summer Claire started using *we* instead of *I* when she talked about traveling. *We.* For Pres, that tiny word transformed the whole future into a hot little secret between just the two of them.

The summer seemed full of secrets. In the moonlit forest, blimps were being built for reasons that, though clearly explained by the city's naval officers as part of a national "contract," still were hooded in mystery. Every few months another blimp emerged from the woods, glided over city hall, and moored on the high school baseball field for a brief celebration. The blimps had sum-mery names: *The Mayfly*, *Honeysuckle Rose*, *The Raindrop*. That one boasted a cabled observation basket that could lower from the clouds. Another—*The Roost*—had a ladder hanging from its cabin that airplanes could cling to in midair like trapeze artists. No one knew for sure where the blimps flew off to afterward; some people said to a naval base in New Jersey, but others claimed out to sea.

The blimps' architects and engineers had come from Germany, and in the spring the city's naval officers had moved them into a house on Jemmison Street, right near the city center. They were large, blocky men, these Germans, broad-shouldered as umpires. And yet they seemed so helpless, so lost all the time, startled by the passing clatter of a police horse, frightened into apologetic fits of nodding and waving by a simple hello from someone passing on the sidewalk. One of them, a man named Heitmeyer, never went anywhere without a parasol to keep off the sun. Pres knew his name because he'd gone into the diner right behind Heitmeyer one morning and seen him write it in the guest book. As Pres ate his breakfast, he kept glancing over at Heitmeyer, who sat in a booth against the far wall. He was studying what Pres guessed was some kind of blueprint spread before him on the table. Every now and then Heitmeyer took up his pencil and began working on whatever it was, bending close to the paper, creating a little fort around it with his arm. Pres got so curious that he pretended to have to go to the men's room just to catch a glimpse. What he saw, though, when he passed the booth wasn't a blueprint at all, but a drawing, a fanciful sketch of a sky filled with blimps of all shapes and sizes: fleets of blimps layered one on top of the next, stretching up into the atmosphere. An elegant network of ladders and rope bridges and spiraling tubes connected the blimps, creating a city in the sky, a floating metropolis protected by a vast, blue moat. How wild to get to live someplace like that, Pres thought. But even as the sketch disappeared behind Heitmeyer's arm, Pres found himself wondering how great it would really be. What if lightning popped one of the blimps? What if they ran out of fuel? What if someone living up there wanted to come down?

There were other secrets that summer, too. More people than ever before were going over the falls. For years no one had done such a thing, simply stepped into a barrel and shoved off toward the rapids, but now there were jumps all the time. The jumpers were always local people, too, not daredevils from Buffalo or Albany, not publicity hounds or stuntmen, but people everyone had known for years: Gideon Wells, who delivered milk and ice and butter every week, and pretty Laura, who kept minutes at city hall. No one knew why they did it, but all around the city, people wondered who would be next.

Claire loved Pres's stories of working on the patrol. She loved them so much, it made him blush with pride there in the pine-scented darkness. Over and over he told her about Pipe Island, where he worked, a slender strip of land shaped like a corncob pipe at the edge of the falls. He told her about the squat stone tower at the bowl end of the island, where he spent his days scanning the river for barrels. He even taught her how to spy jumpers. First thing, he explained, laying his head on her leg, was to watch the shore. Barrels were cumbersome, and the hedging along the river-banks was leafy even in winter. More often than not, people could be spotted before they made it within a hundred feet of the water. It happened all the time, he said. He'd be looking through the binocu-lars, scanning the American, then the Canadian side of the river, and he'd catch a rustling in the bushes near the top of one of the banks. All of a sudden, a lady in bathing trunks and a frilly swim-ming cap would be rolling a fat, brown barrel down the bank and splashing it out into the river. Occasionally, though, the barrels were already in the water by the time he saw them rushing toward him.

I'll bet you think that barrels float, he said, that they bob along like corks. Well, they don't, not at all. In fact, he told Claire, they tumble forward underwater, hardly ever rising to the surface. They would come at him like mice moving beneath a carpet, little swells in the current. Winter was even worse, he said. The barrels often drifted beneath ice floes headed downriver and were only visible as shadowy spots on the white plates of ice. And once a jumper made it past the patrol, chances were no one would ever see him or her again; the jumper would just vanish into the white curtain of the falls.

He told her everything. Staring up at her from the cushion of her lap, the stars visible behind her head, he told her about Dexter, his partner, the boulder of a man who always sat smoking at the tip of the island, with the long, hook-ended metal pole across his lap. Dex, whose son had been killed overseas, in the Argonne Forest. Dex, with that sad look to him, sitting there staring at the passing water all day. Pres explained how, when he did see a barrel coming, he'd ring the bell and Dex would spring to his feet and ready himself, holding the pole tightly in those hands of his, pouched and leathery as baseball mitts. While Pres radioed the crew of the *Maid of the Mist*, trolling below the falls, and warned them to prepare their rescue gear just in case, Dex would wait like that—pole across his thighs, feet planted at the rocky edge of the island—until the barrel was close enough to be seen. Then, in one swift motion, Dex would thrust the pole out into the driving water and yank it back, catching the hook deep in the wood.

"Is this kind of how he hooks them?" Claire said calmly, before lunging at Pres, digging her fingers into his ribs, making him squirm and laugh.

Lying chest-to-chest beneath the blanket, the two of them spent long hours wondering why people went over the falls at all. For the life of him, Pres couldn't figure out why anyone would do something so foolish, why they'd let themselves be so charmed by what amounted to a simple drop in the river. He told himself it was nothing more than hysteria. After all, he'd lived less than two miles from the falls his whole life and he'd never felt the slightest tug. But even so, Pres found himself deeply troubled, as though his failure to understand the lure of the falls pointed to some larger flaw.

"Maybe they just want to go somewhere," Claire said one night toward the end of summer. "Like an escape. Maybe they don't think about it."

Pres was now deeply in love with her. He wanted to tell her so, but he refused to say anything until he could compose an adequate description of his feelings, which, frustratingly, he never felt able to do. The best comparison he'd come up with involved an exhibit on hydroelectricity he'd seen at a fair downtown when he was a child. The exhibit's main attraction was a clear, life-size figure, a glass man filled with miniature wheels and paddles and belts hung with tiny wooden buckets. When water was poured through a hole at the top of the man's head, the machinery inside him whirred to life and one by one a series of bulbs strung through his legs and arms and head lit up like the points of a constellation until, finally, a large heart-shaped bauble of glass in the man's chest flickered on and shined brighter than the other lights, so bright that Pres was forced to shield his eyes. Best he could figure, that was how he felt for Claire, how he would always feel, aglow.

Pres brushed his fingers over her thigh. The hangar walls flashed, illuminating the figures in the trees.

"Maybe they just look at the falls too long and get hypnotized, like by a snake charmer," Claire said. She put her arms out in front of her and stared at the blinking hangar like a zombie. Seeing her like that—her gaze focused yet eerily vacant—sent a slight chill through Pres's chest. He didn't like the naturalness of her pose or the facility with which she'd assumed it. It was how she'd appeared when he first laid eyes on her back in the wax museum; when, no matter how he tried to hold her eyes with his, they'd looked past him. Even as he was thinking this, though, she broke her pose, grabbing him and pulling him to her.

Pres woke to find the map illuminated in front of his face. It had somehow tumbled up from the backseat and spread itself flat against the windshield. The early sun lit the paper as though it were stained glass. There had been no sign of the blimp in Gum Junction and now he was two days' drive outside the city limit, though where exactly he didn't know. He'd fallen asleep while driving again, just passed out of consciousness. Since he didn't feel ready to look out the windshield and find the car hammered into a tree or teetering on the edge of a cliff, he just sat and stared at the map for a while. Each of the forty-eight states was a different hue—Arkansas crimson, Texas mint-jelly green. The sun projected the map's colorful design onto Pres's chest and face. He found his pen lying against the inside of the door and drew a heavy black check mark where he assumed Gum Junction, Arkansas, to be.

Neighboring mountain towns like Holly and Bonanza Springs were rich off their mineral springs, so Pres had been surprised to find Gum Junction a shabby and cheerless place, as though the town's own mountain were a sharp knee over which it had been snapped. The only building open the evening Pres arrived was the public bathhouse. When he opened the door and stepped inside, he'd found a single steam-clouded room lined with changing stalls. The wooden floor was pocked with deep holes fizzing with bubbling water, and inside each hole was an old man. Some, submerged up to their chins, bobbed up and down, their beards and the tips of their long white mustaches dipping in and out of the water. Others were spilling water over themselves from jars of poor-quality purpled glass. To Pres's eye they looked like a garden of ruined fountains.

"Excuse me, sir," Pres said to the man nearest him. "Did you happen to see an airship pass by here a little while ago? A flying machine?"

The man was frail, his chest kicked in by time. "You ought to wet those down, boy," he said, gesturing toward Pres's hands. When Pres looked down, he found that his hands had clawed up from gripping the steering wheel.

"Go on," the man said. "It only costs to take it with you."

"Six cents for the glass," said a man in a hole near the window.

Pres knelt down and dipped his hands in the water. It was a hundred and fifteen degrees, easy, and within moments he felt the tightness in his knuckles melt away.

"Feels good, don't it?" called a man too far back to see, a shadow behind the steam. "That's arsenic and iron working on you."

Pres nodded; the water felt so good he thought he might cry.

"What's this airship look like?" said the man nearest him.

"It's a long balloon with a kind of cabin attached to the bottom," Pres said.

"A cabin hanging from an observation balloon?" said the man near the window. He was smirking in a way that made Pres's heart sink; it was clear that these men were about to laugh at him. He'd been laughed at by so many people in such a number of places that he could feel it coming by now, could sense it rumbling up through a person before it erupted.

Pres sat back and studied the map for signs of where the blimp might go next. The few places he'd seen the blimp himself he'd dotted with a check on the map; everywhere the blimp had been spotted by others he'd talked to along the road, with a question mark. Still, the pattern eluded him. He'd chased the blimp down the icy New Jersey coast by trail of rumor, spotted it once near the Virginia border, rising from a marine hangar floating out in the middle of a lake, and assuming it was going down to the Carolinas or maybe even to Florida, he'd rushed south and overshot it, getting himself lost for nearly two weeks in the lush jumble of the Great Smoky Mountains. He finally caught wind of it again near Nashville, where he wound up spotting it near two in the morning, tunneling like a whale through the starry sky, the fins at its tail a spacey blue in the moonlight, only to lose it again in the bubbling hot springs towns of the Ozarks.

Pres traced the marks with his finger. Once connected, the sightings formed a kind of quivering, larger check mark starting high in the Northeast, dipping through the southern states, then swooping back up toward the country's middle. But would the blimp continue north toward the Dakotas, or plunge back down toward the striped canyons of the western desert? What if he couldn't find its trail again?

Worse than all this, though, was the plain fear that the blimp would make it to the West Coast ahead of him and head off over the Pacific, to Europe or Asia, somewhere he'd never be able to follow. And he knew somehow that this was its course, that it was trying to get to the ocean before he could catch it.

Pres steeled himself and tore the map away from the windshield. He found that he was parked in an endless sea of yellow grass. It fanned out from the car in all directions—no trees, no buildings, just grassland, flat and golden. He felt a twinge of fear: this had to be Oklahoma; so far west already. He started the car and searched until he found a trampled path, then drove on into the baking afternoon.

The world was level forever. Pres felt like he was negotiating the arena of a giant board game, his car a luckless charm. Every few minutes a solitary farmhouse appeared in the distance, and at each one he stopped to inquire after the blimp. He asked through doorways held open just wide enough to see a wife's frightened eye peering out. He asked men in heavy gloves, rolling barbed wire out against fence posts beside the road. He asked children playing with a spotted frog on their porch steps, tying its feet to the ends of a scarf and then tossing it so high that the scarf filled with wind and the kicking frog floated out over the yard before being rocked back down to earth.

Eventually, the houses stopped coming altogether and there was nothing to the landscape but Pres and the occasional prairie dog poking its head up from the ground to look quizzically at him. The expressions on their faces were hardly different than the ones he encountered everywhere he told his story. *Why are you still chasing her?* the eyes said. *Why go on?* Even after he'd stopped mentioning Claire altogether, everyone he spoke with seemed to know that he was chasing after a woman who'd left him, a woman who probably didn't want to be found.

But that's not how it was, Pres thought as the grass changed to dirt beneath the wheels of the car. He might not know why Claire had left, but what he *did* know, beyond a doubt, was that she wanted him to bring her home.

Since that first summer on Pipe Island he'd watched a number of jumpers pulled live from their barrels, and it always went the same way. First, the lid would come off with a suck of air not unlike a gasp, and Dex would reach into the barrel and try to loosen whoever was curled up inside. He'd gently take them by the elbows and hoist them up, blue-lipped and blinking in the sunshine. Then, *whap!* He'd slap them across the face with those enormous hands of his, and again: *thwap!* After that, Dex propped them on their wobbling feet, still in the barrel, while he and Pres waited for the thank-yous to start.

Because no matter how hard the jumpers had tried to make it over the cataract, once caught, they were grateful. Days after the person had recovered and resumed teaching chemistry or policing the streets, Dex and Pres would invariably receive a note or gift or even a visit at the falls. Joe Greeble had sent them hats from his men's store. Mrs. Mishara had met them herself on the rickety hanging bridge to Pipe Island—she still had stitches above her eye where she'd taken a bump in the rapids—and she'd kissed them both and taken their hands and blessed them right there, with the same water that had almost killed her rushing not five feet beneath the bridge's creaking boards.

When Pres turned his thoughts back to the road, he found that the prairie had become endless desert, the grass cooked down to a fine pink sand. The sky was powder blue, too bright to look at. A hot wind kept up outside, butting against the car, rocking it on its wheels and causing it to give off frightened squeaks. Pres realized he must have been staring into the light for some time, as a steady rain of colored spots was falling at the edges of his vision, drops of blue and orange and black. He kept his hat low and drove on, ignoring them until only one lingered in the corner of his eye. He glanced at the spot, figuring it would scatter or vanish altogether, but it remained fixed on the horizon. He turned the car toward it, and still it stood its ground.

The air swayed with heat, but as Pres approached, the spot took on shape: it grew a boxy frame, its roof rose in a point. He knew what it was, the thing in the distance. A chill climbed the knuckles of his spine. A fence appeared around the property—a sign warned that the site was still under construction—but the gate stood wide open, and Pres raced through. Though he'd seen two hangars so far, he was never able to get close enough to get a good look. From a distance, they'd all looked the same to him, like giant barns or garages. But the binoculars hadn't accounted for their sheer size. As he neared this hangar's gaping entrance, its true proportions became apparent and he found himself trying to blink away his incredulity. It was at least fifteen stories tall, the highest structure he'd ever laid eyes on. There were no other buildings around, save some shacks out back. No trees in the area, just scattered bunches of desert four-o'clock and some tongue leaf cactus.

Pres skidded to a stop just outside the hangar's mouth. High, spidery scaffolding buttressed its walls on both sides, and though there were no men working now, Pres could see pails and rags scattered along the planking. A pair of overalls draped over a banister whipped back and forth in the wind. Pres pulled his suspenders up over his undershirt and slipped the .38 into his pocket.

As soon as Pres stepped into the hangar's shade, he was hit with a soft shower of water. He glanced around for a leaky pipe or someone hosing down a piece of machinery, but when he looked up, he saw that above the hangar's highest rafters there floated a soupy gray cloud from which a quiet rain was falling. Dex had shown Pres postcards his son had written from Europe, in which he told of churches so tall that air sometimes condensed up in the rafters and created miniature clouds, but Pres had not been able to picture such a thing.

He looked around and noticed some heavy fans aimed up at the cloud from the catwalks zigzagging the hangar's walls. Whoever was working on the hangar must have been taking a break while they waited for the moisture to dissipate. He stared at the square of clear blue sky framed by the doorway at the other end of the hangar, at the shacks and tents burning with light in the distance, but he saw no one. He wondered if the hangar was even operational yet. He didn't see any hydrogen or helium tanks, no main line anywhere. A runway of mooring rings had been anchored in the cement floor, but there were no cables hooked to them. Perhaps the blimp hadn't come this way at all. For the thousandth time in the last couple of months, the picture of what it would be like to return home without Claire crept up on him: opening the door on a dark house; finding her dresses still hanging in the closet, her empty side of the bed, a hair curled up on her pillow. He forced the image from his mind and headed through the rain toward the far end of the hangar. He would get some information from whoever was working there. He touched the cold bulge in his pocket. He could taste his sweat through the sweet water running down his face.

Something twinkled from the ground, catching his eye: when Pres walked over, his heart seized: Claire's compact. He picked it up and held it in the palm of his hand for a moment. He'd bought it for her six months ago, after hers was stolen at the museum. Claire had been sitting on her bench, powdering her forehead, when a girl came around the corner and surprised her. Claire had been forced to quickly resume her pose, hands gripping the edge of the bench, frozen like that, neck craned down the tracks. The compact fell to her lap, and the girl snatched it up and ran down the hall before Claire had time to react. So Pres had bought her this one. It was white with gold webbing and shaped like a mitten. He'd picked it because it reminded him of winter, which was when they were going to be married. When he flipped it open now, a tiny puff of powder rose from its dish, and for a moment he could smell Claire in the hangar with him. Behind the puff he thought he saw a design in the powder well. At first he figured it was just a smear left by a quick dip of the fingers, but no, it was a traced letter, a V or a W, he was sure of it. Suddenly, though, a fat raindrop hit the compact, and then another, and before he could snap it closed the compact was a puddle of cream. No matter, he thought, racing back through the hangar to the car. The message had been a *W*, for west—there was no doubt in his mind.

Pres had been working at the falls the afternoon Claire vanished. The day was clear and bitter cold, with chunks of ice spinning through the black water. He and Dex sat at the island's rocky tip, waiting for the ambulance to appear across the bridge and take Dex to the hospital. Dex had fallen into the water making a grab at a girl floating by, and though he was calm, he could not stop shaking beneath his heavy blanket. He refused to let Pres move him inside the tower. "I'm fine, Pres," he said, his voice ragged with tiny gasps. Frost sparkled in his beard. "Let's just wait here by the falls."

"Your funeral," Pres said, and clapped Dex on the back. He knew that the water here was shallow, and he knew that Dex was too strong a swimmer to be pulled far from the shore. But no matter how many times he watched it happen, seeing Dex fall into the river never failed to terrify him. It was the moment just after Dex hit the water that always scared him most, the instant when the current first tugged Dex toward the edge of the rock as though he were the one being hooked. But the falls could get you like that, Pres thought. He looked at the southern shore where a tree had been grabbed by the ice and moved fifty yards downriver, just plucked out of the ground with its roots intact.

"I took a couple swallows of that water and I can feel it sitting right here," said Dex, moving his trembling hand to his stomach. "It's like a frozen pond at the bottom of my gut." In Dex's lap was the girl he'd saved from the river, who, it turned out, wasn't a girl but a girl's doll. She had three faces, and they turned beneath a wig fastened in place: happy, sad, and tired, with her eyes drawn half-closed.

Looking at the doll now, Pres could hardly believe that he hadn't seen it for what it was. But he'd argued with Claire until late the night before and he was exhausted; his eyes ached in their sockets. The fight had erupted over a present. Their wedding was approaching, and as a gesture of congratulations, Claire's old boss, Earl Flatt, had offered to use the two of them to make molds for a new pair of background figures at the museum. Pres was excited about the idea.

"It'll be nice," he said. "Like a portrait of us made of wax." They were lying in his bed, cupped together to keep warm. Outside, the tree branches creaked with ice.

"I don't know. The figures always turn out sort of weird-looking," said Claire.

"They might come out all right," said Pres, though he agreed that Flatt often mixed too much fat in the wax, which made the faces look eerily translucent. "I'm sure you'll look beautiful."

"I'd feel too guilty," said Claire. "I don't think I'm going to go back and work there again in the spring, and Earl puts a lot of effort into those dummies. He sticks in each hair himself with a needle. He orders the glass eyes special from a hospital."

The wax museum had closed for the winter, and in the meantime Claire was working at a gift shop in town. The shop's staple was its glass figurines, which the owner, Becca, fashioned in an upstairs workshop; glass men and women in all manner of activity: walking hand in hand, dancing, bowing to one another. Becca had taken a liking to Claire, and was teaching her how to craft the figurines herself. For the time being, she had Claire sculpting glass infants, as they were the simplest figurines the shop sold. Claire's hours there were surprisingly long; usually she didn't get home until after dark. It felt to Pres as though they were spending less and less time together every day. He tried to ignore the smell of the torch gas on her skin as they lay in bed.

"It'd be romantic," Pres said. "We can go back when we're old and see ourselves when we were just starting out."

"You have to stick your face in plaster for an hour. Plus, it's creepy. It's like having yourself stuffed and mounted."

"Jesus. You make it sound so morbid. Fine, forget it."

"No, we can do it if you really want to."

He turned away from her. "Drop it," he said, surprised at his own anger. Next to the closet was a box of her clothes. She'd moved some things over in anticipation of their wedding, but it had been sitting there, sealed, for over a week. Just looking at the box made Pres's face go hot. He thought about Earl, waiting for her to come back to the museum in the spring, standing there on opening morning, smiling, scanning the street for her, checking his watch.

She laughed and pressed herself to him. "Oh, come on, don't be a grump," she said.

"Get off," he said, pushing her away.

"Are you serious?"

"Did you hear me?" he said. "Leave me alone. Get lost!"

She turned away from him. After she fell asleep he moved closer to her, hoping she might find him during the night, but she stayed away and he drifted off alone, staring at the population of lopsided glass babies on the night table.

"My feet are hurting now. They're coming back." Dex flexed his toes, which Pres had earlier cut loose from his frozen shoes with a scaling knife. "When my son, you know, Dennis, when he was just five or six, some girl gave him a doll like this one." Dex turned the

doll over in his hands. "For weeks he dragged it with him everywhere."

Pres had seen photographs of Dennis. He was a large, solid boy
with a heavy brow like Dex's. An image of him came to Pres then:
he saw Dennis standing at the edge of a wooded shore, on the rocks
leading down from the forest into the water. Dennis wore his fatigues and carried his duffel bag on a sloping shoulder. Behind
him, other boys in fatigues wandered through the pines, calling out
names. Some were dragging duffel bags on the ground. Dennis
peered out across the water at Pres, confused and frightened and
wanting to come home.

"It was peaceful," said Dex. "Being washed along on the current
like that."

"Washed away," said Pres. "You're lucky you came to your damn
senses." He took the doll from Dex and tossed it back into the river,
where it quickly vanished beneath the dark water. Pres waited to
see it sucked over the long fangs of ice hanging from the lip of the
falls, but it never reappeared. He wondered if the doll would end
up as part of the blue yodel the city was having that winter. A blue
yodel was what people called it when a number of fish swam too
close to the falls and were swept against the ice piled up at the cusp.
The current held the fish there until they froze, and then slowly,
as the ice pushed forward, they were rolled over the edge of the
falls and worked down through the glassy stalactites in spiraling
columns. All sorts of fish hung in the giant icicle closest to Pipe
Island: perch and rainbow trout, sturgeon. None of them looked
old, or sick. They were large fish with wide red gills. It seemed to
Pres that they could have easily escaped the current had they
wanted to, but there they were.

He looked at the falls. The afternoon sun had burned off the mist, and Pres saw the cascade of Horseshoe Falls curving toward shore, a bow of light sparkling across its apron. For a moment he could almost imagine how a fish, or a person, might be drawn in, romanced by the sheer rumbling beauty of it. There was something romantic about just offering yourself up like that, about surrendering so fully to magnetism.

He thought of Claire—Claire running her wand through a spout of blue flame and then touching it to the end of a glass pod, teasing out a foot, another foot, then the top of the baby's head—and he suddenly understood that what had caused his anger the night before was worry. Having the dolls made would be like one more promise to each other that they'd endure. But how many promises did he need from her?

Below the falls, the ice floes had been pounded into a great arched bridge spanning the whole river, and people from town were strolling across this new promenade of brilliant ice. Children sledded from the center down to the bank on either side, and here and there, girls sold hot chocolate and apple cider from propped-up cardboard booths. Pres decided he would take Claire here after work. He'd buy her a candied lemon and tell her he was sorry for acting so ridiculously.

A shadow enveloped the island. Pres looked up and saw a blimp passing overhead, floating in the direction of the baseball field.

"That's a pretty one," Pres said. "Some I'm not fond of, but there's real beauty to that one."

"Pretty until wartime," said Dex. But Pres could tell that Dex found the blimp attractive too, with its white fins and silver body. He considered leaving early and going to the festival—he knew Claire would take off work and go with her friends—but then he thought better of it. The baseball field would be crowded and loud. The naval officers had recently begun letting people from the audience climb aboard and tour the insides of the blimps. A few celebrations ago they'd invited a group of men and women up to play tennis on the blimp's fins. At the most recent, they'd even offered to give a few lucky people short rides over the city.

Pres heard voices from below, and when he glanced down he saw everyone on the ice bridge waving and cheering at the blimp. He turned and waved at it too, until it disappeared behind the trees.

Pres drove on through Arizona. The heat was terrible, the day a clay oven; he could feel his sense of things evaporating inside the car. The land was ringed with all the colors of sunset and the sky showed a deep green. Though the ground around him seemed static, bleached and splintered towns kept sliding past, one after another, and eventually Pres became quite sure that the car, while anchored in one place, was actually dragging the towns to it, reeling in the land's fabric with its spinning wheels. But the texture of the land was nothing like fabric, he thought. It was pocked and pitted like a fruit skin, and in his mind he was suddenly an ant crawling across the rind of an enormous blood orange. Then he was a tiny crab scurrying across the ocean floor. On all sides lay tremendous pieces of red coral, and far above, huge white jellyfish gently pumped through the water, dragging tendrils of rain behind them.

Then he saw it, and everything became clear again. He was in western Arizona. Those were clouds. These were formations of rock, nothing more, and that was the blimp's silver nose peeking out from behind one of them. He opened his mouth to scream, to laugh, but his throat was too parched. He swung the Ford around toward the stone tower and stomped on the gas. The car gunned forward. Claire's compact slid off the dash and fell into his lap. He would sneak up on the blimp from behind. He would surprise it! The steering wheel rattled in Pres's hands as he roared around the back of the rock tower. He could see the blimp clearly now, hovering just above the cracked, red dirt.

Beneath the blimp's nose, a small crew of men had just finished drawing water from a stone well. Pres could see some of them winding in the snake-like tube of an electric pump from the well's mouth, while others carried plump, jiggling sacks of water over their shoulders toward the blimp. Pres did not know whether the water was to be used for ballast or coolant or just for drinking, but he knew it wasn't going to reach the blimp. He grabbed the gun from the passenger seat and fired it out the window at the line of trudging men. The crack echoed off the rock walls. The men dropped their sacks and ran for the blimp's folding staircase.

The blimp was right in front of him now, just yards ahead. He was near enough to see the men's frightened faces, the gold stripes at the cuff ends of their tan shirts and pants as they rushed up the steps. The last of them disappeared inside the blimp just as Pres skidded to a stop beneath the massive tail fins. He jumped out and ran between the mooring ropes toward the staircase, which was already drawing up into the cabin. The muscles of his legs burned.

"I'm here!" he screamed as the stairway panel clicked shut above him. "Claire!" He pounded on the hatch with the butt of the gun, smashing dents in the wood planking. He rushed over to a curtained window and raised the gun again, but the hot blast from the blimp's engines knocked him backward, whipping and cutting at his arms and neck. He tried to shield his eyes from the storm whirling around him. Then came the horrible tearing noise as the mooring rings ripped loose from the ground, each one dangling a crumbling heap of earth. Pres glanced above the crook of his elbow at the blimp. His hands shook with panic as he saw the cabin rise away from him. He grabbed at a nearby mooring rope and clutched it as tightly as he could. The blimp's nose tilted down slightly, and then it began to glide forward. Pres ran behind it, clinging to the rope, but it soon picked up speed and before he knew it he was being dragged on his belly through the dirt. Pebbles flayed the bottoms of his arms. The friction stung so badly that he thought he wouldn't be able to hold on. Then he was being peeled up, lifted into the air as the blimp ascended.

Pres crossed his ankles around the rope, tightening his grip. He looked down at the landscape falling away beneath him, at the wrinkles in the red earth, the torched heaps of rock. He glanced over his shoulder and saw his car, his battered Model T, growing smaller and smaller until it vanished in a whirl of sand.

Pres turned back to the blimp. He knew that all that stood between him and death was his grip on the cable, and yet even as he clung to its steel braiding a strange calm came over him, an almost restful feeling. Things were out of his hands now; he was being carried toward the end of his journey by the blimp, which he now saw was called *The August*. The name was printed in fine gold lettering over the cabin's rear window.

The air thinned and grew cold and Pres began to feel lightheaded. His shoe fell off and tumbled through the sky. Breathing became an effort. Soon he could feel the blood coursing up his arms. But he would not let go. The rope felt a part of him, the blimp too, and for a moment when he gazed up at its body, sunlight gleaming off its silver skin, what he saw floating up there was not a blimp at all but an extension of himself, his own heart, swelled to bursting and released from his chest. His heart, swinging him through the sky. He thought about all the places and wonders he'd seen these past months, and felt a strange gratitude toward Claire for taking him all this way.

He turned back to the cabin and tried to focus on the word *August*. It was just the right name, Pres thought as a falcon whirled past him. As a child, he'd always thought of August as a time of rousing, the month when everything was rustled awake from the bright dream of summer. And that was just what he was going to do for Claire. He looked at the curtains blocking his view inside the cabin. They were purple and velvety, but they did not look so heavy to Pres. He could push them aside with one hand.

Happy Fish,
Plus Coin

ONCE LIVED NEXT TO A MAN WHO WAS INDESTRUCTIBLE. HIS name was Gay Isbelle and he cheated death three times—twice before I'd met him, and then once in my company.

It was important for me to be around someone like Gay at that point in my life, someone invulnerable, as I was scared and lonely and hiding from my family, which was, and still is, one of the wealthiest in the country. Their money goes back to the days of gas and steam, and the root of the family name means both "vision" and "light" in a language that will not be revealed here. They had detectives out looking for me, detectives with real means, but in Florida at that time, for a short, wonderful period not too long ago, it was easy to find employment without identification of any shape or sort. It seemed you could open a police station with just a few phony papers to tack on the wall. You could become whoever you wanted; that was Florida right then. I had a book of over fifteen thousand baby names, and I changed mine whenever I felt like it.

Gay and I both lived on the second floor of the Shores Motel, which sat on the outskirts of Orlando, near the trashiest of that neighborhood's three convention centers. This particular convention center didn't even have a name; it was simply marked by a sign over the interstate exit that read CNV. CNTR. #16, as though it wasn't even worth plugging vowels into. It only hosted the most dismal conventions—gatherings for the fan clubs of otherwise long-forgotten stars; reunions for high school classes that graduated three, even four generations back, so long ago that only a few ancient people showed up to wander beneath the wrinkled balloons. Whenever a convention came to Cnv. Cntr. #16, most of its attendees washed into the Shores, and it was during one such convention that I met Gay.

I never found out what, exactly, the purpose of the convention was, but that weekend the motel was full of people with all sorts of pigmentation disorders. I saw a woman by the ice machine with skin spotted like a cheetah's. In the elevator, a man with a purple face nodded at me. A little boy splashing around in the pool was covered from head to toe in a dazzling flock of red butterfly-shaped splotches. I'd never realized how many different kinds of albino existed, but here they all were: some just a shade too pale, others with flesh as white as lobster meat.

The afternoon I met Gay, I was in the motel's restaurant bar, a Chinese affair called the Happy Fish, Plus Coin. A young albino woman from the convention was eating dinner in the booth across from me. Her eyes were pink, and her hair was as clear as water; it hung down her back in a transparent braid. I couldn't stop staring at her. She looked just like my sister Melanie, or what I imagined Melanie would look like as a ghost.

Growing up, most of my brothers and sisters were fiercely competitive, even cruel. But Melanie acted different. Though she was older by a full five years, she took an interest in me; she started protecting me from the others. She taught me things—how to trip someone bigger than myself, how to sneak out of the brownstone (climb out the easternmost kitchen window and lower yourself down onto the patio wall. There, now you know too!). Melanie was small and clever and quick. She never looked pretty in photographs, but in real life there was something especially beautiful about the true expressions of her face—the way only one of her eyebrows arched with her smile, the dimpling of her chin when she scowled.

The school she went to forced its students to wear a uniform that included a red blazer embossed on the chest with a gold crest. In all my memories Melanie is wearing that red blazer. She had a friendship with one of our family's drivers, an older Portuguese man named Julius, and she would have Julius secretly drive us places after school: to Chinatown, or to Coney Island, where we'd walk along the pier and watch the families fishing for crabs with plastic baskets they'd stolen from the supermarket.

Once in a while Melanie had Julius take us to the train station, where she'd buy herself a ticket on a northeasterner, a ticket that she said would take her away for good. This was back when I was eight or nine and she was in her early teens. I'd walk with her to the platform, where she'd kneel down and put her hand on my shoulder or my cheek and say something like "Listen, little man. I'm taking this train all the way to Toronto, understand? That's in the country above us. When I get there, I'll find someplace awesome for us to live and then I'll send for you, secretly. You'll get a letter in the mail with no return address, and when you open it, it'll just be a train ticket. That'll be your cue. . . ."

She'd give me a long hug and hand me something of hers—one time she gave me her watch; another time a pen with a tiny cityscape inside, complete with a ferry that slowly sailed from end to end—and then she'd board the train car and I'd stand there at the platform and watch as the train huffed to life and then made its way down the long tunnel and out of the station. I'd watch until the train was just lights, a swirl of vapor, nothing.

After that I'd walk through the station to the taxi stand, where Julius would be leaning against the car waiting for me, brushing lint off the bill of his driver's cap. He'd wink at me and nod to the passenger door and I'd get in and together we'd drive alongside the train tracks to Ruppendale or East Hunting, whichever suburb

Melanie had actually bought a ticket to. If she didn't get off at one, we'd drive on to the next, and as we did, no matter how often this happened, part of me always became frightened that this time she wouldn't get off the train, that today she'd keep on going and ride it farther than Julius and I could follow. But she always *did* get off somewhere nearby, and when we pulled up to the station she'd be waiting for us, sitting on a bench in those high gray socks and that red blazer of hers, its crest like a wax seal stamped over her heart.

My father moved Melanie out to the West Coast just before my tenth birthday. I was at school and never got to say good-bye. When I got home, my other brothers and sisters were packing her belongings into boxes. She works for our uncle now, and spends most of her time on a plane, traveling between offices. It's large, but it has pontoons and can land as gracefully as a seagull on the water. There's a plane waiting for me, too. My real name is painted on both engines.

I've seen Melanie just once in the twelve years since she was sent away, at one of our brothers' weddings, which I'd gone to only out of hopes that Melanie would attend. She acted fidgety and nervous and seemed extremely agitated by me.

"That's disgusting. What is that?" she said when I showed her a lock of her own hair she'd given me before one of her train rides. She was pregnant, but the rest of her was thin and elegant. An Arabian man was helping her into her coat. "Get it away," she said. "Why are you showing me that?"

So that afternoon at the Happy Fish, Plus Coin, I was staring at this albino girl from a corner stool, this phantom Melanie, when I began to cry. I don't know how long I was crying, but at some point Gay appeared and said, "I think you and I are the only ones in this motel God painted by the numbers."

Something to know about Gay: he had a smile on him. Thirty-two perfect teeth set in twin rows, like two lucky horseshoes dipped in white paint. Also, he had been in some kind of fire, that much was clear: his skin was pink and shiny, like melted wax, and his hands had been baked down into little flippers. His head was hardly more than a hairless knob with a slot for a mouth and one usable eye peering out. And he was paralyzed from pretty high up, his chest, maybe even his neck. He sat buckled into a motorized wheelchair, which he controlled with a reed that extended from a small panel up into his mouth. Still, when he smiled at me I hardly noticed the surrounding mess. I couldn't stop myself from staring at his mouth, at that grin.

He took the reed into his mouth and maneuvered his wheelchair a little closer. "Hey," he said. "What are you, gay?"

"No," I said.

"Well, I am. Gay Isbelle. That's my name. Isbelle is French."

"What's Gay?" I said, glad to be talking to someone.

"What do you mean?" he said. "Gay is just gay. It can mean homosexual or happy. I'm old-fashioned, so I think 'happy' when I think of gay."

"Me too," I said.

"Well, why aren't you gay now, chief? You were crying a second ago."

How to describe that voice? There was a musicality to it, a sing-song quality that made me feel safe. It made me want to talk to him, to tell him all about my problems, my family. I hadn't said my last name out loud in over six months.

"I lost my job yesterday," I said instead, which was also true. I'd been working in baggage at Orlando International.

"Is that all?" he said, looking up at me with his one good eye, which was plain brown, nothing dashing about it. "Jobs are easy enough to find around Orlando right now. What a time to be living in Florida!"

"I need something sort of low profile, though. I'm watching out for some people."

"The police?" said Gay. "I don't hold things like that against people. Know that." Gay's nurse, a portly Hispanic man, came over and told Gay he was going to the bathroom. "That's fine, Edward," said Gay. "I'll be right here, with my new friend . . ." He gazed at me, waiting.

"L.J.," I said. This was the name I was using right then, after a character I liked in a musical film.

"I'll be right here with my new friend L.J. when you get back," Gay said. Edward nodded at me and then walked off. "So, who is this you're hiding from, L.J.?"

"Just hiding," I said, though by now I wanted badly to confess. His smile alone was nearly enough to make me do it; it was that glorious, his grin.

"Come on, now. If you're hiding, something has to be looking for you, right? What is it, girl trouble?"

When I opened my mouth to speak again I had every intention of telling Gay the truth; I was going to tell him who my family was, and about how I'd been running from them since just after my nineteenth birthday, nearly one thousand days. I was going to tell him about how they'd nearly caught me in Seattle, then inside a library in Tuscaloosa; about the female detective in Santa Fe whose leg I may have hurt badly with my car. About how they were surely hunting me right then—about how, at that very moment, they might be jabbing flashlights all over central Florida. I had a pair of earrings hung on a lanyard around my neck—ten-carat pear-shaped diamonds. I'd stolen them from my oldest sister the night I left.

They were for an emergency. I thought I'd show them to Gay as a way of starting to explain, but looking at him made me really think about that word, *emergency,* and instead what came out was "Yes, girl trouble. I'm having trouble with my girlfriend."

"Right. Your girlfriend . . ." He waited for me to go on.

"Nancy?"

"Nancy, right. What's the problem?"

"She's mean to me?" I said. "She acts like she hates me."

"Like she hates you, right," Gay said. He continued smiling, but held me with his stare for a long moment. So long, in fact, that I became sure he'd seen right through my lie. I felt confident that in a second he would spit in my face and leave me there. And I didn't want him to leave. Just then, Edward returned from the bathroom. He glanced at Gay, and then at me in a suspicious way, before asking what was up.

"I'll tell you what's up, Edward," Gay said. "What's up is you and I are going to help our new friend L.J. find a job."

When I was born, my father gave the doctor a tiny golden spoon to use to scrape the mucus from my mouth. It had a handle of braided ivory, and in the eighteenth century it had been used by a British nobleman to feed the blood of game animals to his baby hounds. There's a photograph of the doctor leaning over me, pressing the bowl of the spoon between my lips. The picture frame has a special glass compartment for displaying the spoon itself. To this day, I sometimes taste the bowl of that spoon in my mouth. I never know when it's going to happen, when the salty, bitter sting of it will well up, but when it does, the only thing that helps is to suck on something sweet. I once dated a woman staying at the Shores for a candy sellers' convention who made giant gummy animals—bats and rats and even gummy beetles as big as my foot. Her name was Rita Beet, and for a while she worked at a Gummy World at the north end of the Galaxy, the area through which Gay and I were now driving, prowling for employment.

The Galaxy was a ten-mile strip along the interstate that housed all the seedier tourist spots, each one a world unto itself: Gator World, Flea World, Orange World (housed inside a huge graying orange), Orlando's Pawn World, World of Thrills, World of Tees, Scary World (which was nothing more than a plaster cave with a few plastic skulls glued on). As we drove down the strip, though, I started to like the idea of working at one of these places. They looked discarded, like giant, mangled toys flung out a car window. No one would come looking here.

Gay sat propped in the passenger seat with a stack of my résumés on his lap. Whenever I slowed down too quickly, Gay's head lolled forward, and Edward leaned up from the backseat and righted it for him. "Thank you, sir," Gay said each time. "Thank you kindly." Whenever I got out to inquire somewhere, he said, "L.J., this is the one. I feel it. You're just what they've been waiting for."

This was a better day than I'd had in a long time and I was cheerful at first, but after we'd tried some places with no real luck, I began to grow nervous. I started glancing around at other drivers, worrying about my family again. Edward was watching a football game on a cheap, handheld black-and-white TV, and through the static I kept hearing the words *catch* and *caught*. At one point we sped past a dead deer that had been knocked against a tree; it was sitting with its back to the trunk like a person might, staring out at the highway with its front hooves in its lap. The way the deer seemed to watch us as we passed felt accusatory, damning.

"Are you okay, L.J.?" Gay said, staring at me. "Do you want to talk about Nancy some more?"

I turned to Gay, but suddenly he looked so small and helpless sitting there with Edward's hands propping up his ruined head. How could he help defend me from my family?

"Nancy's nasty to me. She . . ." I tried to go on. My heart beat wildly; I was sweating. I was sure that any moment now a carload of my brothers would roar up alongside us.

"I have an idea," said Gay, smiling warmly at me. "Let's talk about green. The color."

"Green?" I managed.

"I try to wear as much green as possible. It's the color of longevity. As in the crocodile, or the turtle, which outlive animals twice, even three times their size."

I noticed that Gay's shirt was green, with dark green diamonds up the front.

"Hey, look. I didn't notice that. Your eyes are green," he said. "You like green, right?"

"Yes," I said.

"Well, just think of green. Think of yourself in cool, dark green."

"Green," I said, closing my eyes. I pictured myself in a deep green jungle, hidden beneath huge, green, umbrella-like leaves. A cool breeze washed over me. My breathing started to calm. I began to feel in control of myself again. I was suddenly overwhelmed with gratitude for having stumbled upon Gay. I felt like he was something conjured up by my imagination, a friend that didn't really exist outside my own mind. I was afraid that if I looked over at the passenger seat, he'd already be gone.

"Gay, what is it that you do? For work, I mean."

"*This* is what I do, L.J. I talk to people. I teach them how to turn bad luck into good. You should come see me live in concert sometime. I speak at churches, meetings, that kind of thing."

"Where are you from, if you don't mind my asking?"

"I'm from a long ways away, L.J. Let's just leave it at that," said Gay. "Because right now I think you should pull over and try asking for work in this place here. I have a good feeling about this one."

I parked and went inside a blinking complex of rides and arcades, where I was hired to work at an attraction called the Home Wrecker, the world's largest inflated house. Imagine a multiroom home that was essentially an enormous balloon for kids to bounce around inside of; picture one of those puffy castles they have at every fairground in America, but four or five times larger and shaped like a house. My job would be to accept tickets from the kids and then point them toward the Home Wrecker's entrance, a dark, rectangular hole in the front of the house, quivering with the efforts of children already inside.

The house itself had five rooms, all equipped with the appropriate inflated furniture—the bedroom had an inflated bed; the dining room, an inflated table and an overhead balloon chandelier; the living room had an inflated TV set with a clown painted on the screen. The points at which these things were attached to the walls, the floor, or the ceiling were actually openings into the larger balloon that was the house itself. The same gas pumped through the whole thing; it was all one bulging organism. Seeing the way the kids tumbled around inside, you'd think that it would topple, maybe even pop. But the house was tough. It was held in place by steel cables, and made of the same rubbery material firemen use to catch falling people.

Gay and I became fast friends. The Shores had a pedestrian overpass, a little walking bridge that cars drove under upon entering the parking lot, and we began meeting up there in the evenings. I always brought a beach chair and an ice bucket filled with the beer we liked to drink, which was rare but popular just then in Florida. It came from the Caribbean in wooden boxes. The bottles were made of thick black glass and had no labels.

It was on that overpass that Gay first told me about his ordeals, which is what he called his brushes with death. This was about a week into our friendship. Night had already fallen. Truck-shaped strings of lights moved back and forth along the distant interstate.

"The first ordeal involved fire," he said. Empty beer bottles lined the tray on his chair. "Our house burned down when I was a baby. That's how my skin got this way. How I became paralyzed was a plane crash, the second ordeal, but that was much later, when I was a teenager. There were other people in the plane with me, but I was the only one who lived. It was the same in the fire. Everyone in the house died but me."

He paused here and took a sip of beer through his straw. A cat came sniffing out of the scrub by the edge of the parking lot. Somewhere a car alarm went off, then stopped.

"It's funny, L.J. You're not supposed to remember things from when you were a baby, but I remember the fire better than the plane crash. I remember being naked in the sink with my mother standing over me, cleaning my heinie with a wet rag. She had a clothespin between her teeth. The phone rang and my mother let it ring. Once, twice, three times. Then on the fourth ring a tiny blade of flame shot out of the phone jack at the base of the wall and sawed its way right up the wallpaper to the phone, which suddenly became this hissing white fireball. The last thing I recall is the fireball hitting my mother in the side of the head. Not like a flame, but hard, like a punch. I could hear it hit her. *Thwap!* Like that. And then she flew out of my line of vision. The wet towel she was using to wash me landed on my feet when she fell. They're the only part of me that didn't get burned. Go on, take a look."

I bent down, my head spinning from the beer, and removed his sneakers. He had two perfect feet at the end of those ruined legs, creamy and white like a girl's, but with patches of golden hair on the toes.

Gay and I took to spending our breakfasts together, too, at the Happy Fish, Plus Coin. Gay loved the name. He supposed it meant "good fortune" in some other language, but figured the expression didn't translate well. "That's what I like about it, though," he said. "I like that the restaurant's owner just kept the phrase exactly how it went in his language, no matter how it might sound to people here. It's like he trusted other people to understand, even if it sounded strange at first. I think I'm going to start ending my letters like that. Instead of 'take care,' or 'best of luck,' I'm going to write 'happy fish, plus coin.' "

Often I tried to pay for our meals, but whenever I laid the money on the table he got a waitress to come over and give half the money back to me. Sometimes, if she was taking a while, I'd push the bills at Gay, slowly, though—I'd creep them toward him like a spider crawling across the table. "Waitress! Waitress!" he'd yell, both of us laughing now, and when the bills were close enough he'd try to blow them back at me, huffing frantically. Gay kept a billfold in his breast pocket and he always paid for exactly half the meal, even if mine was more expensive, which was usually the case.

"I enjoy your company, L.J.," he'd say. "I'm paying for half of the good time being had at this table." He was always saying things like that, things that swelled the tubes of your heart.

Occasionally we took trips together. We drove down to the Everglades, saw the alligators and weird swamp birds. We went to Miami and sat on the beach, which was white and soft as flour. I dug a chair in the sand for Gay while Edward walked back and forth along the lip of the surf in his sneakers. We visited the many amuse-

ment parks—one of which my family had helped finance—getting
to skip the lines for rides and food because of Gay's condition. One
morning we went to Ripley's Believe It or Not!, and Gay became
taken with an exhibit on a man from Iowa who'd been struck by
lightning seven times over the course of his life. Gay kept coming
back to it, asking me again and again to push the button that caused
the tiny thunder sounds and sparked off the lightning.

What we did most of the time, though, was talk about Nancy, the
girlfriend I was supposed to be escaping from at the Shores. Nancy,
who yelled and screamed and mistreated me in more ways than I
even knew existed. She was beautiful, but in the worst way—a clean,
sharp-edged kind of way; beautiful like frost in the corner of a window. She worked as a realtor for a condominium, one much nicer
than the complex we'd lived in together, and she was always having
affairs with the men she showed apartments to. Sometimes, when I
was telling all this to Gay, I actually got angry thinking about her
letting them do it to her on the floors of those empty apartments,
or pinning her against the blank walls. She laughed at me when I
confronted her. She said I was worthless. Did I want to see the hand-
print on her thigh? The tooth marks on her breast?

I couldn't make her bad enough. Every time I started in about
her, I wanted to stop and tell Gay the truth, but I could never get
over my fear that he'd laugh at me, that he'd say, "Look at me. Look
at what I've lived through. You're going to stand there and tell me
that *that's* what you're running away from? *That?*" I was afraid that
he'd tell me to just go home already, to go back to my big house and
my rich family and get out of his sight for good.

It's a difficult thing to explain, hiding from a family like mine,
a family most people would give anything to belong to. The truth
is that sometimes, when your name precedes you—when it actually
appears to you as an overgrown twin, forever loping ahead of you,

shoving open every door it passes with its hip, announcing your arrival with its ape-like hands cupped to its mouth—all you want to do is outrun it. But after a while you find that there *is* no outrunning your name. Sooner or later you find that the only thing to do is run away.

Occasionally I went to hear Gay talk at a nearby church or old age home, and every time, as soon as he finished, the entire audience would line up to meet him. They'd tell him how inspiring it had been to hear him talk; they'd hug him and kiss him on the top of the head, give him little tokens of affection—flowers or maybe a box of clementines. Of course, they all wanted him as a friend. Twice the universe had arranged itself into a great instrument of death and bore down on him, but how did he feel about it? Lucky. Not just for having survived his ordeals, but for the *ordeals themselves.*

"They taught me who I am," he said. "They gave me a calling that makes me happy every day. For that I feel like the most fortunate man alive."

He made me think of fairy tales, of those creatures who swoop in and save you at the last minute, who become your closest, dearest friends, and then, once your problem is solved, vanish. Just like that. So Nancy got worse and worse; the picture darkened every day. One evening I revealed that she'd thrown a steaming iron at my head. The next I told Gay about how I'd woken up in the middle of the night not long ago to find her standing in the doorway of my bedroom, holding her cuticle scissors and just staring at me. Nancy became a bogeywoman hiding in my curtains, grinning at me from behind the clothes hanging in the closet.

"You have to end it once and for all, L.J.," Gay would say. "You don't need someone who doesn't love you. Abuse isn't love." Or "L.J., I want you to call Nancy tonight—no, right now, and tell her it's over. Tell her good-bye. Period." And then Gay and I would head to my room and I'd take a deep breath and call my own extension and tell the busy signal that I had too much respect for myself to go on with it anymore.

Sure enough, though, that night or the next, Nancy would call and tell me that she loved me, that things would be different, and I would usher her right back into my life.

Out of every thousand children who came to the Home Wrecker, nine hundred and ninety-nine were simply out to have fun—to bounce and flip around inside—but there was always that one with a different motive: to try to pop the house. Like I said, this kind of child was rare; they appeared once a week at most. Some of them were what you'd expect: teenagers with shaved heads or colorful, weapon-like hair. They went at the house's rubber walls with penknives or box cutters, nothing that could do much damage. The really dangerous customers were of a different sort altogether. These were children with fury in them, real fury. The first one I encountered was a young boy, ten or eleven, with neatly parted blond hair and skin red and scaly with sunburn. He wore slacks and a tie and carried his folded jacket under his arm like a book. As he handed me his ticket, I noticed something sad in his face, a sort of trembling despair around the mouth. Eventually I'd come to watch for exactly this kind of thing, but at the time I just waved him toward the entrance. He offered a quiet thank-you and then vanished inside. I paid little attention at first. I watched the go-carts race around the track. I heard a girl scream at someone for stealing her golf ball and decided that, later that day, I would tell Gay about the time Nancy had hit a golf ball at me inside our apartment and punched a hole in the kitchen wall.

Suddenly the front wall of the house dented out farther than I'd ever seen it stretched—the cables holding up the house vibrated—then it ricocheted back into place. A few moments passed, and then something barreled into the wall again, hitting the rubber so hard that it whitened up like fist knuckles at the point of impact, before springing backward. I walked over to the door and looked through.

The boy stood with his back pressed against the far wall, sweat running down his neck, his mouth hanging open. His tie lay on the floor. He stared at the front wall for a moment longer, braced himself, and then ran toward it, his head down, his piggish arms pumping. He hit the wall with everything he had, hurled himself so hard that when it rebounded he was thrown backward through the air almost five feet before bouncing across the floor. He staggered to his feet and backed up to the far wall. Again he flung himself at the front of the house with no success. He was crying by now, sobbing. Peeling skin dangled from his arms. I couldn't help but cheer him on. *You can do it,* I thought as he readied himself for another go. *Penetrate! Penetrate!*

Part of me rejoiced each time ones like him showed up, kids who refused to believe in a house that couldn't be knocked down or even hurt, a house that looked like it was giggling, like it was shuddering with delight when they threw themselves at it. *Do it,* I'd whisper to myself as they charged. *Do it!* Harder and harder they banged into those walls: *whump! WHUMP!* And with such hatred in their faces, as though that house contained the very hex of their lives.

Sometimes, seeing these children leap and plow into the walls, I would think about Gay. His room was down the hall from mine, and every now and then in the middle of the night I'd hear him scream in his sleep, howl and shriek until Edward finally shook him awake. Gay was tough, but watching the walls fling child after child back down to the floor, I had to wonder if there weren't things out there more resilient than he. Bad things. I did not want to know what they were.

One evening, about a month into our friendship, there was a commotion in the Happy Fish, Plus Coin. I was talking to Gay about Nancy over dinner, but by this time, I was running out of things to say about her. I could feel my imagination stalling, circling back over the same territory. But this only made my talk about Nancy more insistent and compulsive, more desperate. Lately, I'd been waking up with a hint of the taste of that spoon in my mouth. By the time I sat up and searched for it with my tongue, though, it had always disappeared.

That night at the Happy Fish, Plus Coin, I was telling Gay about how I was sure I'd seen Nancy's brother's car trolling around the parking lot the night before.

"I know it was him because of the fact that one of his headlights flickers on and off," I said. "I could see it winking around out there. And I thought I saw an arm holding a bat hanging out the window."

"You better call her," Gay said distractedly.

"Call her? Gay, are you listening to me?"

"What? Oh, I meant call the police. L.J., do you hear something?"

I listened: somewhere in the restaurant, a girl was crying softly to herself.

"I don't hear anything," I said. "So you really think I should call the cops?"

"L.J., someone is upset. Can you see who it is? They're right behind us."

I craned my neck to see. A few booths back from ours, a girl was crying. She looked about nineteen and was tall with muscular shoulders and arms. Her face was mannish, made even more so by her hair, which she wore in two fist-like buns. She was rummaging through a tote bag with the name of a radio station on it. I recognized her from around the motel. She had come with a singing troupe that had stayed at the Shores for an a capella convention the previous weekend. Gay and I had heard them practicing through the doors to their rooms, their voices weaving in and out of each other. Looking at the girl now, I recalled seeing her argue with the troupe leader in the parking lot one evening when I was out on my balcony. She'd been crying then, too.

"It's nothing," I said to Gay. "She's fine. Listen, I think that calling the police on Nancy is the wrong move."

"Let me see what's going on. Turn me around, L.J.," Gay said, but I made no move to do so.

A waiter approached the girl, but this only made her more upset.

"Hey, behind me!" Gay yelled, sitting there in our booth, limp as a puppet. "Excuse me!"

"Gay, the waiter's got it under control," I said. "Gay! I'm talking to you!"

The waiter continued to speak to the girl, until she said, "Fine! Of course!" She threw some money on the table and then got up and headed toward the door. She was even taller than I'd thought, over six feet.

When she approached our booth, Gay said, "That's a lovely bag, miss."

She glanced at him but kept walking.

"I'd love to hear you sing sometime," Gay called after her.

Once she was gone, Gay shifted his gaze to me. "Why didn't you help me, L.J.?"

"I didn't hear you. I was thinking about Nancy."

"You should have turned me around," said Gay. "She's obviously in need of some kind of help."

"I'm sorry," I said, ashamed and eager for the incident to be over.

Gay sighed. "That's all right, L.J.," he said. But there was a sadness in his voice, a tiredness. He asked me to help him into his chair, which I did.

"Now, where were we?" he said as I unlocked the brake.

I tried to remember what I'd just told him about Nancy. My mind scrambled to come up with something, but I couldn't bring myself to say one more word about her.

I glanced at Gay. He was watching me, his gaze sympathetic but also strangely appraising, almost judicious. I had the sinking feeling that this would be my last chance to tell him the truth about my family. I reached into my shirt, but just as my fingers closed around the earrings, the sun came out from behind a cloud and light poured in through the window, bringing Gay's face into harsh relief—the pits, the knots and whorls of scar tissue—and my fears returned. The earrings felt warm in my fingers. I had them pinched all the way up at my shirt collar, dangling right there at the base of my neck. "I have an idea," I said. "Let's go up to the overpass and have a drink."

Gay sucked air through his teeth. "I wish I could, L.J., but I should get some rest soon. I have time to talk a bit, though. Were you about to say something?"

"You're heading to bed? It's only six o'clock."

"What I meant was that I have to practice my speaking a little, in my room. I should lecture the mirror for a bit. Unless there's something else you want to tell me about?"

I was still holding the earrings. "No. I was all done."

As we left the restaurant I took the earrings from around my neck and slipped them into the pouch on the side of his wheelchair. I don't know what I hoped to accomplish. Maybe I thought he would find them and it would force the issue. Maybe I wanted to give him something, a gift to keep him my friend. "Gay, listen," I said, but he was already pulling away from me and heading toward the elevators.

After he'd gone up to his room, I sat alone in the lobby for a long while. I watched people check in, check out. I know I might have made it seem that only strange people lived in this area of Florida, but it wasn't so. There were plenty of plain men and women, children too, living and visiting. But detectives are very plain people, the plainest of all. You might imagine them hunching around in rumpled trench coats, their faces always surfacing through cigarette smoke, but they are dull almost to being invisible. They look like your mother with no makeup, or your uncle.

Gay started spending less and less time in and near Orlando; he left to speak at places farther away, in Velusia or Delans, and he wouldn't come back for days at a time. More and more often, I'd return from the Home Wrecker and find his room locked, find it dark. My fear was that I'd return one afternoon and see it being vacuumed out, or even worse, rented to someone new. One evening, as I drove toward the Shores, I spied Gay up on the overpass with that girl, the one from the a capella troupe. He was beaming at her from his chair, smiling as widely as I'd ever seen him smile. I pulled to the side of the road and watched. Even from far away I could hear her singing. Her voice sounded beautiful and deep; so deep in fact that it seemed more like a low vibration than an actual voice, the kind of voice that moves beneath the other voices in a choir like a current on which everything else floats.

I began to have trouble concentrating on work. There was no joy in it. I changed my name to Mel Captiol, then changed it again, this time to something very close to my given name. One afternoon, just before closing, a massive girl came into the Home Wrecker. She wore a sleeveless dress and her arms had to be two, even three times the size of my legs. She had it *in her.* I could tell. She lumbered up to me and pulled her ticket from her purse, all the while staring at the house, which rocked gently against its cables in the wind. I took her ticket and she thanked me and then went directly inside, no hesitating at the door, just right on in. I hurried over to watch.

The girl marched around for a minute, sizing everything up, poking at this and that with her shoe—the coffee table in the living room, the refrigerator. I looked on from the doorway, excited. She carried her purse in a tight fist. She sank up to her shins in the balloon floor each time she took a step. The whole house shook with her, as though terrified. She was the one. I knew it. She was going to bring the place down. I could almost feel the heat coming off the back of her neck. The flowers on her dress were red on red.

Suddenly she flopped down on an inflated sofa, took a book out of her purse, and started to read. I was stunned with disappointment. There was nothing to do but stand there and watch as her eyes scanned the pages, her book propped on her chest, her crossed feet wagging from side to side.

When I got home, I went straight to Gay's room, but he wasn't there. I sat outside his door and waited for a long time before finally heading to my room. As soon as I entered, a detective gently shut the door behind me, just slid it closed with his loafer. There were five of them sitting calmly about, waiting. A woman with a cast on her foot had already gone through my clothes and stacked them neatly on the bed. Her blouse was the exact color of the walls. Another one had dragged the safe out of the closet and onto the balcony, where he was banging on its bottom with a wedge and hammer.

Normally at this point I would have fled, maybe fought, but I felt so defeated, so run-down. One of them was sitting on the air conditioner, his T-shirt tucked into his bathing suit. "You can run if you want," this one said. "We'll just find you again."

"Your family's worried about you," said the woman, yawning.

"They want the best for you," said another.

"No, they don't," I started to say, but my tongue felt big. The bitter taste filled my mouth. "I'll give you money if you leave," I said, though I'd tried this with them before. *All* of this had happened before.

"We don't want money. We want you," a familiar voice said from the balcony. Then it called me by my real name. Melanie came in through the curtains. Her hair was pulled back in a ponytail, the same way she'd worn it when we were kids. She had on jeans and sneakers and a sweater with a row of crowns across the front. For a moment I thought she'd come to save me.

"It's been so long. I missed you," she said, and gave me a hug. Her hair smelled both lemony and strangely medicinal. When she pulled away, she kept her hands on my arms. "How have you been?"

"I want to stay here," I said.

"Please don't," she said, smiling at me, her hands still gripping my arms.

"I don't want to go back," I said.

"Well, I'm afraid you don't have a choice in the matter, okay?" she said. "You know you can't just gallivant around forever. Don't you ever think about how it reflects on Mom and Dad and the rest of us? Believe me, you're lucky we found you before you did anything to attract bad attention. I know. You don't want to see what happens to someone from a family like ours when they screw up."

"Melanie, I won't embarrass anyone. I just want to—"

"No. All right?" she said, her voice growing strained. "I'm sorry. I am. But I'm too tired to start arguing. I want to get back home." There was something a little anxious about the way she said all this, almost frantic. "Now, where are the earrings?"

"I gave them away," I said.

"Don't give your sister a hard time," said the man in the bathing suit. "You should be grateful to her for coming all this way."

"Plenty of people in this world have no family," said the woman.

"They're out on the street," said another. A hot breeze rolled over the balcony. I felt myself growing small, weak. I looked desperately at Melanie, but she stared right back at me with her own great need.

"Are you going to open the safe or not?" said the man behind me.

"No," I said, though I felt tired enough to do it.

He slipped me into a nelson.

"Don't hurt him," said Melanie, reaching for me, then pulling back.

"I'll have this cracked in a minute," said the man on the balcony with the safe. "It's a cheapie." He put down his hammer and hefted the safe onto the balcony railing. He had it lying on its side so the bottom faced us. "Knock it on the screw there," he said to the one in the bathing suit, who picked up the hammer and began pounding away at the bottom of the safe. The noise traveled through me in waves. I thought I might pass out.

"Melanie, please help me," I said.

The man holding me tightened his grip and a web of pain spread through my shoulders. "Enough from you, kiddo," he said.

And then, out of nowhere, Gay's voice: "What's going on up there? Are you all right, L.J.?"

"Gay!" I shouted, writhing. "They're taking me back!" I managed to maneuver the man holding me out onto the balcony. Gay was with Edward, stopped just below my room.

"Who is that down there?" Melanie said, coming out onto the balcony.

"Well, well. I thought we'd never get the pleasure," said Gay. "I have a bone to pick with you, Nancy."

"Is he talking to me?" Melanie's eyes darted back and forth between Gay and me. "Please go away!" she called down.

"Not until you leave L.J. alone. He's through with you. You and your family are out of his life forever."

"Please, this is our business!" she said.

"No, Nancy, it's *my* business when your goons treat my friend like he's your property! It's my business when you stop my friend from making his own decisions!"

"Who is he?" Melanie said to me. "How does he know about our family?" She had the wild look on her face of one of those children at the Home Wrecker.

"Shut up, gimp!" said the man holding me.

"You watch your mouth!" said Edward.

"How do you know what's best for him?" said Melanie. "He doesn't even know what's best for *himself* right now!"

"He knows what's *not* best for him," said Gay. "And that's enough for me."

"We're his family," said Melanie, her hands gripping the rail. "We love him. We're bringing him home because we love him."

"If you really loved him you'd let him go."

That's when the safe went over. I don't know whether the man pushed it or it simply slipped from his hands. All I saw was it going over the railing: tipping forward, sliding a little, and then falling. It didn't tumble. It didn't spin or flip in the air. It just dropped.

The rest seemed to happen in slow motion. First there was a terrible crunching noise as the safe hit. The wheels shot off Gay's chair and bounced across the parking lot. One hit a car with such force that it shattered the driver's-side window. The chair tipped over backward and Gay was slammed against the tar, the safe on his chest. There was a popping sound, and then came the sparks, pouring right out of the underside of the chair. Gay's perfect feet stuck up in the air—one of them had a sandal on it, but the other was bare. Then Edward was shouting for an ambulance.

Some old people came hurrying out of the lobby. There was a pounding on my door. Everyone but me was rushing about the room, blurred and moth-like. I heard one of the detectives ask another for a knife and a towel. I saw my clothes being stuffed into a garbage bag. Then, when the man holding me let go, I rushed out the door.

"Get him!" I heard behind me. "Grab his arms!"

I muscled my way down the hall, now crowded with curious people. I pushed inside the stairwell and took the steps a flight at a time, but as I reached the lobby, I started to gag, to wretch on that taste welling up at the back of my throat. I could hear the detectives on the stairs. I stumbled through the lobby and then I was out in the parking lot, kneeling next to Edward, above Gay's shattered body.

Gay's face looked peaceful; he appeared strangely content, pinned to the tar, gazing up at the darkening sky. His breath came in little hisses of air. I could smell oil leaking out of the chair. One of his eyelids kept winking.

"Go, before it's too late," said Edward. "He'd want you to."

I looked around at all the people encircling us, staring. I couldn't tell which ones were the detectives; their faces all looked menac-ingly familiar. A woman in a sun hat with a fan on the brim. An old bearded man with a pack around his waist. A man in shades talking into a plastic walkie-talkie. The taste was still there, pooling in my mouth. I was too frightened to move.

"Go!" said Edward. But I couldn't.

Then, above all of this, I saw Melanie. She was standing on the balcony of my old room. She smiled sadly at me. "Run," she said, and I did.

I called the hospital round the clock, every day for the next four weeks. It got so I knew all the nurses on Gay's floor by name. Every time I called they asked me if I wanted to leave a message for Gay, and each time I said no. I didn't know how to talk to him. One day, though, I called and, instead of picking up, a nurse put me through to Gay's room.

"Hello? Gay Isbelle," he said. "Hello?"

"Gay?" I said.

"L.J. Wow. I was hoping you'd call."

"Gay, I'm so sorry about what happened. I should have—"

"Before you start apologizing, let me say something. First, there's nothing to be sorry about. I have some healing to do, some bumps and scratches, but I'm okay. In fact, I'm glad things happened the way they did. I wouldn't change a thing."

"You wouldn't?" He had suffered four broken ribs, a punctured lung, and some nerve damage to the right side of his face.

"Not a thing. This was my third ordeal, L.J., this bout with Nancy. I've dodged the bill three times. That's something."

"Gay, I have a confession to make. That wasn't Nancy at the Shores. There is no Nancy."

"I know that," said Gay.

I paused. "You do?"

"Sure."

I didn't know what to say. In the background I heard the chatter from Edward's portable TV. "Gay, I want to come with you when you go speak," I said. "I want to be your assistant."

"My assistant? God, I don't know," he said.

"Please, Gay. I want to go with you to talk to people."

"Geez. I guess that'd be all right. My assistant, L.J. Yes, I like that."

I laughed. My body felt light with joy. "L.J., your assistant!" I said.

"Come by tomorrow and we'll talk about what you'll need to do," he said.

I arrived at the hospital well before visiting hours the next day. I brought a bouquet of flowers and a bright green pillowcase for Gay. For myself I brought a legal pad to take notes on. But when I was finally allowed up, I found Gay's room empty, his bed stripped.

"Are you L.J.?" said a nurse whose voice I recognized as Gina's. I told her that yes, I was. "He left this for you," she said. She handed me an envelope, then left me alone in the room.

I sat down on the bed and turned the letter over in my hands. The trunks of palm trees wound upward past the windows. A skywriting plane began to write something, but quit after a few letters and flew off.

Finally, I opened the envelope. Inside were my sister's earrings, and a note written on a piece of hospital stationery:

To my friend L.J.,
 Happy fish, plus coin.
  Gay

———

It's been over a year since I left Florida. I live up in the cold, blue Northwest now, in a small town with rivers on both sides. All I'll say is that I work in a store that sells antique maps and globes, from when the world was not so sharply in focus. There are chimes made of tiny glass guitars over the door. I go by a new name now, the whole thing just two syllables, so quick you might miss it. My favorite things in the store are the copies of sixteenth- and seventeenth-century globes, which are guides to the hopes and fears of people back then more than they are actual globes. Huge blue-and-white tigers stalk the icy regions to the north; sea serpents slink through the oceans; the eastern shore of a misshapen North America is marked by a freckled ear of corn.

Most of these globes don't show Florida at all, but a few do, usually as a long, squiggly tube, like a deflated party balloon. On one such globe there's an oval of sunshine painted over Florida and the Gulf below, a faint golden spotlight. When I think of Gay, I like to picture him under just such a spotlight, sitting in his chair with Edward nearby, talking to an audience. In my mind he's speaking mostly to old people, but also to people recovering from disaster and misjudgment and heartbreak. He smiles at all of them out of the good side of his face as he talks. His eye is so sensitive now—I picture him wearing sunglasses if the floors are waxed too well and have a high sheen. Sometimes I imagine him wearing a wig with sideburns that never stay completely stuck to his temples; other times not.

What Gay is always talking about, when I think of him, are the moments right before his ordeals. Sometimes he talks about ordeal number one, the fire; other times number three, at the Shores; but mostly he talks about ordeal number two. He sets the scene: he says, "There was a click as the glider was released, as the bigger plane towing us let go. But there wasn't any drop or jolt. Our glider just hung there, suspended at the center of this wide ring of clouds. Then the glider dipped a bit—it nosed down the way they can—and all of a sudden the whole green mass of the Arkansas marsh rose into view. My girlfriend at the time, Julie, was seated just in front of me. She was the daughter of a nurse at the clinic I went to for my skin grafts. At one point she looked at me over her shoulder and pointed down at this one patch of marsh that was bubbling and fizzing like crazy. Boiling almost. 'Frogs,' Julie mouthed to me. It was frogs breathing at the bottom of the swamp. I remember her mouthing it to me like that, 'Frogs,' even though it was quiet inside the plane."

Right here is when he smiles biggest, despite the torn nerves, the damage; he smiles and everyone listening smiles too, because they think he's remembering that last, fragile instant up there in the plane before the crash. They never guess that he's smiling because of what he's going to say next.

About Face

MADE A MISTAKE, IS HOW IT ALL STARTED. IT WAS A SIMPLE MIS-
take, the kind anyone could have made. It was dark out, and it
was hard to see. But the city of Glens Creek did not think the
mistake was so simple, and so, to make up for it, the city decided
that I should be given a job. I was thrilled. A job! I couldn't wait to
see what it would be. I left my schedule wide open, open enough for
anything.

All summer I waited to hear about my new job. June came and
went. Then July. I tried calling the courthouse, but they always told
me the same thing: Be patient. Be patient. So I tried to do just that.
I was living with a cousin of mine named Ronald at the time. His
house was on the northern outskirts of Glens Creek, out where the
suburbs gave way to farmland. There wasn't much to do around
there, and so the waiting was painful. Ronald suggested I get a job
in the meanwhile, but I didn't want to complicate things. I was being responsible, for once.

August came and the levee dried up and then the summer was
over. Fall arrived, but everything stayed very warm. In fact, they
said on the news that autumn was turning out to be the region's
warmest since 1956. It was amazing to be a part of. Like living in
a child's drawing of autumn: the sun was everywhere at once. A
giant, shattered wagon wheel of light. The streets were painted
with fallen leaves. Wherever you walked, plump acorns fell from

the branches and hit the sidewalks with a joyous sound, a noise like people clapping in church.

I went for walks in town. I took long drives around the countryside. I became reacquainted with Ronald. He was poor, but, I learned, serious about golf. He coached at a nearby golf resort and each of his clubs had its own little suede hat the wintery green of a crisp dollar bill. Though he was only twenty-five, a few years younger than me, Ronald was quite a wonder at coaching. People called the house all day and sometimes late at night to schedule appointments with him. One of his clients, an old Pakistani gentleman, was so grateful to Ronald for his instruction that he gave Ronald a horse, the offspring of an actual prize Thoroughbred. Ronald's horse was named Captain Marvel, and though he'd been born with a leg injury that would keep him from ever racing, he was a glorious animal, gray with a blindfold of black spots across his eyes.

Ronald grazed Captain Marvel in his own modest backyard. There wasn't much room, certainly not enough for a proper barn, but Ronald was industrious and built a small wooden shelter for Captain Marvel at the yard's far end, a shelter not unlike a giant doghouse. Ronald painted the walls of Captain Marvel's house bright red, with a little golden lightning bolt over the arched entrance.

Ronald made all kinds of efforts to care for that horse. He ordered bunches of sweet green hay from a nearby farm. Once a day he offered Captain Marvel milk from a child's plastic bucket, milk with electrolytes in it, which I imagined as tiny electrical charges that I could almost see firing along Captain Marvel's ribs, popping and sparking up and down the carved muscles of his legs. But for all the power coursing through that horse, he had little opportunity to run, to really bolt. Ronald had purchased a cheap horse trailer, not much more than an aluminum crate on wheels, and once in a while, whenever he had time and could get permission, he'd drive Captain Marvel to the local high school after classes were finished and ride him back and forth across the soccer field. Captain Marvel's hooves pounded the earth so hard I could feel the thuds all the way from where I stood on the sidelines. But as I said, Ronald was a wanted man at the golf course and could rarely go galloping like that. So Captain Marvel spent most of his days in the yard, waiting inside his little red house for his chance to explode through the world. Which is how I felt too, living with Ronald, waiting to be given my job.

Just when I began to worry that the city had forgotten about me altogether, the call came.

"Miles 'Nunce' Fergus," I said into the phone. Nunce was my horn name. It's what people used to call me on trumpet.

During this phone call, I was told by a man named Sergeant Eugene Brill that my job would be to help out at About Face Juvenile Boot Camp, five miles up Route 17 from my cousin's house. He said to drop by the office sometime that week, whenever I was free, to be oriented. I drove up the next morning at dawn.

Before I left I took precautions to make sure I made a good impression. I showered and shaved; I even used some of Ronald's gel, slicking my hair back from my face. By the time I started up the car, my heart was beating hard. I sat for a moment and stared at Ronald's long, winding driveway. My new job awaited me just a few miles away. Mist was evaporating all along the driveway, being burned off by the rising sun, and as I watched, I couldn't help but feel a great hope rising in me. I turned the key and headed down to the road.

The ride to the About Face Juvenile Boot Camp was quick. As I drove, I wondered what they'd have me do. I knew about places like About Face. There was a juvenile boot camp near Roaring Green, New York, where I'd grown up, a retreat for kids who'd gone bad. It was called Rooden and my mother had always made me hold my breath when we drove by.

"For the criminals of tomorrow," my mother said.

And as I neared the port of entry to About Face, I was struck by how much the camp looked like a prison. A high fence surrounded the property with gleaming loops of razor wire on top. The buildings were blocky and fortress-like. Watching the facility loom up in the windshield made the skin on my arms and neck tingle with excitement.

At the gated entrance booth, a guard took my name and ushered me into the parking lot. I pulled in between two dark blue vans and began the long walk across the lawn. To the west lay the barracks and to the east stood a set of obstacle courses. Rope bridges and ladders, tires chained together over pits of mud.

As I neared the main office, I saw an elephant of a man standing in front of the entrance, smoking a cigarette. He smiled and saluted me. "Mr. Fergus?" he said. "We spoke on the phone. I'm Eugene Brill, the camp director." He wore fatigues and a tented hat that reminded me of paper boats I used to float down the gutter.

I saluted back. I'd worn a sleeveless shirt to suggest an air of toughness. I'd always considered myself leanly muscular, but standing here next to Sergeant Brill I realized that I was just plain skinny.

"The drive up all right?" he said. "We've had a problem with deer in the road. That's an interesting hairdo you have."

As for my general appearance, I am a white, plain-looking person. Dark eyes. Average height. The only thing abnormal about me is my head. I have a small shock of white hair in the center of it.

"Sir, this is from scar tissue, sir," I told him.

"Well, allow me to remove my foot from my mouth and apologize, Mr. Fergus. And you don't have to call me 'sir.' You're a drill instructor now. You're Sergeant Fergus. As per the city, you're supposed to work here at least three days a week. If you want, you can work up to five. You've got seven hundred and sixty hours to fill. 'As per'? Is that the right expression? 'As per'?"

"Can I work seven days straight through?" I said.

Sergeant Brill smiled. "Judge Neal said you were raring to go. He told me you called his office near twenty times between June and August, asking what your assignment was going to be."

"I won't let you down."

"I know you won't, Sergeant Fergus," said Sergeant Brill. "As you probably know already, around here we basically specialize in this. Boo!" He suddenly contorted his face into a thing of horror: lips peeled back from his clenched teeth in a terrible grin, his bottom jaw humped out like an ape's, his eyes wide and bulging, smoke curling from his nose.

"See that? See how you jumped back a step, but then stood tall quick? Tells me a lot about you, Sergeant Fergus," said Sergeant Brill, his face having returned to normal. "Quite a lot. Tells me that you're a little nervous, a little scared, but that you're also determined to stand up for yourself, to prove yourself. Tells me you're eager. Am I right?"

"Yes," I told him, and he was right. I was scared. And I was determined to do well at About Face. I saw it as a last chance of sorts. Because at twenty-nine, I was no Ronald. No one was calling the house asking for me. I had no degrees. My longest stay at any one job had been six and a half months. But what I hoped was that About Face would be my chance to get back in the race, to redeem myself. After all, the camp was designed to help children get their lives on track, and I'd been a child myself when things had spun off course for me.

"You crack through a person's front when you scare him, Sergeant Fergus," said Sergeant Brill. "You penetrate his personal facade. His true colors come out when he's afraid, who he really is. You can work with that. That's what we do with these kids. We scare them straight, as the old expression goes."

"Get their true colors out in the open. Then work with that," I said, nodding.

He laughed. "Don't worry. That stuff isn't going to be your department."

Not my department? I felt the tightening of disappointment in my chest.

"I hear you play the trumpet," said Sergeant Brill.

I told him I played clean, hard trumpet.

Sergeant Brill picked up a drawstring sack sitting on the flagpole's marble base and handed it to me. "This belonged to a friend of mine."

I opened the bag and found a trumpet inside, a Blessing with a five-inch bell. I fingered the valves. They were stiff, but pumped smoothly. The last trumpet I played had been played before me by a seal at an amusement park. What I mean is that I hadn't touched an instrument as nice as this one in over six years.

"That's half your job there," said Sergeant Brill. "You'll play reveille in the morning to wake up the cadets, then taps at night to put them to bed. Right now all we've got is a recording. Piece of shit. Sounds like a someone whistling through a toilet paper tube."

I asked him what the second half of my job was going to be. I wanted to do more.

Sergeant Brill stubbed his cigarette out on the ground and then picked up the butt and slipped it into his pocket. "The second half of the job is my daughter, Mr. Fergus."

"Sir?" Behind us, the sprinklers started up, ticking graceful arcs of water over the lawn.

"My daughter, Lexington. Lex. She was born with her kidneys gummed up. The last few years she's started having health problems, real ones. I don't want to get into it. Believe me, it's heartbreaking stuff. You know what dialysis is? That's the second half of your job. To drive her up to the hospital in Albany three times a week to get her blood cleaned."

Take the girl to get her blood cleaned. I liked the way that sounded. It had a vaguely heroic quality to it, and I began to forget my disappointment over not getting to work with the cadets.

"Hey, be nice to her," he said, looking down at his boots. "All this dialysis stuff depresses the hell out of her. It's made her into an introvert. She's shy—I mean, she doesn't have any friends."

"When do I start?" I said.

"Hell, today," said Sergeant Brill. "Right now."

At eleven o'clock that morning, after filling out forms in the office, I set out with Lexington in one of the camp's vans. How my life had changed since dawn! I now had on a uniform: a tan shirt with little buttoned flaps on the shoulders, tan army pants, and shiny black boots. I felt like playing my new horn right there in the van, felt like shouting over my shoulder to Lexington that she shouldn't worry because she was in good hands, but she gave no sign of even noticing me; she sat in the back row with her head leaned against the window.

Though Lexington was twenty-one, she looked about four years younger. She was small, hardly taller than five feet, and while she had hips and breasts, there was still a newness, an awkwardness really, to the curves and flarings of her body. She had dark kinky hair with miniature curls, and that first day in the bus she wore Chap Stick with flecks of sparkle in it. The steroids she took made her face overly plump, but in an appealing, pillowy way. Whether Lex had actually stopped aging because of her kidney problems or was simply a late bloomer, I couldn't tell, but there was something both weary and innocent in her face that I found myself immediately drawn to.

Another drill sergeant, a black man named Williams, rode in the passenger seat. He wore tight, wire-rim glasses, and had neatly trimmed his mustache to look like a perfect third eyebrow beneath his nose. Williams was along to make sure I did my job.

"So, where are you from?" he said as we passed a stand where people sold pumpkins and bunches of fresh corn.

"I'm from all over," I said. "I played the trumpet for a long time. I was *a jazz musician.*" I said this very loudly so that Lexington might hear.

"Cool beans," he said. We drove a while longer and Williams told me about his childhood, growing up "on the streets," how hard it had been. The landscape was beautiful. Oak and birch and poplar trees. The sun flashing through the branches. Lex looked so pretty in back. Suddenly Williams paused and turned to me.

"What's that noise?" he said. "Do you hear a whistling?"

"What noise?" I said, though I knew very well what noise.

"I think . . . It's coming from you. From your face."

"Oh, that. Some of the bones behind my nose are a little out of place. The wind can get in there sometimes."

Williams scrutinized my face. "Do you box?"

"No."

"You get in a fight? That why they sent you here?"

I noticed Lexington watching me from the backseat.

"I had an accident when I was a kid," I said. "It was a stupid thing. There are lots of little bones behind your face that you can knock loose pretty easily. The sphenoid bone. The ethmoid. It's a fragile system."

Williams leaned over and looked up into my nose. "Well, that's a seriously loud whistle you got going on in there. It sounds like a kazoo, you know? Like someone honking on a kazoo."

I glanced at Lex and saw that she was still watching.

"Can you hear it yourself?" Williams asked, still peering up into my nose. "It's like *toooot. Tooooot.*"

I rolled up my window.

Williams tried to get me to talk about myself some more, about what had landed me at About Face, but after I dodged his questions a couple of times, he grew bored and turned on the radio. The rest of the drive was uneventful. Lex kept to herself.

When we reached the city limits, I got off the highway and followed the blue H signs to the hospital. I parked as close as I could get to the entrance. Lex climbed to her feet and came toward me down the aisle.

"I'll be right here when you're done inside," I said as she passed.

"It takes three hours," she said. Her eyes were as green as limes. "You should go walk around town."

"What would you recommend seeing?" I said to Lex.

She gave a tired smile. "Anything but the hospital," she said, and then left the van.

I watched Lex cross the parking lot. At one point a car pulled out of a spot in front of her, and even though it didn't come close to hitting her, she gave a little frightened jump, then stopped in her tracks. The car paused and the driver waved her across his path, but she insisted he go first.

"Nervous little thing," said Williams. "So skittish."

I thought about what Brill had said about her not having any friends. Things had been the same way for me at her age. I'd had a hard time of it, and watching her stand there alone and frightened in the parking lot, I felt my affection for Lex bloom.

She glanced over at me as the car finished its K-turn, and I waved and gave her my warmest grin. She smiled a tight-lipped, friendly smile, but even as she did, she crossed her arms over her chest, as though protecting her heart from me.

When I was ten, a bullet came screaming down out of the sky and slammed into the top of my head. I was on my way to school, walking through the field behind the schoolyard. My book bag was on my back, my hair was combed and still wet from the shower. I was already late, but I didn't care. Because the day before, a girl I liked had passed me a note—Stephanie Leroux, I still remember her name. The note said that tomorrow she'd pass me a romance note, and so on that morning I was taking my time getting to school, enjoying my own anticipation. The day was perfect. Warm, with a glowing blue sky.

I remember hearing a faint static in the atmosphere, a kind of electric crackle. The next thing I knew I was lying on the ground, staring up at the clouds with a metal pebble lodged and cooling in my skull.

I learned later that there had been a race nearby, a charity marathon, and that the man in charge had mistakenly fired an actual bullet into the air to get things started. He came to the hospital almost every day I was there and cried into the rumpled edge of my bed. The woman who won the race also came by once, and gave me a trophy with a man on top, a man painted gold holding a ring of laurels over his head like a shield.

The doctors said that I was lucky, that if the bullet had been falling even a fraction faster, it would have pierced my skull, instead of sticking in the bone, and likely caused serious brain damage, if not death. As it was, the injury, while painful, wasn't all that serious. "It's that thick skull of yours that saved you," said one doctor. He chuckled, then gave me a little punch in the arm. I had a seam of staples down the front of my head. Metal wires ran through my face like whiskers.

I was in the hospital only a month and a half, but when I left, I found that I was afraid to go outside. I developed an irrational fear of lightning—I thought I could sense it coiled in the air all the time, even on sunny days—and if I had to travel anywhere uncovered, I'd start to shake and sweat and stutter. My parents walked me around town day after day to help, but nothing changed. Children picked on me at school because of my jumpiness and my new white hair. They called me "skunk," even after I dyed the white patch brown. They beat me up. I became afraid. My parents bought me a trumpet, which I played alone in my room. I was left back once, then twice. After that I left school altogether.

It's funny how a hit like that can be all it takes to knock you off course. Hardly more than a tap or nudge, and suddenly you find that you've become someone entirely new, some dark version of yourself you never thought possible. One minute you're a boy with promise, you're an honors student, you have friends, a future; and the next you're twenty-nine and living in the basement of your cousin's house. Where has your chance at happiness gone? You don't know. Whenever people talk about how the neighborhood has gone downhill, it feels like they're talking about you.

I worked at my father's comic book store. I delivered tanks of carbonated water for a soda company. I played the trumpet around town for extra money. I landscaped. I worked at a warehouse where they used pig fat to make fireplace logs that could burn all day. At night, I often traveled to Albany and drove up and down the fanciest streets, the ones with the most expensive houses, and watched the lighted windows slide by through the darkness like trays displaying all the things I didn't have. Now and then I thought about stealing, about hurting people, but more often I wanted to be the one to catch someone else doing things like that. As I drove, I often fantasized about spotting some catastrophe I could prevent—spying a prowler creeping through the hedge; catching sight of the fire just now starting in the kitchen of that house. I wanted to be there to save someone else from the kind of disaster that had happened to me, because I felt that if I did, maybe I'd get another chance at things. Maybe someone would help steer me back to where I was supposed to be.

Every morning I tell myself that things will turn around, that today will be a new start. I lean in close to the bathroom mirror and say, "Ready. Set. Go."

Though most of the cadets at About Face wanted to improve themselves, there were some, a handful, who went out of their way to be as bad as possible. A few were in gangs and had cryptic tattoos branded on their arms and necks. Some had relatives in prison, so their desire to end up there made at least a bit of sense. But others just seemed to enjoy being cruel. There wasn't much room for them to do wrong, but they liked to throw their weight around. They teased and tried to injure other boys, some much bigger than themselves. They went around jabbing erections at each other, and at the drill sergeants. One cadet, a boy named Unger, refused to march in step; he'd stagger this way and that like a drunk, or shove the boy ahead of him and try to topple the whole line. Another, a Spaniard from New York City, kept hitting other boys in the groin with his belt, even after Brill punished him with fifteen-, sixteen-, even eighteen-mile marches around the grounds. The one that worried me most, though, was a local boy named Haden McCrae.

McCrae didn't act out the way the other boys did; he didn't fight or misbehave, but there was a lazy, unworried way about him that troubled all the drill sergeants. He always looked at us in a sleepy, heavy-lidded manner—he looked at us like he'd seen it all before. It was this calmness in the face of authority that made him so popular with the other cadets. This and the fact that at sixteen, McCrae had pulled an old man from his car, robbed him, and kicked him in the head until he was near death. Now, at almost eighteen, he was one of the oldest boys at the camp. McCrae was tall and lanky and pale, his face covered with thick, brown smears of freckle. His hair, before being shaved when he arrived at About Face, had been bright orange, and I could always spot his head from far off, glowing like a hot coal among the others.

Most of the grounds at About Face had an air of the military about them: everything sheared flat and laid out at right angles, as though plotted on a grid of crossed sabers. But below the camp lay thick woods, woods that suggested play and joy and mischief. The pine trees stood in bunches, their branches grown together in dark, tangled canopies. The tunnel-like paths beneath them twisted and wound this way and that, past other kinds of trees—gnarled maples and birch tree   with papery bark that unraveled in long, teasing curls. There were jags of rock to hide behind, patches of canary grass high as my waist. And the woods had a downward tilt to them—they sloped down from the camp in a way that implied decline, a kind of crumbling collapse toward Lake Deed, which lay below, and which was black and miles around and always fringed with a foamy white discharge. There were deep currents in the lake, too. If you watched it closely for a long time, you could detect a slow churning motion, a sluggish kind of spinning.

I had my first encounter with McCrae at Lake Deed.

This land below About Face was to be used to expand the camp. Sergeant Brill hoped to get a permit from the state to raze most of the trees by next year, and he often punished the camp's worst cadets, like McCrae, by forcing them to help clear the walkway leading down through the trees to the lake. When I wasn't on trumpet or driving Lex to the hospital, Sergeant Brill had me do menial things around the camp—help dolly boxes of food from the supply trucks into the canteen closet, or restock the bathrooms. But sometimes when he sent cadets down to the lake he had me go with the other drill sergeants "to have an extra set of eyes around," as he said. So I tagged along and watched drill sergeants like Williams tie the cadets together by their waists with a leash-like metal cable and then march them through the locked fencing at the back of the camp and down into the woods. I followed them through the trees and hovered at the edge of the group, looking for any kind of acting out. There was an after-school camp for wealthy children somewhere on the other side of the water, and though we never saw them out on the lake itself, on still days we could hear those other children playing on their beach—the yelps, the laughter, the gasps brought on by the sting of cold water. I often caught McCrae staring out over the dark, spinning expanse in the direction of those voices.

And with such hatred in his eyes! Like if he had a second's chance he'd split their heads open one by one, like pieces of firewood.

Once, during the cadets' lunch hour, I saw McCrae, still attached to the others by the leash, fidgeting with something by the edge of the water. The other three drill sergeants were eating their lunches and talking nearby, and though I wasn't supposed to address the cadets myself, I went over.

"McCrae, what are you up to?" I said in a friendly tone. I never spoke harshly to the cadets. I figured that maybe if I seemed relaxed around them, they might open up to me.

McCrae stood up, but when he glanced over his shoulder and saw who I was, he kept his back to me. I could see that he had something in his hands. "The music man," he said. He had started the cadets calling me "music man."

"Hey, music man," said Cadet Spitz, sitting on a rock by the shore. "You got some bird shit in your hair."

I reached up to feel my head before realizing that he was talking about my patch of white hair. The cadets laughed, the cable between them shaking. Spitz looked at McCrae as though for approval, but McCrae stood facing the lake.

"Funny, Spitz," I said. "Hey, McCrae. What's in your hands there, buddy?"

"Nothing to worry about, music man," he said, his back still to me. The water lapped at the shore.

"McCrae. Do me a favor and show me your hands," I said. Out of the corner of my eye I saw another drill sergeant approaching. I wanted to handle this before he took over.

"Come on now, music man," said McCrae. "Let's not start acting like a drill sergeant."

"What's that supposed to mean?" I said, growing angry.

"It means we all know you were assigned to this job. It's no secret. Cadet Granz over there thinks they sent you here because you're one of those special retards who, you know, can do some things real good, like count or play a instrument. No offense. But I'm of the mind that you did something wrong to end up here, just like us. So what's the story?"

"My story is I'm here to serve my community, McCrae. And as an official drill sergeant I'm ordering you to turn around! Right now!"

McCrae laughed. "Okay, okay. Don't get all riled up."

"McCrae!" shouted the other drill sergeant. "Shut up and turn around!" He grabbed McCrae and spun him around.

McCrae let something flap up out of his hands. It rushed at me, beating its wings against my chest and neck. I grabbed it, and saw that it was a baby loon. How McCrae had managed to catch the bird, I don't know. Attached to its leg was a luggage tag, one of the slips we tied to the cadets' duffels when we shipped them in or out. *Cunt*, it read in McCrae's lefty handwriting.

"Empty your pockets, McCrae," said the drill sergeant.

McCrae pulled his pockets inside out and a dozen little pieces of paper fluttered to the ground. *Ass rape*, said one. *Big diseased cock*, said another.

"That's the end of lunch, then," said the drill sergeant. Then he addressed the other cadets. "Drop what you're eating and get back to work." The boys sighed and swore under their breath, then got to their feet and started working again. As the other drill sergeant pushed him past me, McCrae shot me a sad look, a look that said he was disappointed in me, as though I'd let him down somehow. I looked at the loon, the tag still attached to its leg. I pictured it landing on the other side of the lake, on the beach where the children from the other camp were playing; I pictured it landing right in some little girl's hands.

"Nunce" is short for *enunciate*, which is what people used to say I did best on horn: stepping hard and clear on each note in a commanding, declarative way. But this is a style no one wants to play alongside. It's the style of someone who learned to play alone, not in a band like most people. I'm no good at call-and-response. How I play is like someone talking loudly to himself, yelling at himself.

Each morning at five fifty I took my place beneath the flagpole, dew still beading the grass, the occasional low fog stewing around my ankles, and waited there until it was time to play reveille. I listened to the rope gently bell against the flagpole. I watched a golden outline materialize around the distant treetops. And then, right at six o'clock, I emptied myself into that horn. Sometimes I rang loud enough to knock the birds from the trees. At night, I returned to the spot and played taps the same way.

When Brill didn't need me to do much, I practiced down by the lake. He'd given me permission to use his locker because it was larger than the standard lockers, which wouldn't fit my horn. He was one of the only sergeants with keys to the back gate, so I was always careful when I borrowed them to go practice.

I thought someone might complain about my playing, maybe someone who lived on the lake, or even someone from that other camp across the water, but no one ever did. Even when I played at night, imagining that I was playing just for Lex, no one got upset. In the evenings I tried to play softly, hoarsely. I crooned out songs like "In the Still of the Night" and "Blue Hawaii," songs of romance and longing, coaxing songs, while the lake spun slowly around, black and sparkling as a new record.

Every few days I drove Lex back and forth to the hospital. Rich northeastern forest hemmed the road nearly all the way, and as time passed, I got to watch the onset of the frost, the first snow. Williams stopped tagging along after the second week, so the rides were just me and Lex. She always sat in the last row, the farthest away from me. The first few weeks I tried to make conversation, but she kept cutting me short, answering with a nod or a shake of the head. There was no blaming her. By the time we were off to the hospital, her system was clogged with nearly three days' worth of urea, so much that even from the driver's seat I could see how egg-pale her skin was. It itched her, too. She kept a housepainter's brush in her purse that she often took out and used to scratch herself. I'd watch in the mirror as she feathered the brush up and down her neck and arms and thighs. Occasionally her skin pained her so much that she cried, quietly though, with her head leaned against the window. As winter deepened, the trip grew much longer. Deer appeared in the road more often and slipped and spun on patches of ice while trying to get out of the way. The sky became a gray faucet of snow. I had to drive with caution.

One snowy day in December the drive took an especially long time. Usually the trip took about forty minutes, but that afternoon an hour into the ride we were hardly more than two-thirds of the way there. Lex had given up scratching with her brush and now rubbed her arms and legs with her open hands. Then, without warning, she came up and sat next to me in the passenger seat.

"How much farther?" she said, her eyes desperate.

"At least half an hour," I said. She began to cry.

"I'm sorry," she said. "It just hurts. It won't stop itching. It's like the itch is too deep to get to."

"What can I do to help?" I said, trying not to sound too eager. The windshield wipers creaked as they swatted at the gathering snow.

"Can you pull over for a minute?" she said.

I pulled over to the side of the road and put the hazards on.

"Here," she said, and gave me the brush. "It helps if someone else uses this while I concentrate on blocking the itch out. My dad usually does it for me. Do you mind?"

I told her I didn't mind.

She closed her eyes and rested her head against the seat.

I started stroking her arms with the brush, and tiny flakes of skin, like dandruff, fell to the floor. The hazard lights ticked on and off.

"That feels good," she said, her voice shaky from crying. Her face appeared puffy from the betamethasone, but with the soft winter light falling on her skin, she looked eerily beautiful, like a statue from atop a gravestone.

After a while I laid the brush in her lap and used my hand. I rubbed hard on her jeaned knees, her shoulders. Soon she was able to breathe through her nose and then her breathing evened out, calmed. She kept her eyes closed; her expression was one of resolve. I told her I wouldn't let anything happen to her. I rubbed her neck and told her it would be all right.

When we finally reached the hospital, she asked me to come in with her. A male nurse led us to the fourth floor, where he eventually hooked Lex up to a device that resembled a large beige sewing machine. Two thick tubes ran into her arm. Dirty blood ran out of her through one tube and into the humming chamber of the machine and then out of the machine through the other tube and finally back into her arm. The dirty blood looked no different from the clean; both were a dark, syrupy red. I couldn't tell one from the other.

We didn't say much during that first time. Pop music crackled in from a radio shaped like a cartoon cat perched on the sill. Snow fell past the window, then turned to rain. At one point Lex said, "I heard you practicing your trumpet the other day. You played 'Embraceable You.' That was my grandparents' song."

"That's one of my favorite songs. I love that song," I said. "I learned it the first year I started playing, back when I was thirteen. I was in this YMCA program where coaches taught you a skill or a hobby—you know, to socialize easier? They even had a woman there who could teach you how to ride a unicycle—which still seems ridiculous to me. What popular kid did you know who ever rode around school on a unicycle? Am I talking too much?"

Lex laughed. "A little."

I nodded and was silent for a while. The dialysis machine whirred. I watched her blood slide through the tubes.

"My father told me what you did, you know, to wind up working at the camp."

I felt my face grow flushed. What I'd done to wind up at About Face was try to help someone. I'd been driving along one night, just coasting through the streets, when I spied a man stabbing an old woman in the ear right on her own porch. I watched him take a knife from his pocket and start digging its point into her eardrum. So I did what anyone else would have done. I got out of my car and yanked him off. Then I knocked him to the sidewalk. As the man hit the curb, his arm made a sound like dry pasta breaking over a pot of boiling water. But he hadn't been robbing the old woman. In fact, she was his mother and he'd been testing her hearing aid with a sonic wand.

"It was dark," I said.

"No, I think it's funny. It's romantic, kind of. Chivalrous," she said. "I see you lingering by groups of cadets sometimes. Standing on the sidelines. You really want to help out."

"Yes," I said.

She peeked beneath her bandage. "Sometimes I wonder how well the camp works," she said. "We get letters pretty often from kids who've made something of their lives after being sent to us. Dad puts them up in the barracks. But we also get kids who come back again and again." She nodded at the arm with the tubes in it. "They're like me. You can clean them up, but it's only a matter of time before they go sour again."

"That's not how I see you," I said.

She smiled. Ringlets of dark brown hair hung around her face. "Good. That's not how I see you either," she said.

She slept on the way back. I drove a full ten miles per hour below the limit, my eyes on the road. I felt like everything important was in my hands, which I kept planted at ten and two the entire way.

After that things were different during our trips. We still didn't talk much—on the way to Albany Lex was uncomfortable, on the way back, drained—but the feeling inside the van, the feeling between us, changed. She always sat up next to me, and I often massaged her limbs with her brush. She was like every girlfriend I'd never had when I was younger: fun, playful, patient. I wanted her, and wanted to protect her at the same time. We started listening to country music on the radio together and soon enough we both learned all the popular songs and artists. There was one song we both enjoyed about a man and a woman who were kept apart by their trucking jobs but who talked on the CB all the time. The song was called "It's Not

Over Till It's Over, Over," and there was a part in it when the man's truck and the woman's truck pass going opposite directions in the night and they honk their horns at each other. At that part I'd lay on the horn, or Lex would take my trumpet and blow into it, making a terrible squawk. We found other songs to like, too, but that one was my favorite. I bet they still play it on the radio. I bet if you get up and turn the dial to country right now, you might hear it this very moment. It's that good.

I always stayed with Lex while her blood was being cleaned. I would read her magazines, or if the TV was free in the next room, I'd roll it in and we'd watch a movie on the VCR. They only had a few movies that weren't for children, but I didn't mind. One day, I rolled in the TV and pressed play and a dirty movie came on. Lex laughed and clapped her hands over her mouth, but when I turned it off, which I did right away, she asked me through her hands if I could put it back on, so I did. In the movie a naked man was running back and forth between two women lying on their stomachs. One wore sunglasses and high boots and was demanding, a boss; the other was just a girl, coy and playful, biting her lip and smiling at him over her shoulder. They were both beautiful, though, with their bottoms raised on pillows and rocking back and forth for him. The man's body was shiny with sweat and he kept wiping his brow and sitting down on the floor and panting in an exaggerated, comical way. But then one of the women would beckon to him and he'd struggle to his feet and climb on top of her.

"Oh my God. He only has one thingy. One ball," Lex said, giggling.

"It happens," I said.

We watched for a while, me hesitantly, embarrassed, with a painful erection, and Lex with her eyes glued to the screen. She looked more interested than aroused, though, fascinated in a clinical way.

I wondered if she'd ever slept with a man before. Eventually the movie flickered to static.

"Do you have a girlfriend?" Lex asked quite suddenly, just as I was turning off the TV.

I felt my throat tighten. "No," I said, sitting down next to her.

She began to say something, then stopped. She smiled and scrunched up her nose. "There's a guy I like. I have a crush on someone," she said. "Nobody thinks much of him, but I don't know, he makes me laugh. This is between you and me, promise?" She put her hand on top of mine. Her fingers were hot and clammy.

"I promise," I said, and squeezed her hand.

"It's a guy I've been hanging out with pretty regularly. Do you know what I mean?"

"I think so," I said. Patches of my skin kept giving off shocks of excitement, now at the base of my back, now along my scalp.

Suddenly Lex put her other hand to her head. Her cheeks were red. "God, I'm terrible at this stuff. Let's just forget about it."

"No, go on," I said.

"It's silly. I feel like a teenager." She pressed the button that called the nurse. "I think I'm all done here," she said.

"Wait. You can say it," I said. I could hear the nurse approaching. "Lex. Please say the words."

"Fine. All right," she said. "I have a crush on Haden McCrae. We've been hanging out down by the lake. You can't tell anyone. I'll kill you if you tell."

Haden McCrae. A nauseous feeling descended on me. A week ago I'd found a luggage tag by the lake with *Titty-humper* written on it. I wanted to tell her how I felt about McCrae, and how I felt about her, but I could see how much she liked him there in her expression. Just then the nurse came in to unhook her. She asked me if I'd mind waiting outside.

"Whatever. Sure. You bet," I said, and went out into the hall.

Through the door I heard the nurse ask Lexington, "Is that your boyfriend?"

"Miles?" said Lex. "No, he just drives me here."

"Miles," said the nurse. "I had a toad named Miles when I was a girl. My mom made me throw him out because she said he'd give me warts on my hands. Hmmm."

"Ugh. Warts," said Lex.

I wanted to kick in the door and clap their fucking faces together like blackboard erasers.

A few days later I played sick when it was time to drive Lex to the hospital. I had no desire to talk to her; the thought of hearing about her and McCrae made me sick. I spent the day in the gymnasium mopping up leaks. Snow had piled on the roof and caused some damage. Every now and then a trickle of icy gray water would fall from the vaulted ceiling to the floor. I stood in the corner, leaning against the padded wall with a mop in my hand. Some cadets were engaged in backbreaking running drills on the basketball courts. Others trained with weights over by the rope climb. Watching them sprint and heft and pant, I wondered how many would go home and do well, make people proud, and how many would continue sailing toward ruin. Just as I was thinking about this, McCrae passed into my line of vision. He was inside a grid of cadets jogging across the basketball courts, but when he glanced at me, it was as though he were the only one in the room; everyone else rushed by, but for me McCrae was frozen in place, suspended midstride, his sneakers inches off the ground. He had a look of furious anguish on his face, his cheeks flushed and nearly as red as his stubbled head. Staring back into his eyes, which seemed to radiate hatred for me, I felt I could see his true nature, his black, hidden center. It was like when you put a diving mask to the surface of the ocean and can suddenly peer right into the murky depths with piercing clarity. I could hear him talking to me, saying, "I'm headed toward her, music man. I'm plunging down from the clouds and I'm going to knock her on her ass so hard that she'll never find her feet again. Here I come, music man. Here I come."

All at once I remembered Sergeant Brill's words to me on that first day, about fear being the way to expose a person's true colors, the way to penetrate his facade, and a plan took shape. I knew what I had to do.

I found Lex on the way out of the mess hall that evening. The sunset was gorgeous behind her head, a fiery parachute settling on the pine trees. "How are you feeling? I missed you today," she said. She was shivering a bit; it was the end of February but still hard winter.

"I'm fine," I said. "I'll be up for it next time."

"I haven't heard you play down at the lake the last few nights." She pulled her coat more tightly around her. "I thought maybe you were mad about Haden."

"Mad?" I said. "Not at all."

"He's not the easiest person to like, I know, but he's different around me. He—"

"Really. Haden seems like a stand-up guy."

Lex looked at me for a moment. I tried to give my most convincing smile. Then, thank God, she laughed. "I was all ready to defend him to you. I thought you were going to tell me what a punk he is. He'd never hurt me, you know."

"I don't go down to the lake because I don't want to run into you guys," I said. "Tell me when you head down there, so I can avoid you."

"We only sneak down on Tuesdays and every other Sunday. Those are the nights Fender is off and I can use his keys. Tonight he's here, so we're not going down until Tuesday."

The muscles of my face began to ache from smiling. "I think that's great, Lex. I'm happy for you." Tuesday, I thought. Two days until Tuesday.

"Really?"

"I've got to get back to my bunk. I'll see you soon." I gave her a quick pat on the arm and hurried off just as the last good light fled the sky.

In the couple of days leading up to Tuesday, I avoided Lex as best I could. She didn't have to go to the hospital until Wednesday, so our paths didn't cross. I saw McCrae once, climbing the chain web with some other cadets, but he didn't notice me.

Tuesday finally arrived. I took it as my day off. I spent the day with Ronald: we ate breakfast together, and then we passed the rest of the afternoon at the golf resort. It was too cold for outdoor golf, of course, but the lodge was open, as were the driving cages beneath it. I preferred the lodge this way, with the course closed, as I sometimes felt my old nervousness act up out on the holes with all the golf balls whizzing by high overhead.

Ronald dressed casually, in a college sweatshirt and patched jeans—to look at him you'd think he worked in the kitchen—but as always, almost everyone we passed came up and congratulated me on having Ronald for a cousin. When we sat down for lunch, people wouldn't stop buying us things. Every ten minutes a pair of drinks or a plate of hors d'oeuvres found its way to our table and some couple or other across the room would wave or nod or give us a thumbs-up. Sometimes when this happened I pretended that it was me, and not Ronald, that they were applauding; I imagined that they all knew what I was about to do at the camp, what I was going to do for Lex, and admired me for this.

By the time we got home it was past nine, and I encouraged Ronald to go to bed soon. We were both a little drunk and had early days tomorrow. We should try to get more rest in general, I said, clapping him on the back. Captain Marvel knew something was happening. He kept pacing back and forth in the yard, snorting and pawing up big patties of frozen earth. I was afraid that Ronald might grow worried about him, but he didn't seem to notice. He agreed with me that it had been a long day, and so we said good night and then he headed upstairs to bed. I lay down on the couch and waited. All the while Captain Marvel was trotting back and forth, giving off excited whimpers.

When I was sure Ronald was asleep, I got up and slipped out of the house and into the yard. Captain Marvel reared up a bit on his hind legs when he saw me and then stamped back down.

"Captain Marvel. Stop," I commanded, and he stood firmly on the grass. I went around to the garage, hitched the trailer to Ronald's truck, and drove it around in front of the yard. Ronald had left a cup of coffee in the drink holder and the coffee's surface was skimmed with ice. When I opened the gate, Captain Marvel walked right up the ramp without my having to say a word.

The ride toward About Face was smooth. I drove with the windows down. Deer lined the road like an audience. One appeared every few seconds, standing there with its front hooves on the shoulder. The night air was studded with frost particles that made the skin on my face tingle. A great trill spun out of the cavern of my nose and filled the cab with a high but masculine sound, like the whistle issued from the deck of a warship launching out to sea.

Just before the long driveway up to the camp, I pulled off the road and killed the engine. I got out and opened the trailer gate and down came Captain Marvel, his neck steaming in the cold. I threw the knitted mat that Ronald used as a saddle over Captain Marvel's back and then I climbed on. Through all this, Captain Marvel stood still as an oak, the breath huffing out of his nostrils in spirals of vapor. How tall he was! My feet seemed to dangle two stories off the ground. I patted him on the neck and down we went into the woods.

We wound our way through the pines, surefooted, stepping easily over exposed roots and stones. The night sky was clear, the moon bright. I didn't yet know what, exactly, I was going to do with Captain Marvel when I found Lex and McCrae, only that nobody could experience this horse under me charging straight at him and not be struck with terror. And I knew that, once terrified, McCrae would reveal his true, repulsive self.

When we reached Lake Deed, I steered Captain Marvel out of the woods and rode him along the pebbled shore. The moon cast an eerie light across the lake, and as we moved toward the camp I imagined myself a knight traveling through a barren landscape of ice and stone.

Just as we neared the beach directly beneath About Face, I spotted figures moving down by the water. I sneaked Captain Marvel uphill into the trees.

"Say that again, in my ear, though," I heard someone say.

Then something too low for me to hear.

Next the first voice again. "Keep that up. Keep talking like that."

I peered around the tree. My stomach seized. Lex and McCrae sat on a blanket, facing each other, her legs draped over his. I could see his hands underneath her sweater, mangling her breasts. She had her mouth to his neck. A strange red light coated them both. At first I thought the light was actually emanating from them, from their bodies, but then I noticed two small propane heaters sitting on either side of them, the grilles glowing hot.

McCrae laughed and pulled Lex toward him. "Come here, Lexy," he said. *Lexy!*

I heard her giggle, the exact same laugh she made when I kidded her in the van, and then she began to rub his thighs. His legs were impossibly long, like tongs. Lex seemed enveloped by them. I wanted to rush in and pull her out of those pincers. I knew that all I had to do was give Captain Marvel the slightest kick, just a brush of the heels, and he'd burst from the woods with me on his back. I could see it happening already, see us charging toward them both, tearing down the beach, Captain Marvel's hooves hammering the shore, causing the ice fixed between the pebbles to shatter and spray up behind us. We'd run at the two of them so fast, the wind would blow my hair straight back.

I pictured us barreling toward Lex and McCrae until they were right in front of us, until Captain Marvel's crushing hooves were bearing down on them. Then, in my mind, we ground to a stop, Captain Marvel's chest heaving, and when I pulled on his mane, up he went, rearing high into the air on his hind legs. As he rose, his hoof struck one of the heaters, and its grille exploded in a burst of sparks. Captain Marvel called out, his voice a sound that in years to come I would try to imitate on my trumpet again and again. And when I looked down from the summit of his back I saw—somewhere far, far beneath us—Lex and McCrae crouching in the sand. She was huddled against him, her face buried in his chest, the little knuckles of her spine flashing in and out of view as sparks shot from the busted heater. McCrae was looking up at me with a face split wide open by fear—his eyes wild, his mouth twisted up in a grimace. Then, before he could help it, he did exactly what I'd known he'd do: he pushed Lex away from him, toward Captain Marvel, and scrambled backward, out of the way.

I could see Lex's terror as Captain Marvel's hooves came plunging toward her, her shock, and then relief, as they crashed down on either side of her thin shoulders. When she finally looked over at McCrae, I could see the shame on his face, and the rage at being exposed.

"Lexy, he made me do it. He tricked me," he'd say, reaching out for her.

But it would be too late already. Because Lex would be climbing up behind me, sliding her hands around my waist. I could practically feel the warm pressure of her cheek against my back, hear her saying, "Thank you, thank you," into my jacket. I could see myself carrying her away from him.

I watched them a moment longer from the woods, savoring my own anticipation. I thought again of McCrae's horrified face, the skin pulled tight, teeth bared. An owl hooted and the sound echoed across the lake. Captain Marvel's ribs twitched. I tightened my grip on his mane.

But just as I was readying myself, McCrae jumped to his feet and held his hand out to Lex. She took it and he pulled her up and started leading her toward the edge of the lake. I felt a tingle of worry at the back of my neck. He was going to throw her in. He was going to drown her. I raised my heel. But then, instead of wading out into the water, McCrae stepped out onto its surface, pulling Lex after him. For a moment I was bewildered, but then I saw that the edge of the lake had frozen over. How far out the ice reached, though, I couldn't tell. When I craned my neck, I saw ripples at the lake's center.

Disappointment overwhelmed me as I realized I'd have to wait for the two of them to return to shore before I could make my charge. I watched as McCrae dragged Lex farther and farther out onto the ice. She wobbled clumsily as she slid behind him. At one point she lost her balance and screamed. The sound made me burn to race out there and scoop her up. I knew I'd been wrong to think McCrae would go so far as to toss her into the lake, but still, it was reckless of him to take her out there. The ice couldn't have been more than a few inches thick. Thin as a windowpane. I could practically hear the cracks veining out beneath their feet. How could he be so careless with her? And why was she letting him drag her out there? Then, even more surprisingly, she began struggling to catch up to McCrae, taking quick little steps toward him. Soon she was sliding past him, and now she was the one towing him out toward the lake's center. The sight of her hurrying away with him confused and angered me, and I wondered how McCrae had cast such a spell over her.

They wandered out farther, so far that I could barely make them out in the moonlight. Finally, McCrae began to slow and gesture for her to stop. Lex tugged on him, but he planted his feet wide and held her in place. She yanked on him, trying to pull him farther out, but McCrae reeled her back toward him. Next she made to kick his feet out from under him, but slipped and fell on her behind. Even from that distance I could hear their laughter blowing across the lake.

I watched as they lay down together on the ice. For a while, they lay with their faces cupped to its surface, peering into the glassy blackness. Later, they flipped onto their backs and gazed up at the night sky. Every few moments one of them would point to something that was invisible to me through the branches. I strained to listen to what they were saying, but all I heard was the wheezing of my face. Eventually, McCrae laid his head on Lex's stomach, and for a long time they stayed like that, his ear resting right above those damaged kidneys of hers.

I grew painfully cold. I leaned close to Captain Marvel and tried to warm myself in the vaporous heat coming off his neck. A lone cloud wheeled slowly across the moon. I rubbed my hands together to keep the circulation going.

Finally, Lex and McCrae got up and began walking back toward the shore. I shook the fatigue out of my shoulders and steeled myself. But as they stepped back onto the beach I found that I was unable to charge. I could feel the muscles in Captain Marvel's legs trembling beneath me, tensed and ready. I knew that now was the time. But an image appeared to me and made me hesitate, an image of myself on horseback, hiding in the woods, waiting like a funhouse clown for his chance to jump out and terrify someone. But that wasn't the truth, I told myself. I was about to help my friend. I was going to save Lex. My teeth were chattering now. I felt like the cold was shaking me apart. I tried to conjure up the vision of McCrae ejecting Lex from his embrace, throwing her beneath Captain Marvel's hooves, but it wouldn't materialize. I tried to imagine Lex's grateful smile as I pulled her up behind me.

McCrae came up behind her and wrapped his arms around her waist. I made myself remember those birds, the words tagged to their ankles. I said the words out loud to myself, listing them one after the other, chanting them into Captain Marvel's ear. Each one was an attack on McCrae, an ugly truth about him. I started spouting off new ones.

"Trash," I said as I watched him kiss Lex on the shoulder.

"Reject," I said as she pulled his hands tighter around her. "Piece of shit."

I watched until I couldn't think of anything else to call him, and then I turned Captain Marvel around and tried to find my way back to the main road.

My seven hundred and sixty hours at About Face ended soon after that. For the week and a half until I left, I asked that other drill sergeants drive Lex to the hospital. She came looking for me, but I avoided her as best I could. When we did talk, the feeling between us was different, awkward, and even though she kept pursuing me, looking for me in the lunchroom or out by the canteen, I could sense her growing more and more frustrated by our strained encounters.

In the end, I did little those last days at About Face but play reveille and taps. Sometimes I ran stock. Now and then I worked custodial. When I finally left, Brill let me buy the trumpet from him for a cheap price, and I still have it. It's what I use today. I work at a small museum of natural history near Albany, collecting tickets at the desk. Groups of schoolchildren come by a few times a week and tour the museum with their teachers. Once in a while my new boss, an elderly woman named Reese, has me play my trumpet to let the children know when it's time to return to their buses.

The museum isn't much. The wood floors creak. Some stuffed birds dangle from the ceiling. There's one dinosaur, but it's the size of a chicken and has lovers' graffiti scratched all over its bones. Still, the museum is a quiet, pleasant place to work. Now and then, dust in the air reveals secret scaffoldings of sunlight descending from the windows.

One day, about three months after being hired, I was printing up tickets in the office when Reese came in and told me I had a visitor.

"Tell Ronald I'll be out in a second," I said, separating a sheet of ticket stubs.

"It's not your cousin," she said. "They say they're from a camp? Somewhere you used to work?"

I looked past Reese, at the doorway, but it was empty. I felt the blood rushing to my head. I hadn't spoken to Lex since I'd left About Face. Maybe McCrae had finally done what I'd always known he'd do. Maybe he'd broken her heart and she'd come to say she was sorry. I'd been thinking about her a lot lately, sitting next to me in the camp van, her eyes closed as I painted the brush across her legs. Leaning back on her elbows on the doctor's table, laughing, joking with me while all the blood in her body was being drawn out of her.

I left the tickets on the table and went out to the admissions counter. I scanned the room, but the only person around was a young man standing with his hands in his pockets. He wore an old army jacket and blue jeans and it took me a moment to recognize him.

"It's okay, music man," said Haden McCrae, smiling at me. "I'm not used to me in civvies yet either." His hair had grown into a bright orange shock that he'd wetted and wore smoothed back from his face.

"What do you want?" I said. I felt a liquid heat rising in me.

He dug his hands deeper in his jacket pockets and shrugged. "I don't know. I just came to say I'm out."

"Congratulations. I've got to get back to work," I said, and turned to leave.

"Wait. I want to tell you something," he said.

I stopped and looked at him over my shoulder.

He kicked at the splintered end of a floorboard. "I want to tell you thank you," he said.

"You're welcome. For what?" I said, sensing a trick.

"Lex told me you said nice things about me when we first started up together. She said you told her I was a stand-up person."

I didn't know what he was talking about, and I was just about to tell him what I actually thought of him, right there at the museum entrance, when the memory returned. I had; I'd said he was a stand-up guy the afternoon I'd been trying to find out from Lex which nights they went down to the lake.

I said to McCrae that, yes, I guessed I'd told Lex that.

McCrae nodded. "Why'd you say that about me?"

"I don't know," I said. "You made her happy."

He seemed to think about this for a moment. "I was never really going to let those birds go, you know. I was just tagging their feet to mess with you guys. I thought you all hated me."

I sighed. "I don't hate you, Haden," I said. "Like I said. I think you're a stand-up person."

He smiled at me. "I think you are too, Sergeant Fergus," he said.

I told him I had to get back.

McCrae saluted. I saluted back, and then he turned to leave. "I'll tell her you said hello," he said, and then he was gone.

The museum only has one impressive exhibit. It sits at the back of the third-floor hall, in a square, dusty glass case: the skull of an ancient human, a skull nearly two million years old. The skull doesn't look human. The top of the face looks familiar enough, from the nose up, but the bottom half is monstrous: the jaw is a massive hinge of bone with crushing rows of giant teeth. Under the harsh lighting inside the case each tooth looks mountainous, rising in knobby peaks, pitted with deep valleys of shadow.

The schoolchildren that visit the museum always find the skull soon enough, and even after they've wandered off to see other exhibits, they eventually return to it and look some more. There's a plaque on the wall beside it, which explains that the skull in the case belonged to a particularly unsuccessful species of man, a species that followed an embarrassing evolutionary path. It seems clear, states the plaque, that just before this species evolved, back when man was still a hunched, ape-like creature, a great climate change occurred in ancient Africa, where man was then living. Fruit puckered, leaves shriveled, and a deep frost came upon the land. All at once, man began to adapt, to change into a number of different versions of himself in order to find one that might survive the freeze. Where almost all these new species of man advanced or developed was in the area of the brain: they grew bigger, more complex minds so that they might figure out new ways of getting food. It was one of these species—a species that used its new intelligence to make tools and hunt animals—that would eventually go on to become early modern man, then man of today, you and me. But there was another, lone species, says the plaque, that didn't put any energy at all into developing its mind. (Here you can see the children becoming more interested, straining to read over each other's shoulders, squinting.) What did this species see as its source of promise? Its mouth. It grew a giant mouth so that it might chew up more of the garbage left behind to scavenge, so that it might actually eat up bones, droppings, everything. It's this, a species of ancient man called *Paranthropus*, that the skull in the case belongs to.

There's a drawing of *Paranthropus* next to the display, and in it he looks sadly bewildered, gazing down at a clutch of stringy gray grass in his hairy palm. He's forlorn; he seems to understand that at some point, long ago, he took a wrong turn somewhere, and now he's ended up looking like a fool. From his eyes, though, you can tell that, for the life of him, he can't remember how this mistake happened; he has no idea where or when he made the error. Often, as the time approaches to call the children to the buses, I imagine that it's him, *Paranthropus*, that I'm calling to. Sometimes when I play I close my eyes and I can see myself doing it, aiming the bell of my horn at his ugly face and leading him back this way.

Voodoo Heart

i.

MY GIRLFRIEND AND I ARE NOT RICH PEOPLE. NOT BY A LONG shot. But together we own a mansion—one of the last real mansions in central Florida. It was built by a family of lemon farmers back in 1869, almost one hundred and fifty years ago. We put less than eleven hundred dollars down, hardly anything, but the house has over twenty rooms in all: five bedrooms, a library with a vaulted ceiling, a study, even a garden room that looks out on three full acres of wild backyard.

The morning the realtor first showed us the place, I was sure she'd made some kind of mistake. The other houses she'd taken us to see had been small: one- and two-bedroom apartments mostly. And then, out of nowhere, this.

For a long time, Laura and I stood on the front lawn, just staring up at the house. It had a wraparound porch. There were four stone chimneys rising from the roof. Laura had a good job at the aquarium, and I managed a major wrecking yard, but even so, how could something like this be in our price range?

"I know what you're thinking!" said the realtor. She had to speak loudly to be heard over the persistent buzzing from insects hidden in the foliage. "But the price is just what I said. I'm tempted to buy this one myself."

I studied the house, trying to take in the whole giant sprawl.

Granted, it would need work. The place looked like it had stood vacant a long time, abandoned for ten, maybe even fifteen years. Ferns had sprouted though the slats of the porch. The columns were covered in a scaly silver mold. There were mushrooms growing in one of the rain gutters, a whole row, white with red spots, like tiny blood-stained umbrellas.

The grounds were in bad shape too: everything wild and overgrown, choked by weeds and bramble. Long tatters of moss hung from the trees.

Still, there was no disguising what lay beneath all the disrepair. With time and effort, this could be a wonderland for us.

Laura must have sensed my excitement. "This house is incredible. But it'll be way too much work. I mean, look." She waved a hand over the tall, weedy grass, which came all the way up to our thighs. "The yard alone will take weeks to clear."

"We wouldn't tackle the whole thing all at once," I said. "We could just do a little every day."

Laura turned to examine the house again. I spotted a tick crawling up the back of her shirt and quickly plucked it off before she could notice.

"I don't know, Jake," she said. "If it's so great, why has it been standing here, empty, year after year? What's wrong with it?"

"So," I said to the realtor. "What's wrong with it?"

The realtor shrugged, mopping the sweat from her face. Her name was Joyce. She was an older lady, a grandmotherly type; she wore her white hair in a bun; her sneakers were brand-new. The house had been hard to find. It lay off the main road, hidden behind the old lemon fields. Walking over from where we'd parked had been a big exertion for Joyce.

"Nothing's wrong with this place, love," she said. "People are just afraid of privacy, I suppose."

I waited for her to go on. "You're sure? There's no catch?"

"Fess up, Joyce," said Laura.

Joyce sighed and wiped her glasses on her shorts. "Look. The only thing I can think of that might have kept people away is the camp. There's a camp nearby."

"A camp? Like a camp for kids?" Laura said.

"No. It's a camp for ladies," said Joyce. "It's more like a retreat."

"Like a spa?" I was intrigued; I'd never been to a real spa before. I pictured myself relaxing in pits of bubbling mud.

"Not exactly a spa," said Joyce.

"Not exactly how?" Laura asked.

Joyce picked a daisy from the brush and sniffed the petals. "It's a federal retreat."

"A federal retreat like a prison?" said Laura, sounding alarmed.

"I suppose it's sort of like that," Joyce said. "But it's strictly a white-collar facility. It's not like there are any violent offenders in there or anything. This is a place for society ladies."

"A jail for them," said Laura.

"Laura, it's not something to worry about," said Joyce. "It's practically a resort."

Laura turned to me. "Jacob, I don't want to live near a prison. What if we were here and there was a jailbreak or something? Those women would make a beeline straight for our house."

I noticed a glimmer of excitement in Joyce's expression at hearing Laura refer to the house as "ours."

"You heard Joyce," I said. "It's not that kind of place. It's for society ladies." I made a tea-sipping gesture.

"I've heard of some very high-profile women spending time there," Joyce said, swatting at a cloud of mosquitoes. "Remember Shirley Sayles, the famous golfer? She bet all that money on the U.S. Open? The one she was playing in? She's at the retreat right now."

"Listen to that," I said. "Shirley Sayles."

"Maybe we should look at something else," Laura said.

"Come on." I stepped onto the front porch, which groaned loudly.

"Jacob," said Laura.

But I was already opening the front door.

The inside of the house was dark and cavernous, with a fog of dust rolling across the floor. Trees stood crowded against the windows, their green-and-yellow leaves pressed to the glass like children's hands.

As I stepped into the parlor, I could feel the temperature dropping around me. The room was empty except for a burned-out chandelier reaching down from the high ceiling. I glanced around, examining the peeling wallpaper, the molding sculpted along the ceiling's edge. I already knew that this was the house for us. It had stood for over a hundred years, like a fortress hidden in the woods. Nothing about it was cheap or makeshift. The beams supporting the ceiling looked like they were carved from stone.

It didn't take long for the house to win Laura over, either. The touches were what got her, all the charming details: the claw-foot tub in the master bathroom, cracked but still usable. The carved lemons at the ends of the banisters. The small stained glass window in the parlor door, round as a coin.

What really brought her around, though, was the garden room. It lay at the south end of the first floor and extended out from the rest of the house, overlooking the sloping backyard. The curtains were drawn when we entered, and the room was especially dark, except for a trickle of light seeping in through the far end of the ceiling. I figured there was a crack in the roof, but when we walked over, we saw that in fact, in a certain spot, the ceiling rose and gave way to a small crystal dome. Laura's face lit up when she saw it, the gentle swell of glass, the elegant iron webbing. The dome was filthy with soot, but when she reached up and wiped off one of the panels, a spear of sunlight pierced the room.

"Romantic," said Joyce, and then coughed from the dust.

Of course, even now, six months after we moved in, we still have lots to do. If you came over to our house today, you'd find some rooms fully furnished and others completely bare. If you chose to open the sliding door to the library, you'd find it thoroughly decorated—a sofa by the fireplace, a glass coffee table, the towering bookshelves lined with books. But, on the other hand, if you picked the door at the end of the second-floor hallway to open instead, you'd find a room with nothing in it but an old electric picture of a beach hanging on the wall. When the picture is plugged in, the palm trees sway gently in the breeze, the waves sparkle and roll across the white sand. A flying fish even jumps out of the water, then slaps back down.

There are a few rooms Laura and I haven't even begun yet, storage closets mostly, little side rooms with shelves built into the walls. We leave the doors to them closed for days at a time, weeks. Sometimes we'll forget one exists altogether, until one day when we happen to notice a doorknob sticking out of the wall. Just the other morning I opened the door to a storeroom near the basement and found a dead snake lying on the floor. It must have been there for months; all that was left of the corpse was a skeleton. A winding comb of bones coiled in the dust.

All the space used to make Laura nervous, the empty rooms, the dark door frames. Now and then she'd panic and call to me from wherever she was in the house and I'd have to come up from the cellar, or down from the study, and stay with her for a while.

Recently, though, I bought a pair of walkie-talkies from a toy store, so that whenever we're working on different rooms we can stay in contact. We've started making up tag names for each other, like truckers.

"Kitty Cat, this is Hunka Luv. What is your twenty? Over," I say, the plastic receiver to my mouth.

"Well, hey there, Hunka Luv," says Laura. "I am currently en route to the shower, over."

We sand, and we paint, and we drill, and every day the house progresses. The old layers of wallpaper are scraped off. Little by little the floors brighten, revealing rich swirls and knots in the wood grain. The chimneys are flushed out, and suddenly a cool, sweet draft flows through every room.

Our bedroom is my favorite place in the house. It sits at the top of a wide central tower, and it's round, with shuttered windows that look out over the treetops. The ceiling is high and cone-shaped, pointy as a witch's hat. If we forget to shut the windows at night, fruit bats fly in and hang from the rafters like little leather change purses.

Laura's almost finished with the garden room. She removed the heavy curtains. She cleaned the dome so that the glass sparkles in the sunlight. I told her I'd cut down some of the vines lashed across the windows if she wanted me to, as they obscured the view, but she said to just leave them.

"They make the room feel like a tree house," she said. "I like it this way."

She keeps a bunch of pillows scattered around, big satin pillows with tassels on the corners, and I often wake up on weekend mornings to find her already downstairs, lying beneath the bright dome, reading the newspaper in her nightgown and sunglasses.

I chase Laura up the creaking spiral staircase, laughing, both of us naked. I carry her to the windowsill, her arms around my neck, and I make love to her with the whole blue sky behind us.

Then, when we're done, I'll sit with her while she takes a bath in the giant cauldron of our marble tub, her knees poking up through the water like tiny islands of pink sand. Sometimes I'll read her part of a book or a magazine. Other times, while Laura soaks, I'll amuse her by spying on the women in the prison near our home, the federal work camp. I bought a telescope from an antique store in town and set it up by the window. When I look into the eyepiece, it's like I've been transported right inside the camp among the residents.

Joyce was telling the truth, too. The camp's grounds are beautiful, with shaded walking paths and picnic tables set up beneath the many trees. There's a pond populated by giant goldfish, a vegetable garden that the women tend in the afternoons. The facility is entirely open, too. There aren't any barbed wire fences or guard towers, just a bright green sprawl of grass and trees around which the ladies are allowed to wander freely for most of the day. The only thing bounding the property at all is a bright yellow line painted in the grass along the prison perimeter. The paint contains fluorescent chemicals, and at night the line glows an eerie, spaceship green.

"What are they doing now?" Laura said to me the other day. She was lying in the tub.

I used the telescope to scan the grounds for any of Laura's favorites. The women she most liked to hear about were the high-profile inmates, the society wives and politicians and celebrities who'd lived all sorts of glamorous lives before ending up at the camp. One resident was the owner of a baseball team, another was a restaurateur. There was a famous jazz drummer, the CEO of a baby food company, even a world-renowned eye surgeon. I don't know about Laura, but sometimes I actually felt a strange surge of pride knowing that such a cluster of accomplished women was gathered so close to our home.

I tried to find something interesting to report, but most of the women had headed inside the canteen for supper. A couple of them were jogging along the gravel exercise path. One, the baseball team owner, was reading the newspaper beneath a tree. It was nearly sunset and the line painted around the prison had just started to glow.

"The chef, the really fat lady? She and your favorite girl, Shirley the golf pro—they're fighting it out in the yard."

"Sounds exciting," said Laura. She knew I was lying. Nothing like that ever happened at the camp.

"It's ugly," I said, turning back to Laura. "Shirley just pulled out a shank. Things are looking bad for the chef."

"Her ass is grass," Laura said, smiling.

She yawned and let her head fall to the side and I studied her face for a moment—studied the soft shells of her eyelids; her lips; a tendril of wet, brown hair curled against her cheek. I felt a pull in my chest so hard it frightened me.

"I'm going to marry you in this house," I said. "We can have the wedding in the yard after I clear it out."

Laura wrung the water from her hair. "Is that a proposal?"

"I guess I can do better than that," I said.

She laughed. "I should hope so." Then she closed her eyes and let her body slide down into the water.

"Did you know," she said, "that in exactly one hundred days from tomorrow, you and I will have been together for five years? I was doing the math in the car the other day. Isn't that crazy? Five years."

I leaned over and kissed her on her forehead. "I'll tell you what. If in a hundred days from tomorrow I haven't proposed to you, you can leave me forever."

"Jacob, that's not what I was getting at."

"No, I mean it," I said. "One hundred days."

"This is silly."

"It's not silly," I said, suddenly feeling agitated. "It's not silly at all."

"Are you okay?" she said, sitting up, her skin raw and tender from the hot water.

"I'm fine," I said, but I was angry now. "You deserve someone who'll stick around and commit. Someone who'll love and take care of you. I mean for life."

"Jake . . . you're talking about yourself, right? You're scaring me."

"What do you mean?" I said. "Of course I'm talking about myself. Who the hell do you think I'm talking about? I mean myself. Jake. Me."

My grandfather was a traveling salesman. He met my grandmother in the winter of 1920, while passing through her hometown of Barclay, Virginia. He was twenty-two at the time. She was seventeen.

The way my grandmother remembers it, she was upstairs in her room, doing her homework, when she overheard yelling down on the street. As she came to the window, she spied a young man outside, standing on top of a parked car. He was shouting and gesturing at people, making some kind of sales pitch. A crowd had already gathered around him. In one of his hands he held a little star, which was emitting a cold and piercing light.

My grandmother opened the window to get a better look at the star. She'd never seen light so concentrated before. The little star was shining brighter than all the town's electrical streetlamps put together.

The star, she soon learned, contained something called neon gas. My grandfather was working for a company called Star Neon, the country's first manufacturer of neon lighting tubes. The owners of Star paid my grandfather to drive around the South in a new Ford and do promotional demonstrations about the wonders of neon lighting. Neon tubes were still brand-new in 1920. They were delicate and expensive to construct. Only a few businesses in the whole world had neon signs hanging in their windows, and all of them were located in Western Europe. Hardly anyone in the United States had seen a neon light before.

My grandmother watched, fascinated, as my grandfather continued with his demonstration, making his case as to why neon was *the* light source of the future. Neon was beautiful, he said, holding the star up high. It was enduring. Soon enough, everyone would be using neon to light their homes.

It was at about this point in his speech, according to my grandmother, that he noticed her up in the window and winked at her, making her blush.

Later that night, she snuck out to meet the neon salesman. Less than a week after that, she ran off with him, hopping into his car in the middle of the night and driving off.

The two of them ended up traveling all across the South together. My grandmother learned to help with the demonstrations:

she passed out pamphlets about the science of neon, she gathered names and addresses. They were a team: two kids in love, living in a shiny black Ford, the whole country spread out before them. They kept blankets and tins of food on the backseat, along with a loaded revolver. At night they slept in the car, huddled together. Sometimes, when they ended up parked out in the middle of nowhere, my grandfather would hang the neon star from the rearview mirror and leave it turned on, glowing through the night.

They traveled together for three months before my grandmother became pregnant. They were in Bristol, Tennessee, when she told my grandfather, who seemed thrilled at the news. He took her out to dinner to celebrate, bought them both fried steaks and wine, and then took her dancing afterward. He even rented a hotel room.

The next morning my grandmother woke to find the car gone. No trace of my grandfather anywhere. She waited at the hotel for three days before giving up on him.

The wrecking yard I manage is down on Orange Blossom Road. There's a neon sign in the front window of the office: a big, flashing dollar sign that goes from green to yellow to orange. CASH FOR WRECKS!!! And so on.

Wrecking is a lucrative business in our part of Florida. There are more trade-ins per year here than almost anywhere else in the country. During the week, our yard is always busy with acquisitions and parts cataloging. Still, I understand that managing a wrecking yard, even a huge one like ours—a yard that pays a real salary—wouldn't be enough for some people. I enjoy the work, though. Putting vehicles to rest: rolling them into the lot, dismantling them piece by piece, loading the empty husks into the crusher. I've been at the yard in one capacity or another since I was a teenager, when I spent a summer helping the owner, Liam, with the books. By now Liam and I are close friends. He relies on me.

More than the work, though, I enjoy the yard itself. For all the business that goes on—for all the sawing and loading and jacking, for all the squealing metal and busting glass—the property is generally a quiet and restful place. The lot covers two acres; the maze of wrecks stretches back from the office almost to the interstate. You can spend hours walking its deep alleyways, getting lost, listening to the towers of flattened cars creaking in the wind.

The lot is especially beautiful when it's stormy out. The rain drums and pings off the crumpled metal, making everything glisten for a brief moment. On rainy days I usually give my assistants, Jesus and Marco, the afternoon off and just man the shop by myself. No one seems to want to bring in a car on a rainy day—to drop off their ride and then have to wait in the bad weather for the bus or a cab to take them home. The time drags by. I read or listen to the radio, to the old country station I like. Once in a while a car will glide past on I-35 in a cloud of water. The songs keep coming through the radio: songs full of yodels and whining slide guitar and all the otherworldly sounds I love about that music. Here's a song about a woman who murdered her husband by dipping the mouthpiece of his horn in poison. Here's another, about a man whose wife flew away in a huge silver blimp.

And while the songs come, one after another, I'll examine the neon dollar sign flashing in the shop window, and I'll think of my grandfather; I'll picture him speeding across an open landscape in his Ford Model T, alone behind the wheel.

He came back into my grandmother's life periodically, through the years, haunting her. Out of nowhere the doorbell would ring and she'd answer it and there he'd be, standing on the porch, holding his hat by his side. He'd tell her how sorry he was, how badly he wanted to work things out. If she'd only give him another chance. He'd be selling something else by now, ladies' shoes, or typewriters, or parlor furniture for Beaulieu and Sons. And of course my grandmother would be dating someone new, someone kind and reliable—the type of man her own daughter, my mother, would eventually marry—and even though she knew better, even though she understood exactly how things would unfold, my grandmother would come outside to meet him.

He kept hurting her, over and over. He'd come back and stay with my grandmother just long enough for her to become attached, even hopeful, and then he'd vanish. Poof. Gone.

ii.

LAURA AND I LIKE TO JOKE THAT WE MET ON THE BOTTOM OF THE ocean, that we swam up to each other—just two lonely people drifting along the dark, empty moonscape of the ocean floor—and introduced ourselves.

"Hello," I said, which, underwater, came out more like: "Mebbo." Bubbles tumbled from my mouth as I spoke.

"Hi," Laura managed, her hair swaying around her face.

The truth is that Laura and I met at the aquarium, where she was doing evaluation work for its public relations department. I had gone to the aquarium to see an exhibit that had just opened, an exhibit on deep ocean life that was causing a big stir in the news.

The exhibit was called "Creatures of the Deep: Life in the Bathypelagic Zone," and everyone I knew was talking about it. The opening had been a big event for the state of Florida. Politicians had come, and local celebrities.

The exhibit featured fish from the deepest parts of the ocean, strange, frightening fish that had never been on display before. Until this particular exhibit, no one had been able to successfully bring any bathypelagic fish up from the depths. The captured specimens had always died as a result of the massive changes in pressure that occurred as the traps were brought up toward the surface.

But in acquiring their specimens, the marine biologists at our aquarium had used a brand-new type of trap from Australia called a PrAc, which stood for pressure acclimatization. A PrAc trap gave a fish time to adjust to a low-pressure tank by reducing the atmospheric pressure inside the trap a fraction at a time, over a period of days.

Even Liam was going on about the exhibit. He called me at work to push me to go. "They have weirdos you have to see to believe," he said.

I could hear seagulls behind his voice. Liam owned five wrecking yards around the state and was basically retired. He lived with his wife on their houseboat, which was huge, with three stories, like a penthouse bobbing on the water.

"I'm not much for aquariums," I said. "I'll send Jesus or Marco. They'll report back."

"No. I insist. Take the day off tomorrow and go see this exhibit. It'll clear your head."

"My head is clear," I said.

There was a pause from Liam's end. Just the birds, the lapping waves.

"What?" I said.

"Your head isn't clear," he said. "It hasn't been clear since you broke up with what's-her-name. Angie? Angeline?"

"Anne," I said.

"It hasn't been clear since her."

"I'm fine," I said.

"You're taking time off," said Liam. "Go see some fishes. To-morrow."

So I did. I took the day off and I went through the motions. I drove up to the aquarium, the whole time just wanting to go back to the yard. The exhibit did take my mind off things, though. It was easy to lose myself once I'd made it through the line and down the long, winding ramp leading to the exhibition's main gallery.

The gallery was a world unto itself, a winding maze of underwater glass tunnels and exhibit halls. Behind one window was something called a gulper eel, a black, eight-foot serpent with razor-sharp teeth and a mouth that billowed open like a sack, wide enough to engulf a small child. Behind another window swam a deep-sea angler, a vicious animal with beady eyes, and oversize fangs sticking out of its mouth. From a stalk on its head hung a little lure that glowed bright white, like a bare bulb, swaying back and forth to attract victims.

Then there was a fish that seemed to be wearing all its organs in sacks hanging on the outside of its body. Across the hall was a fish with extra rows of teeth inside its throat. And whipping around in a tank by the water fountain was a slimy, worm-like animal called an Atlantic hagfish.

Also known as the slime eel, read the hagfish's information plaque, *the hagfish eats by burrowing inside of unsuspecting passersby, then devouring them little by little from the inside out.*

The hagfish thrashed about inside its tank, leaving gooey smear marks on the glass.

They were like monsters, these creatures, like things come to life from my childhood nightmares. These were what hid beneath all that beautiful ocean. These were what lurked in the darkness.

I walked over to a bench in front of the angler's tank and sat down. I began thinking about Anne again, and how badly things had ended. How, like always, I'd changed into someone I hardly recognized, someone I hated.

"She's really amazing, isn't she, the angler?"

An attractive girl was standing beside me, twenty-four, maybe twenty-five years old. She was wearing a blue skirt and blazer. A security tag hung from her neck on a chain.

"She's the ugliest thing I've seen in my whole life."

The girl smiled. "Well, granted, she's not about to win any pageants. But the guys like her. See all those fins sticking out of her stomach?"

I noticed a crop of little tube-like shapes protruding from the angler's belly.

"Those aren't actually fins. They're male anglers. The males, they attach themselves to a female and fuse to her body. And then after a while their insides dissolve and they become these pouches of sperm she can use when she feels like reproducing."

"That's sweet," I said.

The girl laughed. "Was that totally disgusting, what I just told you?"

"Which part, the fusing to the female's body, or the insides dissolving?"

Her smile was lovely, almost too wide for her face, with a single dimple in one cheek. "I'm sorry," she said. "You talk to kids all day and you get a little loopy. I'm Laura."

"Jacob," I said.

"So, Jacob," she said. "What do you like best about the new hall? I'm doing a survey."

"I don't know. I've just been in here. The ugly room."

She sighed and shook her head in a teasing way. "Come with me," she said.

I got up and followed Laura through the gallery. Children ran past us, laughing and yelling. I watched her walk, watched the way her dark hair swung across her back.

We came to a room off the main throughway. Like in the others, the walls here were all glass. Behind them hovered schools of differently colored jellyfish. They glowed brilliantly in the dark blue water. Their movements were so elegant, the way their bells expanded and contracted in a dreamy, billowing slow motion. The rhythm was like breathing, like a deep, slow breathing. Then, all at once, the whole bunch changed colors in unison, like the turning panels of a kaleidoscope. The bells went from violet to green to bright yellow.

"Better?" said Laura.

"Better."

"This is my favorite room. Look at that one, over there," she said, gesturing at a lone jellyfish hovering in a tank across the way. It was enormous; it looked like some kind of mutant, with a bell that was at least five feet across. Its huge tentacles lay coiled along the tank's floor. It was hideous but lovely at the same time, a huge upswell of color and light.

"It's amazing how much pressure these animals live under. This jelly, right here—you find it almost two miles beneath the surface. The pressure down there feels like an elephant standing on every square inch of your body. Isn't that wild?"

She waited for me to answer. The giant jellyfish was glowing a pale orange. The light coming from its bell was soft, like firelight, and Laura appeared very beautiful in it.

"Would you like to go out to dinner with me?" I said.

"You're asking me out?" she said.

"Usually, when I find a woman I like I just fuse myself to her body. But I'm trying something new."

Laura laughed. "So, Jacob," she said, holding up her pad again. "What's your favorite part of the new hall?"

"That depends on what you're doing later," I said.

I did my best to win Laura over once we started dating. I liked her right away. She was bright and driven and funny. There was a toughness about her, too, a stubbornness that I found sexy. If she began reading a book she'd always read it all the way through, even if she hated it, especially if she hated it.

"I feel like it got the best of me if I put it down," she said to me one night, when I woke up to find her sitting in the bathroom, on the lip of the bathtub, reading a novel she'd already read once and disliked for its confusing ending.

It made me smile, seeing her in her nightgown, squinting at her book in the bathroom in the middle of the night, so tired, but so determined.

"What?" she said, looking at me.

"Nothing," I said.

"What?" she said again, laughing now. She threw the book at me.

I couldn't get enough of her those first few months. I took her to all my favorite places. I took her to a restaurant out on the pier. I bought her a pair of rhinestone cowboy boots and took her dancing at a place I loved, a country music bar that was located on an alligator farm. To get in you had to cross a rope bridge suspended above the hatchery, with all those yellow, prehistoric eyes staring up at you.

"Okay, I give up. I surrender," Laura said to me, laughing as we left the dance floor and returned to our booth, both of us tipsy. She flopped down and put her cowboy boots on my lap. "Where have you been all my life?" she said.

I pulled a tack from one of her boot heels. "I should tell you something," I said.

She squinted at me. "This isn't the part when you tell me you're married, right?"

"I'm not married," I said.

"You're not in love with someone else."

"I'm in love with you."

"What?" she said. The band had started up again, and she had to shout over the music.

"I'm in love with you!" I said.

She grinned. "I'm in love with you too, fool!"

"Listen, though." I paused, trying to figure out how to put it. An image of Anne came back to me: Anne lying curled up on the bed, crying. Screaming at me through her hands.

"Why are you doing this?" she yells. "Why are you ruining us?"

And I can see myself standing over her, not caring, saying terrible things to her.

"Who are you?" Anne says through the cage of her fingers. "For eight months everything's great, and then, one day, out of nowhere, you're saying these things to me. You're killing me!"

And I don't know what to tell her. I only know that something in me has changed and I don't want to be with her anymore. Instead I want to hurt her, to lash out and cut deeper until she never wants to see me again. I want to tear her apart.

"I have problems, sometimes," I said to Laura. "I have trouble . . ."

"Shh," she said. She ran the back of her hand down my cheek. "We're just getting started, right? Nobody's buying rings yet?"

I felt a tremendous gratitude. "No. Nobody's buying rings," I said.

Coincidentally, though, a week earlier, an aunt of mine had died and I'd ended up inheriting, among other things, her engagement ring—a plain gold band crowned with a one-carat diamond—which I've been waiting to give to Laura ever since.

In our old apartment, I kept the ring hidden in a drawer in my desk. In our new house, I keep it in a small room off the main hallway, one of the dark, empty rooms Laura never goes into. I hid the ring beneath the floorboards—I pried one up and placed the wrapped ring box in the dark hollow. It makes me feel good when we get into bed at night to know that the ring is nearby, that it's tucked like a seed deep inside our home.

There are moments, though, when I'm tempted to throw all this caution to the wind. Moments when I want to just go ahead with it. Laura and I will be lying in bed, talking, or taking a shower together, and suddenly I'll feel this great urge to give her the ring—to go dig it up from beneath the floor and offer it to her right then.

But I tamp the urge down. I remind myself of what can happen when you rush things, when you're not careful. I think of examples, such as a certain photograph Laura brought home from work not long ago. The photograph showed a killer whale stretched out in the middle of a country road. The whale was lying on its side, one fin in the air, the other crushed between its body and the ground.

The picture was taken at the site of an accident the aquarium's transportation crew had. They were driving the whale from a water park in Jacksonville, speeding, and they lost control of the truck. When the cab jackknifed, the whale's aqua hammock broke and the animal came crashing out into the road, tumbling over itself, its bones cracking, before it finally rolled to a stop. The whale lay there wheezing, insects crawling over its skin, for a full hour before the rescue team came. Every now and then it would shriek through its blowhole.

I remember that picture and think: See, asshole? See? That's what happens when you act too fast. When you don't go step by step by step.

iii.

THE HOUSE IS COMING ALONG. IT'S AMAZING TO WATCH THE place change, week by week. Just nine months after moving in, we've finished most of the major work; we scraped the rot out of the second-floor walls, replaced the floor in the basement. Marco and Jesus and Jesus's brothers came by and helped for a fee.

As expected, there are things about the house that will take years to fix: the slight, undulating warp in the upstairs floors, the sag in the attic ceiling. But our goal was to make it livable by the end of the first year, and here we are.

The only thing bothering me is that the prison has turned out to be something other than what Joyce said it was. I've learned that there's more to the place than she originally let on.

From almost the moment we moved in, I made a hobby of studying the prison and its residents—looking up all the women, getting to know who they were, what their lives had been like before they ended up incarcerated. Almost every one of them had an interesting story: the chef had tried to burn down her own restaurant for the insurance money; the owner of the baseball team had been caught trying to smuggle drugs into the country on her private plane.

I enjoyed getting to know them, one by one: finding out about them on my computer at work, looking up their stories, then coming home and getting to watch them in person, through the keyhole of my telescope.

But there was one group of women, a tiny subset, that I didn't become aware of—didn't even see—until long after Laura and I were already settled in. After those first months of spying, I started to notice, every now and then, and only in glimpses, a different kind of resident wandering the grounds: I became aware of a small handful of women who were much older than the rest, actual elderly people, white-haired and wrinkled. There were only three of them on the grounds, I learned after watching the prison more closely. During the summer these women must have been indoors, where it was air-conditioned. But as autumn closed in and the weather grew cooler, they began to come out into the yard, lingering for just a few minutes at a time, smoking a cigarette by the vegetable garden, playing a quick hand of cards at the picnic tables, before heading back inside.

None of the younger inmates seemed to want anything to do with them. At first, I assumed the giant age difference was the reason. It took me a while to learn that they stayed away from the old ladies because they were frightened.

As it turned out, the three old women were transfers from another Florida penitentiary—a real prison, with guard towers and searchlights, bars and razor wire. They were all violent offenders too, killers who'd spent thirty, forty, even fifty years in maximum-security prisons. They'd simply been transferred over to the camp because by now it was assumed that they were too old to do harm anymore. And because at their age they needed certain amenities that were difficult to provide in real jail.

"It's not like there are any thugs in there," Joyce had said. "No real criminals."

But these women were murderers. All three of them had killed in cold blood. Two of them had murdered their husbands. One had done it for money, the other for no good reason at all. And the last lady, the oldest of the three, turned out to be a serial murderer. Her name was Rose Deach, and as a young woman in the 1940s she had killed over thirty people. If the war hadn't been going on she likely would have made national headlines, because her crimes were particularly heinous.

Rose had started out working in the nursery of the Volusia county hospital, up the coast, not far from Daytona. She'd been a physician's assistant, a pretty young girl who watched over newborns until they were ready to go home. Some babies she apparently took good care of. She checked their temperatures, their breathing; she fed them, did whatever she was supposed to do to keep them healthy. Other babies, though, Rose killed by clamping her hands over their faces in the middle of the night.

For three and a half years Rose moved from hospital to hospital, caring for some, killing others. When she was finally caught, she didn't seem to understand what she'd done wrong. She'd only killed the bad babies, she said. She claimed she could tell which ones were going to grow up to be good people, and which ones were bad seeds.

"I don't understand it myself, but it's so," she was quoted as saying from jail in June of 1944.

"I press my hand to a child's chest and right off I can feel what kind of character they've got. Right in my palm. I can tell whether they're going to add goodness to the world, or subtract from it. And so," she said, "the bad ones I go ahead and press out of the world. Who needs them here? Right?"

In the 1940s Rose Deach was a scary story that parents and nannies around Florida told misbehaving children, a fairy-tale villain. Kids used her name to frighten each other.

Rose Deach knows you're a bad boy. She's coming to get you. She's sneaking inside your closet right now, closing the door behind her with those bony hands. She's waiting for you to fall asleep. . . .

I watch as Rose and the other two murderesses emerge from the barracks. I watch them make their way to the picnic table, so skinny, all three of them, shrunken, tiny women, their skin pale and crinkly as tracing paper. The orange jumpsuits hang on them—Rose is so small, she has to wear hers cuffed at the ends of the pants legs to keep from tripping. And as they near the exercise path, I see all the other women part and let them pass.

Who can blame the younger ones, though? I'm frightened myself. It makes me angry to think that Joyce didn't tell us about the murderesses. Laura doesn't seem to understand. To her the murderesses are just three little old women hobbling around. They're harmless. But for me, there's something deeply scary about them. They remind me of a certain kind of car that shows up at the wrecking yard once, maybe twice a year. A kind of car that all of us are very careful around.

Like at most wrecking yards, the majority of the vehicles we acquire we get at insurance auctions. We buy them ourselves, junkers that we purchase for parts. An old Honda or Ford, for example, might have the back smashed to garbage but the front still full of usable machinery—a transmission, a fan belt, a dirty radiator. We're scavengers, for the most part. We buy dead cars and gut them for pieces, catalog them, then stack them on the bone piles, wait for the aluminum prices to go up before selling the scrap in tonnage.

A few times a week people will bring cars to us. A guy looking to get rid of his dead grandmother's clunker. A kid going off to school who doesn't need the old station wagon anymore. But once in a while, someone will come to the yard with a different kind of car altogether. They'll come by with the kind of car that they shouldn't be bringing to a place like ours—nice, new cars with purring engines and smooth, shiny bodies.

Again, this happens three times a year at most. A guy will drive up in an expensive car, maybe a brand-new Cadillac SUV, and when he gets out, he tells us to just take it away from him. Sometimes he'll want us to buy the car for some ludicrously low price: a thousand dollars, a hundred, maybe even less.

"Just give me a dollar and you can have it. Please, get it away from me," he'll say, already walking away from the car. Like it's cursed.

Usually when they come by like this, when they're frantic just to get rid of a car, they want a guarantee that we'll destroy it. They don't care if we gut it for parts, but they don't want the car driving the streets anymore. They don't want to have to see it ever again. One time a woman came by with a '68 Mustang in perfect shape, jet black with a silver racing stripe down the center, and paid a hundred dollars to watch us flatten it in the crusher. Another time, two years ago, I came out of the office to find an empty 1972 Cadillac Eldorado idling in front of the gate. It had a glazed, butter cream exterior, red leather trim. The car was worth at least nine thousand dollars, just sitting there by the curb with the engine purring. A note taped to the windshield read, *Wreck it.*

Marco and Jesus call cars like that Voodoos. They like to try to guess what happened between the cars and the people who brought them in.

"I'll bet it's his lady's car. Probably dumped him in it."

"He was sadder than all that, man. It must have belonged to someone who died. A brother or a sister. Someone he loved. Maybe they offed themselves in it. You saw his face."

Sometimes we dare each other to drive a Voodoo, or to take one home. A 1970 Cutlass SS will come in, triple black, and before we load it into the crusher, I'll tease Marco, who drives a broken-down Chevy truck, about what a nice ride it'd be to bring home to his wife.

"Go on," I'll say. "Take it. You deserve it. I won't tell."

He'll laugh and shake his head. "No, no. You'd look better in this one. A Cutlass is your style."

"I insist," I'll say.

"So do I," he'll say, even as I push the button that starts the crusher.

That's what Rose and the other two remind me of—Voodoos. Cars you know can't really be that dangerous, but you avoid all the same. I look through the telescope at Rose—small, bony Rose, hobbling across the grass, stooped, the other old women at her side—and I am fascinated.

"Jacob, how long have you been up here?" Laura asked.

This was just the other day. I was watching the women get ready to take a sculpture class. There were seven of them sitting around a picnic table with a big bowl of water in the center. In front of each woman sat a gray, brain-like lump on a paper plate.

"Not so long," I said. I swung the telescope to the left a little, to see which one of the women was going to pose for the others, and I spied the money manager already standing on the far picnic table, getting nude. She was not one of my favorites. Young and attractive, she had long blond hair and a slender, graceful body, but even so, there was something slightly repugnant about her. Maybe it was the hint of snobbishness in her face, the upturned nose, the small, darting eyes always assessing people. She'd stolen millions of dollars from her clients, investing their money in risky stocks without telling them. She would reside at the camp for seven more years.

I watched as she stepped out of her jumpsuit, then peeled off her panties. Her body gleamed, so pale in the sun. She was a little small, a bit bowlegged, but her breasts were full, the nipples bright pink. The hair between her legs was trimmed in a perfect diamond.

The telescope went black. I looked up to see Laura's hand clamped over the lens.

"What's the deal?" I said.

"Nothing. I just wanted to talk to you for a minute, that's all."

"The women are taking a sculpture class. The three killers, too."

"Jacob, are you sure you're all right?" Laura said.

"Of course," I said. "What are you talking about?"

"I don't know. You're just a little distant lately. And you haven't been sleeping."

The night before, I'd had a dream about being chased by a man on fire. He was driving behind me on the highway, flames streaming from his eyes and nose and open mouth.

Laura ran a hand through my hair. "And you've just been spending a lot of time in here. You've been spending a lot of time inside your head."

"I'm spying on the prison. I'm relaxing."

She put her hands up. "Okay. Sorry. I was just checking in. Want to eat soon?"

I turned back to the telescope. "Just two more minutes. Roger, Kitty Kat?"

"Sure," she said, waiting there. "Roger." Then she headed downstairs.

I went on watching the women sculpt for a few more minutes, enjoying the last of the sun, the warm breeze coming through the window. Most of the sculptures were hopeless, deformed and mangled, but a couple were quite good. It was a thrill to observe the better sculptors, to watch them slowly draw human figures up from the clay, tease out arms and legs. The eye surgeon was working on a bust that looked more and more like the money manager with every pass of her hands. I was impressed by how carefully she molded the facial features—smoothing out the money manager's brow, pinching up the bump in her nose.

Rose was sitting at the far end of one of the tables. I watched as she molded her flattened clay into a square gray slab, all the while thinking about what those hands of hers had done. As soon as she finished shaping the corners, she began plucking out the slab's edges, picking the clay apart with her spidery fingers. She worked quickly, snatching at bits of clay, now and then shooting a glance up at the naked money manager, studying her.

Soon enough Rose peeled her sculpture off the table and stood it up. It was a twisted shape, almost like a gnarled, barren tree, or a system of veins squiggling off from a single artery. Nothing human to the shape at all. Still, there was something about those squirmy, desperate tentacles that reminded me very much of the money manager standing on the table. Maybe it was the way the sculpture seemed to speak of greed, a kind of veiny, slurping greed. I don't know. But Rose Deach got it right. She saw right through to the money manager's ugly heart.

iv.

THE DAYS SLIP BY. THEY SLIDE INTO ONE ANOTHER AND DISSOLVE. The wrecking yard is only a few miles from the aquarium, so most afternoons I'm able to visit Laura at work for lunch. Sometimes we eat in her office, other times we eat outside, in the aquarium's amphitheater, where the shows happen. Jed, the trainer, rides across a pool on a chariot of dolphins. Baby sea lions tumble through the air like footballs.

I worry that one day soon I'll break Laura's heart. And not by accident either. I'm afraid I'll do it violently, bust her heart wide open.

I've done it before. I've dated a woman, fallen in love, and then turned on her. I don't know why.

It always happens the same way. I'm going along fine with someone. One month goes by, two, six. I'm attached. I care now. I think about her all the time. I look forward to seeing her. She starts leaving things at my house: a hair clip, earrings; she starts bringing things over: a toothbrush, an extra pair of glasses to leave on the nightstand, old sneakers to go biking in.

And wham: I start waking up sweaty in the middle of the night with a strange crackling in my chest; waking up angry, even furious, my fists clenched, aching. And from there it all starts to slide. I feel it happening and don't know how to stop it. The fear and resentment, the rage; I feel them all blooming in me so fast, like something from a fairy tale, a vine sprouting overnight, its black leaves slapping open.

But that's too pretty a way to describe what happens to me. The change is much uglier than that.

Does this ever happen to you? You're going about your day with the person you love, your girlfriend, your boyfriend, your spouse; maybe you're in the car together, on your way to the home improvement store to pick up supplies: paper towels, glass cleaner, lightbulbs, dusting rags, a plunger. You're waiting at a traffic light together. Your person is talking to you, saying something about a musician they like, or a commercial they saw, and you're listening to them, watching them talk, and all of a sudden the strangest sensation comes over you. This feeling of total disorientation, almost like you're seeing your life through a new set of eyes, like you're watching yourself from afar. And what you see is so unfamiliar to you, so wrong. This is you? This is your car? These are your hands on the wheel?

And who the fuck is this person sitting next to you, talking to you? Who are they? Of course you know they're the person you love—*you know that*—but right now, at this moment, they're unrecognizable, a total stranger. Some kind of mistake has been made; you shouldn't be here with them. But they're keeping you here, keeping you from your real life, which is happening somewhere else, with someone more attractive, someone wilder; not in this car, not here, in this line of people waiting for a traffic light, listening to the tick, tick, tick of your own turning signal. And so you hate this person all of a sudden. You want to smash them. Because their face is a trap. Their face is a cage.

But then someone behind you hits their horn and breaks the spell.

"It's green," says your person, who's beautiful to you now. Just as they were seconds before.

"Hey," they say. "You can go."

I understand that moments like this are common enough; that they happen to most people at one time or another. But what if the moment didn't end for you? What if you couldn't find your way out?

That's what happens with me. The feeling hits me and it won't go away. I get angry and mean and, most of all, restless. Everywhere I look I see chances to go back and correct my life, chances to start over alone or with someone new. I see opportunity in the starry night painted across the checkout girl's fingernails. I see it in the cars brought into the yard, especially the Voodoos. The '76 Triumph motorcycle standing in the lot, gleaming beneath the spotlights. The feel of the helmet, the way the world looks through the visor.

There are so many places I want to go, all of a sudden. So many scenarios I want to live out. The feeling is like standing beneath an active electromagnet at the wrecking yard. I don't know if it's the iron in the blood or what, but the magnet creates a sensation like something gently sucking on your insides.

And soon enough, there's my girlfriend, asleep in our apartment, and here I am, drinking with some woman in a bar all the way out by the airport. The woman has a flower plucked from a cocktail in her hair.

But this was all a long time ago, before Laura. I used to move too fast. Let things barrel forward with no brakes. Laura and I have been together almost five years and I understand that she is the best thing in my life. I look at her and I know that. So I'm making sure we're doing things right, building slowly. And I'm close now. I'm almost there. I've taken to carrying the ring around with me during the day, instead of leaving it at home, beneath the floor. I keep it in the pocket of my bag, zipped into the side. I can feel the bump beneath the canvas. I could pull the ring out any day now.

Sometimes I get scared, though. I get scared that something in me will react and change and push Laura away. If the worries get to me, if they keep me up at night, which is when they come most often, I'll go for a walk around the house to calm down. I'll take my walkie-talkie in case Laura wakes up, and put on my robe and creep down the winding staircase, careful not to let the boards creak.

I try to find something active to do, to keep me busy. I'll do push-ups in the den. I'll ride the exercise bike. Most of the time, I do something simple, something quiet. I'll organize our record collection, or riffle through our bills. I'll check the inventory for the yard. Occasionally I end up looking through the old photo books. Laura has a whole book of photographs devoted to her grandparents and even her great-grandparents. Black-and-white images with that silvery gloss to them, the people's eyes blank as old lightbulbs.

I only have three photographs of my grandfather. One shows him posing with my grandmother. He's sitting in a wooden chair on a porch, wearing his suit and tie. She's standing next to him and he's got one arm around her thighs, squeezing her, making her laugh. In another photo, my grandfather is holding up his neon star. He's pretending to shade his face from the bright light.

The photo I like best (and the only one in which his face hasn't been scratched out) shows my grandfather as he was in the 1920s, still a young man, lean with sleek black hair. He's sitting in the back of a flatbed truck, parked at a general store in the middle of nowhere. The sky is huge and cloudless. In the corner of the picture you can see a pair of hands emptying a can of petrol into the truck's tank. My grandfather is sitting on top of a crate of grapes in the back of the truck in his undershirt and suspenders, the sun gleaming on his thin chest. He's grinning, mugging for the camera, holding a grape sprig high over his face, as though waiting for one of the grapes to drop right into his mouth.

I often wonder, as I stare at the photo late at night, unable to sleep: was he content with his life? I ask myself: Did it make him happy—really happy—to always be leaving things behind, homes and friends and girls who loved him, girls like my grandmother, who'd hate him once he drove away? And if it didn't make him happy, why did he do it? Did he leave because he just didn't give a shit about anyone but himself? Because he was a selfish, lusty motherfucker? Or were there other reasons? Did he leave because he was scared? Scared that if he stuck around he'd be an even bigger disappointment to the person he loved? Because he was afraid of hurting her even worse?

The last time my grandmother heard any mention of him was in 1949. A detective called the house where she was living with her new husband and children and told her that a vehicle belonging to my grandfather, a Ford A Roadster, had been found abandoned near San Francisco. The car had been discovered parked on a bluff overlooking the ocean, not far from the Golden Gate Bridge. There was nothing inside it at all, no wallet, no suitcase.

Someone had burned the car, the detective explained. The Ford's exterior was charred and bubbled. The interior was all melted, the seats blackened husks, the steering wheel a drooping mess. The police suspected that the fire had been started by teenagers who found the car sitting vacant at the edge of the bluff, but they weren't sure. It's possible, said the man on the phone, that my grandfather set the car on fire himself. Still, there were no clues. Just a burned-out car sitting on a cliff.

What the police were really trying to figure out, of course, was what had happened to my grandfather himself. Had he committed suicide, jumped off the cliff into the ocean? Had he lit the car on fire and then just walked away, on to somewhere else?

As the detective assumed that my grandmother hadn't heard from my grandfather in some time, he didn't expect her to be much help. But, if she did have any information about my grandfather that might help him with the investigation, she should call him right away. My grandmother didn't even bother to write down the detective's number.

V.

FINALLY, I DECIDED TO JUST GO AHEAD AND PROPOSE.

Enough time had passed. Our days had fallen into a warm, familiar pattern. And I felt good. Everything felt right. After nine months in the new house, it was almost finished, everything except the far portion of the backyard, which was still tangled and overgrown.

I figured I'd make a whole day of proposing. I'd surprise Laura at work, spend the day with her, take her out to a nice dinner at a restaurant on the water. Go dancing afterward at the country music bar. Then ask her to spend her life with me.

The day I chose to do all this was Laura's day-care shift at the aquarium. The day-care center was one of the best resources the aquarium offered to its employees. The facility was small, just one classroom, but it was filled with all sorts of state-of-the-art educational material—computers and electronic toys, a whole library of storybooks. All employees were required to spend at least one day a month helping out at the center, which basically amounted to a day off. You played with the children, read them stories, finger-painted with them.

I'd always liked visiting Laura at the day-care center. I loved the craziness of the classroom, all the noise and commotion, little pumpkin-heads swirling around your waist, shouting and laughing. And it was romantic in a strange way, too. Being responsible for little children with your girlfriend.

I woke full of nervous energy the morning of Laura's day-care shift. She'd already gone to work by the time I got up, so I took my time getting ready. I had an extra-long shower. I shaved with the fancy lotion she used on her legs.

I waited until I was ready to leave to retrieve the ring. As I bent down to pull up the floorboard, I felt a stab of fear that I'd find the hole empty. But as soon as I reached inside, my fingers found the plastic bag with the box inside. The ring looked beautiful. The diamond was small, but it sparkled brightly, slicing the light into pieces. I imagined myself giving it to Laura that night, kneeling down and holding it out to her, looking up into her face.

I put the ring in my pocket and left for the aquarium.

"Delivery for Laura," said Marie, a day-care attendant, as she opened the door to the building for me. "We've got a delivery for Laura."

"This isn't what I ordered," said Laura, coming to the door.

"You want me to send him back?" said Marie.

Laura kissed me. "No, I'll keep him," she said. Then, to me: "What are you doing here?"

"I had a date, but she stood me up." I held up the yellow roses I'd bought. "I don't know. You want to go out with me instead? I mean, I already have these flowers."

She took the flowers from me. "All dolled up and no one to dance with, huh?"

"Something like that." I put my arm around her waist and followed her inside.

The morning went even better than planned. Laura and I had a ball playing with the children, drawing pictures with them, reading them stories. We made crocodiles out of egg cartons with a girl named Lucy. Another child, a black girl named Christina, showed us how to make little fortune-telling devices out of sheets of colored paper.

I touched one of the numbered panels on Christina's fortune-teller.

"G-r-e-e-n, and that spells *green*," she said, manipulating the little paper mouth, making it open and close on her fingers. The fortune-teller finally stopped moving and Christina looked inside.

"What's the verdict?" I said.

She read my fortune. "You smell funny," she said, giggling.

"Let me see that," I said. When I looked, I saw that all the panels said the same thing.

"He does smell funny," said Laura, laughing. "P.U."

Throughout the day we teamed up to help different kids. We read a storybook about a talking coffee cup to a girl named Susan, Laura reading the female voices while I read the male characters. We helped an Indian boy build a birdhouse out of Popsicle sticks and glue. The second half of the day we spent helping to operate the train. One of the women working at the center had a husband who ran a model train shop nearby, and he'd built an elaborate train set for the kids, with tracks that ran around the whole classroom. He'd even designed four different towns for the train to pass through, each town in a different corner of the room. Every town represented a different season of the year, too. One was winter: the yards were snowy; tiny icicles hung from the roofs of the houses. In another town, over by the toilets, it was autumn. Children trick-or-treated. Thimble-size jack-o'-lanterns flickered from porches.

The kids' favorite part of the train set, though, was the tunnel. In one place, near the cubbies, the tracks disappeared into a dark hole in the wall painted to look like an old, rickety tunnel, with little DANGER and ENTER AT YOUR OWN RISK!!! warnings all around the entrance. The kids never got tired of running the train through—steering the engine into the tunnel's dark mouth, watching the cars disappear one by one, then rushing to the tunnel's exit, at the other side of the cubbies, to wait for the glow of the engine lamp.

They made a game of putting notes in the coal car and sending them around to one another. One kid would stand by the spring section of the tracks, the other in winter, and when the first had put his note in the coal car, he'd make a sound like a train whistle and Laura and I would help the second child operate the control box and bring the train around the tracks, through the tunnel, and finally over to us. *Hello, Jim,* said one note. *Good-bye, Carol,* said the reply.

The train tracks were equipped with special hook rails that gripped the engine's wheels, keeping it from tipping over. That afternoon, though, something must have been off with one of the engine's wheels, because it kept derailing. We could hardly get the train around a turn without it tipping over. At one point the engine fell off the tracks inside the tunnel. All the kids crowded around the tunnel's mouth, peering into the darkness. One boy was even trying to stick his head inside the hole.

"Hang on there, Poncho," I said, and pulled him off the tracks.

Laura started toward the cubbies, where the door to the crawl space was, but I told her I'd go instead. The crawl space was just a sealed-up storage area, but it was dusty and cramped and I knew that none of the women liked going back there.

"My hero," Laura said. I struck a superhero pose and the kids squealed with laughter.

The crawl space was narrow, only about four feet wide, and lengthwise it ran for about fifteen feet, like a short, dark hallway. I opened the door and slid inside. The air was cold and musty, and when I tried the lightbulb nothing happened. The two train tunnel openings didn't offer much light, and it took me a good minute of fumbling around to find the engine lying beside the tracks.

"How you doing back there?" Laura called through the tunnel's exit.

"All aboard," I yelled back, righting the engine.

Then, out of nowhere, an idea came to me.

I reached into my pocket and pulled out the ring box. A note one of the children had written lay inside the coal car. I would write a proposal on the other side of the note and then send the train down the tracks.

I glanced down the length of the tunnel at Laura's face, peering back at me. Taking the note, I got a pen from my pocket and wrote on the blank side.

Laura. You and me?

I folded the note and placed it inside the coal car, beneath the ring box.

"Jacob," Laura called down the tunnel. "You get lost?"

I made sure the train was righted properly, my hands trembling a little now. Then I opened my mouth to tell Laura to hit the power. But the words froze in my throat.

"Jacob?" Laura squinted into the tunnel's entrance, searching for me in the darkness. Children huddled around her, tugging and giggling. "Hello?"

The ring box and the note sat waiting in the coal car.

Laura tucked her hair behind her ear. She looked worried. "Should we hit the power? Jake?"

"Hit it," I finally said.

Laura called over her shoulder to the children. "Flip the switch." All at once the current surged through the tracks. The engine began to pull away from me, but I wouldn't release it. I couldn't get my hands to let go. The ring box and the note shook in the coal car. Folded up, the note showed the message written on the other side of mine.

Boo.

A shiver ran through me. I looked up at Laura, at her beautiful face at the end of the tunnel, waiting. I was ready for this. For her. I had to be.

"Jacob," Laura called. "Are you all right?"

The engine's wheels spun, trying to pull away, but I held on. My heart was pounding fast. I glanced behind me, at the tunnel's entrance. The hole opened up on the miniature summertime scene. Tiny children climbed trees bursting with flowers. They chased each other toward a bright blue pond. A girl flew a kite high above the rooftops.

"Jacob," came Laura's voice. "Jacob?"

I felt light-headed. I took the ring box and note out of the coal car and then I let the train go.

When Laura got off work, we went to a restaurant on the shore. It was all the way out on a pier, overlooking the ocean. The table I'd reserved stood at the far end of the room. It was pressed right up against the huge window and the view couldn't have been prettier. The dark blue ocean stretched out forever, calm, flat as a cutting board. The sun was already down; the sky was covered in glowing pink gashes.

Still, all I could think about was what had happened back at the day-care room. I kept wondering what was wrong with me. What was so broken? Laura was talking to me, but I couldn't hear her. Nothing's broken, I told myself, taking a long sip from my gin and tonic. I just needed more time.

But on went the thoughts: What if it's not just about time? What if you're not built for this? What if there is something wrong, something that runs in the blood? What if all you'll ever be able to do is leave? My face felt hot. I mopped at my forehead with my napkin.

Laura put her hand on mine. "Hey. What are you thinking about?"

I took another pull from my drink. "About you," I said, trying to smile.

"I hope not," she said. "You look about ready to kill someone."

"I have a headache from all the kids today. Sorry. All the fucking noise."

Laura looked up from the menu. "I thought you liked it there."

"In doses," I said, finishing my drink. "I shouldn't have picked today to come by." The ice cubes rattled as I set the glass on the table.

"Slow down," said Laura. "We haven't even ordered yet."

I motioned to the waiter to bring me another.

"What is your problem?" Laura whispered loudly, leaning toward me. "What's going on?"

I felt anger coursing through me, building. Part of me wanted to stop myself. Part of me wanted to apologize and start over, go for a walk down the pier together, look at the sunset on the water.

But another part wanted to hurt Laura; hurt her so bad.

"Talk to me. What's wrong?"

"You look really ugly when you make that face," I said. "When you crinkle your forehead up like that. You look about eighty years old."

Laura stared at me. "Jacob. What are you doing?"

"I'm ordering a drink," I said. "I'm a grown man."

"Why are you acting like this? What did I do?"

My drink arrived. Laura tried to grab it, but I yanked it away, spilling some on the table. A couple nearby looked over.

"What are you looking at, fuckface?" I said to the guy.

"Jacob! Stop it!"

"Shut up," I said to Laura. Then I turned back to the couple looking over from their table. The woman had turned away but the man was still watching us from the corner of his eye.

"We're having a private conversation here. Turn that way," I said to him. "Do it. Turn around. Before I stab you with your fucking lobster fork."

Laura got up to leave.

I got up too. "You watch it," I said, pointing at the man at the other table. I took out a bill for the drink and flicked it on the table.

By the time I was out in the parking lot, Laura had gotten into the car.

"Wait," I said, but she was pulling out of the lot.

I stood in front of the car and Laura squealed to a stop.

"Wait," I said again.

She was crying. "What do you want from me, Jake? What?"

"I want you to leave me alone," I said. I could hardly believe the words coming out of my mouth. But right then it was true. All I wanted was to hold her, but at the same time, all I wanted was to rip her apart.

"That's it?" she said. "That's really what you want?"

"That's what I want," I said.

"You don't love me. You don't want to be with me anymore. Just like that."

"I don't love you," I said. "I want to, but I don't. Go find someone else."

She stared at me, her eyes wet and red. "You're lying. I know you are."

"I don't love you, Laura. I don't want to be with you. Go away."

"Jacob, I love you. I don't care if you're not ready for things, the house, or whatever. I just want to be with you. We can work it out."

"Are you deaf? Go. Away. Fuck off. I don't want to be around you anymore. Leave."

Laura waited.

I slammed my hand on the car's roof. "What else do you need to hear, you stupid bitch? You cunt! Go! Get lost!"

Laura shot me a look; her eyes were full of grief and pity. Then she put the car in drive and left me in the parking lot.

I took a while getting home. I stopped at a bar I liked, a small place by the airport called the Fly by Night, and I drank more than I should have. I didn't feel drunk when I left, but by the time I got home, I couldn't walk straight. The front door lock took me three tries to open.

The house was completely dark and difficult to navigate. Gripping the banister for balance, I climbed the spiral staircase to see if Laura had gone to bed. But of course, Laura wasn't in our bedroom. Some of her clothes lay strewn about the floor, and it hit me then that she was truly gone.

I saw one of the walkie-talkies on the floor by the bed and I picked it up and turned it on.

"Laura?" I said into its receiver. "Do you copy? Kitty Kat?"

Nothing. Just static.

I clipped the walkie-talkie to my belt and headed downstairs. The house looked especially beautiful that night. Moonlight poured in through the windows, casting long blue shadows across the walls. The nails in the floorboards gleamed like stars. The tiny faces in the molding looked so alive, they seemed to be watching me as I made my way down the main hallway.

I wandered from room to room, trying to take in the whole house, all the work Laura and I had put into it. So many of the rooms were finished now. I wanted to appreciate every little detail; I sat and smoked a cigarette in the leather armchair Laura had bought for the study. I stared at my own fun-house reflection in the bottom of the glass bowl on the living room coffee table. I ran my hand over the points of the antique pitchfork hanging on the wall of the kitchen.

The garden room I saved for last. As I entered, the view caught me off guard. I'd been in the room at night before, but that evening the yard looked so beautiful through the huge windows, the grass shimmering purple in the moonlight, sloping away toward the old lemon fields. There were only a few small patches of shrub left to clear at the yard's edge. The rest was smooth and clean. I took the machete from the box by the door and headed outside.

The cool air smelled like lemons and fresh-cut grass, and as I walked down the hill toward the far end of the yard I felt invigorated, wild. Just a little more work and the property would be done; I would finish the whole job that night. I walked faster. The machete made a low humming noise as the blade swung by my side.

When I reached the thicket at the edge of the yard I started right in, hacking away, chopping at the dense knots of vines and thornbushes. The machete was dull and it took a few whacks of the blade to cut through even the thinnest brush. Before long I'd sweated through my shirt, but I kept slashing. It was exhilarating, the glint and scream of the blade, the shudder it sent up my arm when it hit. Some of the vines sprayed a sweet, stinking liquid from their severed stumps.

Eventually, I found myself on the other side of the main thicket. The brush began to thin out, and soon enough I could hack through the vegetation without much trouble. I'd never been this deep behind the yard before. The old lemon fields were dried out, but tall, reedy grasses and bulbous weeds covered the area. I could hear rodents moving beneath me, and every few moments the grass rustled with the movements of larger animals I couldn't see.

I walked for a long time, hacking away at everything in front of me. *This is my life,* I thought, and brought down the blade. I slashed my way forward. *This is my fucking face.* I was so busy swinging the blade I almost walked right into the women's prison. I didn't even notice the perimeter until it was in front me, a wide, glowing green line in the grass.

I looked across the line at the prison grounds on the other side. They appeared even more stunning than through the telescope; the manicured lawns glistened. The trees were clipped perfectly. The chalk-white walking paths wound across the grass.

I braced myself for an alarm to sound, and then waved the machete over the line. But nothing happened.

I put one foot on the other side of the line, then the other. Still no alarm. Maybe it was silent, I thought, but somehow I knew that there was no warning system.

I crossed the grass to the main walking path. Up ahead, the barracks rose from behind a line of trees. I headed toward them, the machete at my side.

The grounds were entirely silent. No crickets, no owls. Just the faint crunch of my feet on the path. I passed the jogging track, the small pond filled with koi, the vegetable garden with its little rows of trellised stalks. I passed the picnic tables where the women sat for lunch every day.

When I reached the barracks, I saw that the only thing blocking me from entering was a screen door. Slowly, I pulled the door open and stepped inside.

The barracks were darker than I expected. Small emergency plug-ins lined the base of the walls, casting dim puddles of light along the linoleum floor. All around me, I could hear the women breathing in their sleep. I walked past the first few bunks. I saw the eye surgeon in one of the bottom beds. She looked different in person. She slept on her back, her lips parted just slightly. I leaned over her, examining her face in the faint light. With her glasses off and her features relaxed she looked much prettier than she had through the telescope. Younger, more innocent.

I walked on. I passed the jazz drummer; I passed Shirley Sayles, the golfer, sleeping with a tanned arm thrown over her eyes. As I continued on, I noticed that many of the beds had photographs taped to the headboards. One woman had a picture of a puppy sleeping on a windowsill. Another had a photograph of a little boy with a balloon tied to his wrist by a ribbon. Some of the women had belongings or charms beside their beds, on shelves built into the walls: a stuffed giraffe, a library book, a snow globe with a miniature tropical resort inside.

Then I saw her. Rose Deach was sleeping on a bottom bunk near the window. I could tell it was her by her hair, white against the dark pillow.

I was careful to be quiet as I made my way over. There were no pictures taped to her headboard. No toys or trinkets or books on her shelf. There was just Rose, lying alone in the narrow bed.

I bent down over her, examining her face, which was raked across with deep wrinkles. Her expression was stern. Her lips were pressed tightly together and her brow was creased, like she was thinking hard about something. She had black scabs growing on her scalp, visible through her thinning hair. Her breath came in slow rasps.

"Rose," I whispered, excited now. "Rose." But her eyes stayed closed.

I reached down and opened her hand. Then I placed the machete in her palm and closed her fingers around the handle.

Her eyes fluttered opened. I felt my throat seize. Even through the darkness I could see how yellow her eyes were.

"Rose," I said.

I thought she might start, or even scream, but she just stared at me, blinking away sleep.

She turned her head and glanced at the machete, her thin fingers wrapped around its handle, and then she looked back at me. Slowly, she pushed herself up to a sitting position.

I pointed to my chest. "What do you see?" I whispered. "Here."

She was looking straight at me, but she said nothing.

"Please," I said. I opened my shirt so she could see the space over my heart.

"What do you see?"

Rose just stared.

"I'm begging you, Rose. Tell me." I felt tears forming in my eyes. My voice was cracking. I needed to know.

"Jacob," came a woman's voice. Laura's voice. I spun around, but the hall was dark and silent.

"Jacob. Where are you?"

She sounded close and far away at the same time, like someone shouting through the wind.

"Jacob?"

I realized her voice was coming from the walkie-talkie still clipped to my belt. The red light on the top had come on.

"Jake, I can't find you."

Rose Deach was looking at me, dead-on. I took her hand and placed it over my bare chest. Her palm was cool and rough and sent a chill through my ribs, but I held it against my skin. I stared into her eyes, crying now.

"Jacob, where are you?" said Laura.

I held Rose Deach's hand against my chest. "Here," I said, pressing her palm hard over my heart. "Here."

Wreck

N THE SUMMER, I SIT UP IN MY HUNTING STAND AND WATCH THE children get thin. There's a camp for obese youth just down the road from my house—a fat farm—and from the stand, perched high up in a basswood tree, I have a clear view of the whole facility. I can see the different buildings scattered around the grounds: the cafeteria, the gymnasium, the rows of cabins. I can see the playing fields. I can even see the campers themselves, lumbering about, half-nude and shameful.

The place is called a camp, but to watch the campers is to know that it's a farm. There are all kinds of camp activities: the children go swimming, barging around in a small pond; they play soccer and tennis, even basketball. But they do everything dressed in uniforms, shorts and T-shirts made of a black, rubbery material. The uniforms are designed to absorb the sunlight, to suck it right up and make the kids run with sweat. They have strips of mesh around the belly and down the thighs to let things funnel, and with my rifleman's binoculars, complete with adjustable crosshairs, I can see the sweat draining down the children's stomachs and thick legs, leaving shiny, slug-like trails across the playing courts.

All summer I watch the children run and jump and heave under that fat, watch them struggle to shake it off. Occasionally, they manage it, too. They peel off their uniforms and emerge pale and slender, looking slightly bewildered, blinking into the bright August sunshine. But more often than not they simply achieve weird, un-even forms of fat. One girl last summer lost only the rings of lard around her neck, and another, just the turkey flaps beneath her arms. I once saw a boy who was bony from the waist up, but mam-moth around the ass and legs, like his guts had been stuffed down to make room for something that had never arrived. Always, though, before I'm ready for it, winter charges in from the east, hammering everything flat with cold, and the children scatter, having emptied all they could of themselves into the ground.

Now and then one gets loose. Sometimes a boy, but usually a girl. I'll be outside with my metal detector, sweeping it through the woods by the road, and she'll barrel through in a flurry of snapping twigs. Once, a black boy, about eleven years old, got into my house. When I came home from work I found him standing in my kitchen, cooking popcorn in a pan. He was tremendous, probably twice my weight even though I stood at least a foot taller. He could have car-ried the stove out on one shoulder.

He didn't see me at first. My cat was crouched beside the refrig-erator, trembling. The boy had flung off the top of his uniform and his titanic, black breasts were slick with sweat. A veil of cobwebs clung to his hair. I was amazed and terrified by him, by his need; I could have watched him for hours. He mumbled frantically at the kernels to pop. He talked right into that furious, sizzling pan.

"Come on and pop, motherfuckers!" he said to the kernels, rat-tling them over the flame. Sparks of butter shot from the pan. "Pop! Pop! Pop! Pop!"

But they wouldn't; he'd doused them with too much salt. At the camp, the children weren't allowed to have salty foods because salt made them retain water. So this boy had poured salt all along the floor of the pan, smothering the kernels in it, cooking salt into them until they looked like tiny white baby-teeth burning on the stove.

"Pop!" he yelled again. "Pop up!"

Then he saw me.

I suddenly realized I was caked in salt—dried sweat from being out all day in the July heat.

He stared at me, his mouth hanging open.

"Easy there," I said.

He put down the pan and raised his hands toward me.

"Let's just calm it down, okay? Calm. *Calm!*"

He trudged around from beside the stove. My cat hissed hysterically. I backed into the wall, knocking off a pilot's medal I'd dug up the day before.

He kept coming, those horrible breasts of his swinging from side to side.

"Wait a second!" I said, huddled in the corner. "Stop!" But then he moved past me, out the door, and was gone.

Certain nights, even now, I have nightmares about him, nightmares that instead of leaving the house, he descends on me, clamping down with his hands and mouth. Before I can stop him, he's licking the salt off my body with his giant, monstrous tongue, licking it off my face and my chest; he's sucking it off my arms, off my fingers; and then he's biting at me, eating me; he's tearing strips of flesh from my back with his teeth as I scream and struggle to escape, he's ripping chunks out of my thighs. He eats and eats and eats, in a wild effort to get back the very thing he just spent three hot months trying to lose.

Not long ago, I met a woman who was very famous. I never found out what, exactly, she was famous for, but it seemed everyone knew who she was except for me. I worked in Glens Creek at the time. I sold hunting equipment in the back of a cavernous sporting goods store: rifles and shotguns, but also oddities such as turkey decoys and shrunken plastic flutes that would turn your voice into the call of a lusty mule deer.

She came into the store at the very start of summer. An enormous man walked in behind her. Even in his shorts and flip-flops he reminded me of one of those heroic, iron statues you see in front of museums or military tombs. When I first saw him I thought that maybe he was the one who'd done that to her face.

She wore a baseball cap pulled down low on her head and huge sunglasses over her eyes. But still, there was no hiding the damage. Her cheeks were puffy and swollen, and her eyes lay in deep black-and-yellow webs of bruising. Trails of stitching crossed the skin beneath her eyelids, and her nose had bulged to a shiny mound with one stringy blue vein running down the spine like a river on a map. Beneath her chin hung a rubbery yellow bag, into which some kind of fluid was draining.

"Excuse me," she said to me. "Do you sell archery equipment?" She seemed nervous, jittery. Her eyes kept shifting around behind the lenses of her sunglasses, which were blue at the top, fading to a sparkling gold at the bottom. How wonderful to look out and see the world through those lenses, I thought. Like having a glass image of dawn over each eye.

I took her to the store's archery section, her man following us. As we made our way through the aisles, I became aware that people were looking in our direction, but I assumed this was because of her injuries.

I showed her the different kinds of bows—the longbows, the recurves, the compounds—and I recommended what I thought would be best for a beginner.

"And you find that archery is fun?" she said, looking at me a little intensely. "I mean, it's something you can really get into?"

"If you take to it, I guess," I said.

"But you don't find it fun?" she said, biting her thumbnail.

I shrugged. "Me? Not so much."

She gave a tired little laugh and clasped her hands behind her head, causing her nipples to press at the fabric of her shirt in a way that sent a warm tremble through my stomach. "Okay, here's the thing," she said. "I'm a lady with a lot of time on her hands and I want to find something to do that's private and fun. What do you do for fun around here? By yourself."

"Me? I collect things," I said. "If you're staying nearby, you should get yourself a metal detector and see what you can find in the ground. The woods up the road from town used to be a kind of dumping area."

A man carrying a Big Wheels box stared at us as he slowly passed the entrance to our aisle. The woman shot a nervous glance over her shoulder. "Go looking for things in the ground," she said.

"It's what I do alone," I said.

She looked down the aisle again, but it was empty except for the two of us and her man. "All right, you've sold me," she said. "Where are your metal detectors?"

I suddenly realized we didn't sell them. I told her so, but offered to lend her one of my own. "I have two," I said. "Just tell me your address and I'll drop it off."

"My address?" she said. She looked at me for a moment. Behind her, her man took a canteen from the rack, unscrewed the cap, and peered into the empty calfskin pouch.

"Listen," she said, "you seem like a nice guy, but let me just emphasize what an evil person it would make you to put me through anything while I was in this kind of condition, okay?"

"What do you mean?"

She sighed. "What I mean is, I wouldn't even have come to town, but I feel like I'm going stir-crazy sitting in my house all day," she said. "What I mean is, look at my face."

She lifted her sunglasses to give me a better view of her injuries, but all I saw were her eyes. They were the lightest blue, almost white. Tiny blue rafts in that storm of a face.

"Your eyes are pretty," I said, before I could help it. As soon as the words were out, I felt my face go red. I'd never said anything like that to a woman I didn't know well.

"My eyes are pretty?" she said, staring at me. For an awful moment I thought she was about to call her man over to destroy me. Instead, she laughed, causing the bag beneath her jaw to jump around in an oddly pleasant, girlish kind of way. Then she took a pen from her pocket and wrote down her address. "It's Saturday tomorrow. If you're off, come by in the morning, around ten, and you can show me how to use the metal detector."

I told her ten would be fine.

"I'm Grace, by the way," she said, and put her hand out.

I shook it. "Wade," I said.

"This scavenging better be fun, Wade," she said, smiling and pointing her finger at me in a playful way. "Don't let me down, now." Then she turned and left, her man trailing after her.

As soon as she'd gone, Haymont, my supervisor, hurried over from behind a rack of animal urines. "That was her, wasn't it?" he said, breathing fast. "I'd heard she was staying somewhere nearby, but I never thought she'd come in here. I can't believe she talked to you of all people!" He laughed. "You're probably the one person on earth who hasn't heard of her."

"Who?" I said.

"Christ, Wade," he said, already rushing to the window. "If you don't know, I'm not going to tell you."

My cat is blind. There's nothing wrong with his eyes—his eyes are perfect—but they've been disconnected from his brain. I found him through an ad in the paper. The university used him in a lab test, is why he's blind. As soon as he was born, the people in the lab sewed his eyes shut and kept him like that for three weeks. Finally, after all that time meowing in the dark, they plucked out the stitches and pried open his little eyelids. And what they found was that although there was nothing wrong with his eyes anatomically, they didn't work anymore. The doctors tried it again and again with other kittens, and every time the same thing happened. What they proved was that if a cat doesn't learn how to use something during that first, critical period—not just its eyes, but its ears or even its voice—it never will. The critical periods for some kittens are very short. They only last a matter of days, a matter of hours.

My cat's name is Sonny. He's gray with orange stripes and I try to take him everywhere with me. The morning I set out for Grace's house, Sonny lay curled up beside me on the passenger seat of my truck, his face resting on his paws.

The address proved difficult to find. The house was set back from the main road, at the end of a long, rutted dirt path that wound deep into the woods. When I finally arrived, the size of the house surprised me. It looked like an old hunting lodge, with log walls and high chimneys of piled gray stone at either end of its mountainous roof.

Grace emerged from the lodge's front door wearing a tank top and shorts made of a pink towel-like material. Her whole body was tanned a rich, buttery brown and streamlined in a way I'd never encountered in real life.

"So, this is your weapon of choice, huh?" she said as I pulled the metal detector from the truck. The bag beneath her chin was empty today. It looked like a yellow rubber bib.

I showed Grace how to work the detector, how to hold the neck close to her stomach so as not to hurt her back, how to wave the pan over the ground in slow, wide arcs. I explained that fast clicks meant precious metal, and that lesser kinds like nickel or steel caused more of a low, static sound. I tossed some coins on the ground so she could hear the chatter.

"I don't know, Wade. I lost something at the beach once when I was a kid and they looked for it with one of these things . . . to *no* avail," she said, smiling at me with exaggerated skepticism as she slowly moved the detector over the coins.

"If you don't like it, I'll bring over the archery equipment to-morrow," I said, and then started back to my truck.

I was about to tell her good-bye, when she said, "Hey, Wade, why don't you come along today?"

I hadn't considered this. I tried to imagine spending the af-ternoon with someone. The last time I had real company was months ago.

She glanced at her man. "No offense to Petyr, but I could use a fresh face around here. And you're not a weirdo, right?" she said.

I told her I wasn't a weirdo.

"Good. It's settled. Let's start scavenging."

And so we did. I let Sonny out so he could rest in the shade be-side the truck, and then the three of us set off into the woods be-hind the house, Petyr walking behind Grace and me.

At first I felt nervous, being around someone new, but the day was ideal, warm and sunny, and soon enough I began to relax. The metal detector gave off gentle, bird-like clucking noises as we walked. A soft breeze blew up from town, causing the Indian grass along the forest floor to sway back and forth and tickle our bare legs.

As we made our way deeper into the woods, I explained to Grace about the surrounding land, about why it was so rich with collectibles. I told her about the air force base that used to exist ten miles west of town many years ago, back during the two World Wars. And about how the air force men of those days believed that, upon returning from combat in foreign lands, it was good luck to throw something out of the plane just before it touched down, some token of your time overseas. "If you did," I explained to Grace, "according to the superstition, you wouldn't be haunted by anything you'd seen or done while you were away. The person you'd been couldn't follow you home."

"What kinds of stuff have you found?" Grace asked. A jay flapped up behind us and I remembered Petyr. Despite his size, Petyr was unusually stealthy.

"All sorts of things. Lockets, watches, bullet casings. Last month I found a toy train, a little windup engine. There's an antique store in town that takes almost all of it."

"You don't get lonely living out here all by yourself?" she said. "Alone in the woods? No people to talk to?"

"I talk to people at work," I said, helping Grace over a log. "And I talk to the old man who runs the antique store when I bring things in. Mr. Gourd."

"Mr. Gourd?" Grace said, and chuckled. "What are you, Wade, twenty-eight? Twenty-nine? Don't you have a girlfriend? Some friends our age?"

People were always asking me things like this.

"I like my own company," I said. "I'm not lonely."

And it was true: I wasn't lonely. I had never been lonely. I had no real friends, no family, but I didn't long for any of that. Alison, the last woman I'd dated, had left me because she felt that I acted like I didn't need her, like I didn't need anyone at all.

"You don't relate to people, Wade," she'd said the day she left. It had been scorchingly hot. We were sitting naked on the kitchen floor with the refrigerator open behind us, its vapor cooling our backs. Behind Allison's head were bags and jars of uneaten food. "It's like you don't know how and you don't care to learn. What happened to you? Who fucked you up?"

But nothing had happened. No one had done this to me. I had never been any other way. If anything, it was living here, in this place, that made it hard to become attached to other people. No one stayed around very long. It seemed that, eventually, everyone moved away. In their old age, residents left for warmer weather, as my parents had done. And most young people took off for big cities to start careers and families as soon as they finished high school. Over time I'd come to think of this area, my home, as a kind of port that people stopped at for a little while, a port in which to do a bit of maintenance before piloting off.

I understood why no one stayed, too. The land here is unattractive. It's frozen and bare nearly ten months out of the year. The frenzied parade of summer comes and goes before anyone can really enjoy it. Flowers huddle in frightened little bunches. The trunks of too many trees are knotty with tumorous black burls. Even Alison herself wanted to leave. The whole time we were dating she kept talking about getting out, going somewhere exciting.

But there are things to like around here. It's quiet and peaceful. In the winter the ice is so thick it glows blue. You can hear it slowly rolling forward at night, splitting and pushing on, making noises like grinding teeth.

The metal detector gave off a burst of sharp clicks. "Yay!" Grace said, and laughed. She laid the detector on the ground and took a garden shovel out of the pack around her waist. Petyr came over and offered to dig for her, but she said she wanted to do it herself.

I sat beside Grace as she dug. Whenever she hit a rock, I scooped it out and tossed it to the side. As she worked, she passed in and out of a patch of sun that caused her hair to change color. In the light it shined up to a brilliant red, in the shade it became a dull brown. Seeing it shift back and forth like that, I felt as though she were sharing something special with me, letting me get a glimpse of some secret part of herself. It was noon by now, and after a few minutes of digging, she took a break and we sat back on the grass. The sun felt wonderful on my face and chest. High above us, the pine trees creaked back and forth in the breeze like the masts of ancient ships.

"What was it you lost at the beach?" I said. "When you were a kid. The thing the metal detector couldn't find."

"What? Oh, it was nothing," Grace said. "Just a piece of metal."

I waited for her to go on.

She laughed, but it was a sad hiccup of a laugh. "It's dumb. It was the latch to the mailbox of my mom and dad's house. This little tin ladybug you flipped down to keep the mailbox door from falling open. I took it with me when we first left for California. I know. It's stupid."

"I don't think it's stupid," I said.

Grace pulled her knees to her chest and smiled at me. "Thanks, Wade," she said. "I was pretty hysterical about losing it at the time." She took off her sunglasses and wiped them on her shorts and there were those eyes of hers again. The stitches beneath them looked like extra sets of curling eyelashes. I felt myself staring, so I glanced at Petyr, who was lying beneath a tree with his eyes closed. A bright green leaf had landed on his giant chest and rose and fell with his breath.

"Look at him," Grace said. "I should probably just let him go, now that I scare everyone away myself." She pointed to her face and laughed, but then she looked away, at the pit she'd dug in the ground.

"I find you very beautiful," I said, which I knew then to be true.

She blushed. "You know, I didn't do this to look younger or anything like that. I was in an accident. I don't want to talk about it," she said, touching the bag under her chin, which now had some liquid in it. "I'll tell you a secret, though, since I was so nosy before." She leaned closer and I could feel the warmth coming off her body. "I poke at it sometimes, at my face. I know I'm not supposed to, that I'll scar it, but I do it anyway."

"Why?" I said.

"I don't know," she said. "Maybe I'm just not ready to go back home yet."

"Everyone around here leaves sooner or later," I said.

"Well, who knows? Maybe I'll be a 'later,' " she said.

Grace and I started spending time together regularly after that. Sometimes she'd meet me at the store and Haymont would let me go—would, in fact, nearly push me out the door after her. Other days I'd drive out to her house after work. I'd pull up with Sonny and find her waiting for me on her porch swing, or on her stomach reading in the tall grass, the sunlight fanning over the backs of her long legs. Petyr hardly ever joined us. Grace told me that his sister was having problems with her husband, who coincidentally was also a bodyguard. Petyr had a high, soft voice, a soothing voice, and he spent long hours walking around the lawn with his tiny silver phone, talking patiently to one of them, then the other. At night he retired to the guesthouse, a cabin at the edge of the yard with vines strangling it.

Grace and I spent most of our time loafing around that cavernous house of hers. She had movie players that could hold up to two hundred movies at once, and a huge flat-panel TV that hung on the wall like an antique mirror, but we never used any of that. Grace left it all unplugged. She made a bed for Sonny on the movie player out of an old, glittery dress, and he took to lying there nearly all the time. We drank beer and played board games. We built an intricate model of a French church that I had bought in town. At night we lit fires in the massive stone fireplaces—fires nearly as big as me, fires that sounded like war and lit the whole house with smoky orange light. There was a pool in Grace's basement—or rather, her basement was a pool. You walked down the basement steps right into a long, tiled alleyway of water. The pool was rich in minerals and smelled like clay, and when Grace lit the porthole lights along the walls, the water glowed a luminescent, milky green, like the color of a potion from a children's book.

As the summer wore on, Grace's manners relaxed. She started teasing and joking with me, ribbing me about how out of touch with things I was, but in a way that let me know how much she liked this about me. I set up a hammock on the balcony and we often lay in it reading or talking or napping together. We cooked meals out of a glossy cookbook. Sometimes we went to my place and watched the children down at the fat farm. We picked one out and followed her progress through my binoculars. She was pretty in an exotic sort of way, with olive skin and soft black down on her arms. We named her Patty. She kept her hair in two braided loops that hung from either side of her head like giant earrings. Patty's favorite activity was tennis, and Grace and I would sit up in my stand and watch her clomping back and forth along the baseline. It felt so calming, observing Patty from high in the trees, so fulfilling. It was like we were her parents and she was our daughter, and I felt proud of her for working so hard to achieve her goals.

On days that were cool or overcast, Grace and I went scavenging. She held the metal detector and I walked out in front, scouting, wearing those sunglasses of hers, my head angled so that the horizon always stayed balanced along that narrow band of clarity between the darkening planes of gold and blue.

As we walked, Grace told me things about herself. She rarely talked about California or her life out there. Now and then, though, a certain worried look would appear on her face and I understood that she was thinking about having to go back. Petyr knew not to put calls through to Grace, but I often spied little sticky notes that he left for her clinging to things around the house like insects. They always had names on them, with messages written beneath, like *Again* or *Twice today.*

Sometimes, as we walked, I wondered about Grace's life before the accident; I wondered what it was that she did out in California— was she a singer? An athlete? A businesswoman? What had made her so famous? More than that, though, I wondered about the little things that made up her life out there, the details. I wanted to see the view from her front door. I wanted to know what the inside of her car looked like. To see the magnets she kept stuck to her refrigerator.

We never talked about her accident. Over time, though, I came to understand that whatever had happened to her had involved glass. Because every now and then—no more than once every couple of days—a piece of glass would emerge from her head. These weren't big shards that came out of her; they were tiny specks of glass, just particles. Apparently, when she had her accident, some glass had gotten lodged between the two layers of muscle tissue around her head, and now they were slowly working their way out of her. Mostly the glass came out through her hair follicles. But on a couple of occasions, pieces of glass exited right through her face. Once I saw one come out of the corner of her eye, a tiny shard, no bigger than a snowflake. I watched as she calmly plucked it from beneath her lid as though it were a stray eyelash.

Even though Grace didn't talk about her current life during our walks, or about her accident, she still managed to tell me all kinds of intimate things about herself. She told me about her parents, her childhood. She told me about how, as a little girl, she'd wanted to be a policewoman, then an acrobat, then a deep-sea fisherman. She told me about her mother, about how she'd made Grace beg for change when they first moved out west, beg everywhere from the boardwalk to the bus station, where a man had once thrown a penny right into Grace's mouth.

No one had ever talked to me in such a way before, never so openly. It was weirdly arousing. It felt like watching someone undress right in front of me; it felt like standing next to them and being handed layer after layer of clothing. And the more she talked, the harder it became for me to ignore the need for her I felt building in me. I tried, though, because I understood that she was here with me only for the summer, just until her face healed. And it was healing all the time.

By the second week I knew her, a kind of settling process had already begun. Her features, the ones that were swollen and bulged out of place, had rapidly started taking shape, gathering ominously toward the center of her face. But part of me refused to see these changes. Part of me already believed that something would happen to stop her from leaving. Something miraculous, or even terrible.

Here's what Grace told me on one of our walks: one morning,

while she and her mother were wandering on the beach, they found a dollhouse washed up on the sand.

"It was so creepy," she said. "I'd been asking for a dollhouse—it was like the one thing I wanted for my birthday that year, my eighth birthday—and suddenly here one was. Just sitting there on the sand in perfect condition. Even the tiny windowpanes were intact."

We were walking along the edge of a brook that had long ago dried to chalk. It was three weeks to the day since I'd met her. The wind blew strongly. The shadows of clouds kept skating over us before we saw them coming.

"My mom and I had this game," said Grace. "Whenever we found something washed up on the beach, we would try to guess whether it was flotsam or jetsam. Flotsam is what gets washed overboard in storms—it's things swept away by the sea. Jetsam is what's thrown overboard if a ship is in distress. What people get rid of to make the ship lighter so it won't sink. There's really no way to tell which is which after the fact. I mean, if the ship wrecks, everything gets mixed up together, the stuff people wanted to keep and the stuff they got rid of. It all becomes the same thing."

The metal detector gave a few clicks around a patch of scrub. I rooted around for a moment but couldn't feel anything substantial, so we went on.

"So my mom wanted me to guess which the dollhouse was," said Grace, "flotsam or jetsam, but I didn't want to. The idea of some girl my own age on a ship about to sink was really scary to me, you know? And then, right as I was looking at it, the whole house just fell in on itself. It collapsed in a heap on the sand."

Grace's calves moved up and down in gentle swallowing motions as we walked. "Keep talking to me," I said. "I love listening to you."

She smiled at me over her shoulder. The light that afternoon was kind, and her cheek looked like a smooth, snow-covered field broken only by the wiry black fencing of her stitches. "It's easy to talk to you," she said. "I like who I am with you. I love her, actually."

"Can I try kissing you again?" I said. We'd kissed a few times before, but it had always hurt her face too much.

"Stay still and let me kiss you," she said, and then she leaned over and brushed her lips against mine, first the top one, then the bottom. Next I felt her tongue tracing my lips, gently sliding between them. Before I knew it she was kissing me harder, really pressing her mouth against mine. I kissed her back. Our teeth kept clicking together. I felt the bag beneath her chin bulge as it was squeezed between our necks—the liquid inside felt warm and viscous—and I worried that it might pop, but she kept at it, pushing harder now, hardly kissing so much as driving her mouth into mine, wedging and ramming. When she finally stopped and pulled away I saw blood inside her mouth.

"I'm sorry," she said, and wiped her lips with the back of her hand. "I didn't hurt you, did I?"

"No," I said.

"I just don't want to go back yet," she said. She tugged on the collar of my shirt. "And I like you."

"Kiss me again," I said. And she did.

To this day, I remember everything she told me. I even remember exactly what we found scavenging each day. The afternoon Grace told me about the dollhouse, we discovered a bottle cap, a green stone she thought was pretty, and the horn from a phonograph, smashed so badly you wouldn't believe music had ever passed through.

———

By July we'd started making love, but rarely, only once every few days. Grace wanted to more often: she asked me to, but I had to be careful; it would have been too much. Already I couldn't sleep without her. When she wasn't with me, my house seemed to buzz with silence. I tried to keep some distance between us, but she began talking about driving with me back to California. We didn't have to stay out there, she said. We wouldn't. We'd just hang around long enough for her to settle some things, some business matters, and then we could go anywhere we wanted—we could even come back here. She said she loved me. I couldn't stop myself from being hopeful, from expecting things. I bought a book on driving across the country and drew little stars next to all the places I wanted to take her.

But her face was taking shape. The drainage bag had vanished, along with the stitches beneath her eyes, inside her mouth. All that was left of the face I'd known was a ghostly blueprint of white scars, and even that was quickly melting into the fresh pink skin underneath. At certain moments she looked like someone else entirely, someone strangely familiar whom I'd seen or met many times over, but somehow managed to forget. At first she acted as frightened about all this as I was. Not just frightened of what was happening, but also of what I'd think about her. The day the last of the stitches came out, I had to convince her to come out of her bedroom.

"It doesn't matter what you look like," I said into the keyhole.

"You'll see why I don't want to go back," she said, crying. "You'll know what I used to be like."

"I know what you're like now," I said. "That's all that matters."

When she finally opened the door and I saw those flawless crescents of flesh beneath her eyes, I felt my blood drain. She'd become beautiful to a degree that felt difficult for me to understand.

Her face didn't look like a face anymore. It was like a sail she'd raised between me and her real face, a tall white sail that could carry her anywhere she wanted to go. And as much as I didn't want it to matter what she looked like, as much as I told her so, it *did* matter, and I wanted the healing to stop, to slow down at least.

But of course it didn't slow down: her skin tightened, her cheekbones surfaced. Streaks of copper appeared in her hair. I tried to ignore it, but sometimes looking at her made me so sad that I could barely speak. Grace began to make arrangements. She started taking calls from Petyr. At first she spoke in a brief, clipped manner, but soon she began to really *talk* into the phone. She joked and laughed and wound the cord around her finger. Occasionally she used a miniature phone hooked up to her ear by a cord, a phone that left her hands free and made it look like she was talking to an invisible stranger in the room with us.

I began to think of California as a weak but constant force pulling on Grace, a growing undertow. I was certain that if I didn't go with her, I would lose her altogether, that she would just vanish behind its long curtains of sunshine. Sometimes, at night, watching her sleep, I wished for her face to go back to how it had looked when I met her. I actually fantasized about changing it back myself.

All of this happened in a matter of weeks, not months. It felt like it happened as fast as I'm telling it to you.

Near the end of July, just a couple of days before we were supposed to leave, I took her to the yearly picnic to celebrate the end of the tourist season. I warned her that a lot of the town would be there, that people would probably come up to her, but she insisted. We could bring Petyr, she said. It would be like our first real date. Food. Dancing. Romance.

I went out and bought a new pair of shoes and a tie with tiny downhill skiers on it. I asked a woman in town to make me a little ladybug out of tin, which she did, cherry red and covered with shiny black dots.

On the day of the picnic, Grace, Petyr, and I drove down the hill and into town in my truck. Before we even got within five blocks of the picnic, though, it became evident that everyone in town was attending. Parked cars lined the avenue, some up on the sidewalk and others left right in the middle of the street with the keys on the driver's seat.

The picnic took place on the lawn behind the mayor's house. He'd set up tables on the grass, which were already filled by the time we arrived. There must have been five hundred people crowded on the lawn, not counting the many children threading their way between the knots of adults, giggling and swatting at one another.

I felt Grace tense up at the sight of all those people—the joints in her arm locked—and I grew nervous too.

"We don't have to do this," I said.

She gave me a kiss on the cheek. "I want to show you off," she said.

A band from Canada played country songs in French beneath a tent at the edge of the lawn; couples had already begun to dance in a loose ring. As we crossed the lawn to the food, I felt Grace beginning to relax, but my own anxiousness only grew worse. People were staring. Most of them tried not to be obvious about it, but I could feel them looking at us, at Grace.

"Wade, are you all right?" said Grace.

I told her that I was.

"Hey, they're all staring at me, not you, okay?" She took my hand. "They're wondering how I landed the hottest stud in town."

"Grace . . ."

"Come on, let's dance," she said. Before I could refuse, she kissed my hand and led me toward the tent.

We stopped at the edge of the moving ring of couples. I put my hands on Grace's waist and pulled her close as we entered the flow of people and began to dance across the grass. Her skin was a deep brown and smooth as the underside of a shell. I felt my heart relaxing. I caught sight of Petyr standing by the edge of the tent, and I watched over Grace's shoulder as he tapped one foot in time to the music. Every few moments he'd let himself be swept along with the couples; he'd post his arm as though he'd found a partner and take a few graceful steps in the direction of the dance before hurrying off the floor and returning to the spot where he'd begun.

"I want to fly away with you in a blimp," I said to Grace. Everywhere, hoppers leapt out of the yellow grass. The feeling was like dancing across the surface of a fizzing glass of champagne.

She laughed. "A blimp? Like a zeppelin?"

"A blimp. I want to fly across the country with you in a blimp. Just coast, the two of us weightless up there."

She put her head on my shoulder and we kept dancing like that, swaying back and forth, while the other couples moved around us in unison, spinning, rising and falling like the working parts of a carousel. I kissed her neck and closed my eyes.

"Wade!" said Haymont, dancing next to us with his little daughter standing on his toes. "I didn't think you'd come today. You two about make the cutest couple here."

"I don't know how that's possible when you've got the prettiest girl around," said Grace. She winked at Haymont's daughter, who pressed her face into his belly.

Haymont laughed. "She's a shy one tonight. She's actually a big fan of yours."

Grace thanked him, though I could tell that, as always, he was making her uncomfortable.

"So, a little birdie told me you're taking Wade away from us. I get such a kick out of picturing him out in California," he said, and gave a big coughing laugh that nearly shook his daughter off him. "Wade driving down Hollywood Boulevard with the palm trees whizzing by. Waving to the stars." He laughed again, staring too hard at Grace.

"Let's go, Daddy," whined Haymont's daughter.

"Bailey, don't be rude, now," Haymont said to her. "Daddy's having a conversation here." But when he turned back to us, Grace had already put her head on my shoulder.

Haymont waited a moment. "You two have a good night, now," he said, finally.

We thanked him and he waddled off, maneuvering his daughter like a marionette.

"Not all of California's like that," Grace said into my neck. "That's just a small part. Besides, we're not going to stay."

"I know," I said, but as we made our way around the ring, Haymont's words stayed with me. I could feel him watching us, feel other people watching too. Making no bones about it now, just staring from their tables. And I knew so few of them. I could hardly pick out a familiar face. I saw a young girl whisper something to her mother and point at us. I saw her mother laugh into her napkin. I realized that this was what California was going to be like. People I didn't know gawking at us, laughing. Laughing because it was funny to see someone like me with someone like Grace. I caught sight of Petyr again, dancing alone by the edge of the tent, and a series of images flashed through my mind, images of myself alone in California, alone at all the places I'd read about in my guidebook.

On the beach. On the pier beneath a swarm of seagulls. At the aerospace fictitious museum, standing before an enormous, dangling model of the moon. I held Grace tighter against me, but even as I did I grew angry. It seemed like too long ago that I'd been happy alone, that I'd preferred it that way, and now I was suddenly following someone to the other side of the country. Someone I'd only known a matter of months. Someone who was just vacationing in my life. Someone who would leave me; who, in her own mind, had probably already left.

"Grace," I said, "I need to talk to you about California."

"I know. God, we're leaving so soon and we haven't ever really discussed my life out there, have we?"

"No," I said.

"It'll be difficult. But I'll only need a couple of weeks. I promise."

"I think you should go without me," I said.

Grace pulled back. "What are you talking about?"

"I think you should go to California without me. You could fly out and get done what you need to get done and I could stay here until you get back. I'd just be in your way out there."

"In my way? The whole fun was going to be driving out together. I thought you wanted to go with me."

"I did. I do. It's just that hunting season is about to start and Haymont needs me at the store. He'd never say so, but I know he does. I can tell."

The song ended and everyone bowed and curtsied. When the music began again, we continued around the ring.

"I don't want to go without you, Wade," Grace said, and laid her head on my shoulder again. As soon as her face touched my shirt, the sudden, overwhelming feeling shot through me that I was making a tremendous mistake. I had a stinging urge to tell her that I loved her, that I *needed* her, but I couldn't do it. In my mind, I begged her to ask me to come with her. I pleaded with her to ask me just once.

"I guess it would be easier if I went alone. It'd make things simpler to deal with," she said. And then, as though she *could* hear my thoughts: "Wade, you know I'll come back, don't you?"

"Yes," I said, already trying to memorize the sound of her voice, the feeling of her back against my hands.

"I mean, I'll only stay out there as long as I have to."

"I know," I said.

Grace's eyes searched mine. "Wade. I will. I'll come back."

I kissed her. "You'll come back," I said.

Later, while Grace danced with Petyr, I walked to the edge of the lawn and tossed the tin ladybug into the woods, where it was quickly swallowed by the ferns.

Grace called three times from California. The first call came just after she'd landed. I got home from work and found the light blinking on the machine. I could hear the slowing whine of the plane's engines in the background of her message. "Well, the eagle has landed," she said, "and all she wants to do is take off again and fly straight back there. Ugh, Wade. Get me out of here. I wish you'd come with me. I miss your tummy. I'm going home to take a nap, so don't bother calling. I'll try you tonight. Kiss Sonny for me."

I went to work and tried to keep busy, but I couldn't keep my mind on anything. Twice I almost gave equipment away for free.

I told myself she wasn't going to call. I told myself I didn't want her to.

But that night, when no call came, I couldn't sleep. I stayed up and watched the fireflies waste themselves against my window.

She didn't call the next morning either. I assumed she would call sometime that day, but instead of waiting around, I went scavenging with Sonny. I took him with me in a small pouch I'd bought, a pouch I could strap onto my back. We walked for hours, just the two of us. We hiked deep into the woods, deeper than I usually went, and late in the afternoon I found an amazing thing. A baby shoe dipped in copper. But I wasn't as excited as I knew I should be. I wasn't excited at all. Instead, the whole idea of being out in the woods, hunting for buried junk, suddenly felt ridiculous. It felt like a waste of time.

When I got home that night there was still no message from Grace. I felt a bubble of anger rise in my stomach.

I called the number she'd left, but all I got was a recording telling me that she was out of range. I called again, but the same thing happened. I called the office number she'd given me.

"Hello, Wade," said the office woman before I even opened my mouth. Her voice was hoarse and grating. "Grace gave me your number. My phone has it memorized. I'll tell her you called, okay?"

Again that night I couldn't sleep. The air crackled with her absence. I tried Grace's personal phone number again and again, into the early morning hours, but each time I got that same recording. Sometime around noon, I fell asleep by the window. I woke with a throbbing sunburn on half my face. The light on my machine was blinking.

"Wade, I'm so, so sorry I didn't call earlier," said Grace. "I know you've been trying to reach me. Don't worry, though, all right? Nobody's going to kidnap me or steal me away. You don't have to keep calling. We'll be all right. I just have a million things to do. Miss you. I'll try you tomorrow."

Three days passed with no word from her. I thought about flying out there. I thought about tracking her down.

Finally, the phone rang.

"Hello?" said Grace. I could hear car horns and voices in the background. "Hello, Wade?"

"Grace?" I said.

"Wade, are you there? Hello?"

"Yes! I'm here!" I said, both furious at her and panicked she'd hang up.

"Jesus. Hang on a second."

A rustling sound came from the other end, then things quieted down.

"Yikes. Sorry about that," said Grace. "I had to get away from the tables."

"I miss you," I said angrily.

"I miss you too. I'm sorry things have been so crazy here. The web is more tangled than I remembered."

"Grace, I want to come out there."

"Hon, that's not a good idea. I'm running around like a chicken with my head cut off and I—"

"Please, Grace. Just let me."

"Wade, I can't talk about this right now. I'm at a restaurant and the person I'm meeting just walked in."

"Who are you meeting? What's going on?"

"Just calm down, Wade, all right? You're acting silly."

"Don't tell me to fucking calm down! I want to come out there."

"Stop it, okay? Stop! Take some time and cool off. I'll call you when I get a moment."

The line went dead.

I tried to call her back but all I got was that recording. I called her office but no one picked up. I called twice more, and on the third try, a recording told me that my phone had been blocked by the number I was trying to reach. My face and hands pulsed with a painful heat.

I looked around my house at all the things I'd collected over the years. The trinkets and baubles and junk. I ran my arm along a shelf, knocking everything to the ground. I tore the shelf off the wall and threw it across the room. I smashed another shelf, and another. Soon the room was littered with broken things. I got in my truck and gunned it into town.

It was dark by the time I arrived at the store. Haymont was just locking up. I pushed past him and made my way to the counter, where the phone was kept. I dialed Grace's office.

That same woman picked up. "Put me through to Grace," I said.

"It doesn't work that way," she said, and hung up.

I called again and a recording told me that all phones in my area code had been blocked by the number I was trying to reach. I was about to slam the phone to the ground, when I remembered the one other number I had. I dialed.

"Hello?" said Petyr.

"Petyr, it's me, Wade," I said, overcome with gratitude. "Please. I need to talk to Grace."

"Grace asked me not to accept any calls from you, Wade," Petyr said in that quiet, soothing voice of his. "I have to go now. I'm hanging up. I'm sorry."

The line cut off.

"Are you all right?" said Haymont.

I looked up at him standing by the counter with his tie slung over his shoulder. I was about to yell at him to call Petyr for me, but something about the way he was looking at me caused me to stop. His eyes were fearful and he was shying away, almost cringing. I stepped forward to hand him the phone and he actually flinched. It reminded me of how frightened I'd been of that boy, the one who'd appeared in my kitchen long ago, so ravenous. I thought of how I'd recoiled as the dimpled black meat of his arms came toward me.

"How about we relax, Wade, all right?" said Haymont. "Please."

I put the phone down and drove home.

Eventually, as the weeks passed with no word from her, I came to understand that I would never see Grace again. This knowledge left me feeling both empty and strangely calm. The days grew quiet and dry. The August heat finally broke, causing leaves to crack and fall to the ground in brown particles. I decided to build a new hunting stand. I placed it farther up the trunk than the old one, up in the highest branches. I went scavenging with Sonny until late in the day, until it was nearly dark and our shadows stretched deep into the woods.

One morning, I woke to the sounds of going home. I realized, as I climbed from bed, that this was the day all the children were leaving for the winter. I fixed myself a coffee and headed out onto the porch to watch the buses take them away.

The day was very bright. I had to put on Grace's old sunglasses to be able to look at the camp without my eyes hurting. So many of the children were slim this year. There was hardly a fat one among them. I watched as they scurried around, hugging each other good-bye and exchanging numbers and addresses, loading their bags and duffels onto the buses. I went up to my stand to get a better view.

As I made my way up the rungs, though, I became aware of a creaking above me. I glanced up at the stand and saw that someone was already up there.

I froze halfway up the tree. Grace. She'd come back.

A breeze washed over me. I began climbing again, my hands

almost trembling. What would I say to her when I reached the stand? Part of me wanted to hug her. Another part wanted to hurl her to her death. When I neared the top of the trunk, though, I saw that the person in my stand wasn't Grace at all.

I pulled myself up onto the platform.

"You can see the whole camp from up here," said Patty. She was sitting cross-legged at the platform's edge. Her hair was finally loose. It hung down her back in a shimmering black fan. She was much smaller than she had been at the start of the summer, but she was by no means thin.

"You're going to miss your bus," I said.

She glanced over her shoulder and studied me a moment. "I pictured you different," she said. She spoke with a slight, lovely accent. "I thought you'd be older. Scarier."

"You should go. You're going to be left behind."

But she didn't move, just sat and stared at the camp, where the buses were already loading up. I sat down beside her. How strange she looked, part fat, part thin, like someone caught between two versions of herself. Her legs were almost slender, but there were crushed black veins in her ankles. Her neck was thin but her face was puffy and shiny with sweat.

Down at the camp, the buses began shuddering to life.

I noticed a chunk of something resembling a moon rock in Patty's lap. "What's that?" I said.

She glanced at the rock, turning it over in her hands. "It's salt. Rock salt."

She brought the rock to her mouth and bit off a piece. She sucked and chewed it. "See?" she said, and handed me the rock.

I took it and bit off a hunk. Immediately my tongue began to burn. Chewing it, I felt as though my teeth were cracking and shattering against its surface. My mouth filled with liquid.

Patty smiled at me. "Stings!" she said. Her eyes were bloodred from tearing. Drool leaked from her mouth.

Wiping her chin, she inched closer to me, and together we sat and watched the buses pull out of the lot. Counselors stood in the grass, waving good-bye.

I wished that Grace was there, that she was sitting beside me in my stand, watching the children leave for home. I could almost see her next to me instead of Patty, sitting at the platform's edge in her jeans and T-shirt, her hair pulled back from her spoiled face. I could practically feel her there, pressing against me. Her head was on my shoulder now, her hair soft against my neck. I smiled, staring out at the sloping woods through her old sunglasses. Because everything was all right. She was back with me. The sky was the bluest of blues, and the land was rich with gold.

Dumpster
Tuesday

Part One: The Two Ferns

THE RULE FOR GUARDING THE DUMPSTER WAS SIMPLE: NO ONE, under any circumstances, takes anything out.

So imagine my chagrin when I woke to the sounds of someone rummaging around inside the dumpster's hull. I wiped a porthole in my fogged-up windshield and saw that it was before dawn: the sky dark, the mist still clinging to the palm trees. I fished around until I found my spear gun and got out of the car.

"Time to quit that," I said, and banged on the dumpster's side, sprinkling rust everywhere.

The noise from inside stopped.

"Out," I said.

A man peeked over the lip. He was older than I'd expected for a thief; he looked to be in his seventies, skinny and bent, with unkempt hair and a dirty white beard.

"What seems to be the problem?" he said.

"Scat. Now."

"All right. Fine. Goddamn." The old man swung his leg over the top of the dumpster and lowered himself to the ground with surprising agility. He wore no shirt, just a pair of cutoff jeans shorts with long, fraying threads hanging off the ends. Spatters of pink spots dotted his chest and shoulders from years of too much sun. In his hand was a duck with part of its beak blown off.

"That goes back in," I said, and gestured to the duck, an old, wooden hunting decoy.

"Oh, come on, son," he said, tucking the duck beneath his arm. "No one's going to miss this thing."

"I'll miss it," I said. "My boss will miss it."

He shot a quick glance at the hedges beyond the lot. I could almost feel him doing the math, calculating his chances of getting away if he made a break for it. I tightened my grip on the spear gun and made sure he saw. The gun was a 24″ Blue Reef Special. My boss, Orlando, had let me borrow it from the pawnshop for the night, to guard the dumpster. The Blue Reef was a long and mean-looking gun with a razor-sharp harpoon sticking out from the barrel. Professional fishermen used it to bring down large deep-sea fish—marlin and jackfish. Fish much faster and tougher than the old man standing by the dumpster.

He adjusted the duck beneath his arm. "Just hear me out. My son, he gave this to me for my birthday a few years back. It was a gift from my boy. It means something to me."

"See these?" I said. "See those?" I gestured at the flyers taped up everywhere—on the chain across the entrance to the parking lot, on the window of the pawnshop, on the front of the black, barge-like dumpster itself. The fliers explained that to remove anything from the dumpster was strictly illegal, as the dumpster was the collective, rented property of the neighborhood's four pawnshops, including Orlando's Pawn World, where I worked. On Dumpster Tuesdays, the first Tuesday of every third month—March, June, September, and December—the local pawnshops got together and rented a dumpster to use to clean out all the merchandise that had gone unsold for too long. The dumpster stayed in one of the pawnshops' parking lots for ten days, and then the rental company would come and pick it up.

This time around, the dumpster was in our parking lot, outside Orlando's. We took turns guarding it at night: me, Orlando himself, and four or five guys from the other shops. It was my first Dumpster Tuesday.

"But no one bought this thing," said the old man, holding fast to the duck. "You tossed it out."

"If everyone who pawned something at our shop waited until we tossed it out and then just came by and got it out of the dumpster, no one would bother buying anything from us, would they?"

"Friend, I'm an old man." He smiled at me; I saw he was missing some teeth on top. "Memories is almost all I got left. And this duck brings up fond memories for me."

"Like what?" I said.

"Pardon?" he said.

"I mean, what memories does it bring up for you? Name one."

He studied the duck in his hand. "Well," he said, "it makes me think of this one time my boy Jerricho and me, we went duck hunting together? We used this very decoy. And I'm saying, the boys couldn't stay away from her. Thought she was a regular Marilyn Monroe." He nodded at the duck. "She did her job that day. Yes, sir." Then he turned back to me, waiting.

I stared at him.

"Aw, come on already," he said. "Give me a break."

"Sorry. You missed your window. You should have bought the decoy back from us while it was still in the store. Better yet, you shouldn't have pawned it in the first place if you cared about it so much."

Suddenly his eyes brightened. "Hold up, hold up. I know who you are," he said, pointing at me. "You're the guy who had all the problems with that country singer. I heard about you on News Twelve."

I felt an uncomfortable tingle at the back of my neck. "Back in the dumpster," I said, meaning the duck.

"Tell you what, it sounded like you was about ready to murder that poor cowboy. Following him around, threatening him and all. Not that I blame you, though. After the trouble he caused you? Bringing down a shit-storm like that?"

"I don't know what you mean," I said. But I knew exactly what he meant. And I knew exactly who he was talking about.

"Listen," he said. "It's all right. I can't stand that guy. Dick Doyle? I don't like his songs. I don't like his singing. Hell, I don't like his whole, you know . . ." He waved the duck in the air.

"Act," I said.

"Right," he said, pointing at me. "That act he does. I mean, how in this day and age, with all our knowledge and computers and whatnot, can people still fall for bullshit like that? What a fucking phony, correct?"

The person the old man was talking about—the person who'd apparently brought a shit-storm down on me—was a country singer named Dick Doyle. Dick was the flashy kind of country singer, the type that wears the big white Stetson, the colorful suit with rhinestones sparkling all over the lapels. The big belt buckles. The cowboy boots with pointy silver caps on the toes. In the past couple of years, Dick had managed to become something of a local celebrity. He was always playing clubs and events around central Florida; he went on tour a couple of times a year, up to the Northeast or across the Southwest. He'd even been featured on some national television shows. None of this success had to do with actual talent on Dick's part, though. No one paid to see Dick Doyle because he was a great songwriter or musician. People were interested in Dick only because of the bizarre circumstances surrounding his act.

"I don't have any problems with Mr. Doyle anymore," I said.

"That's good. Because folks are going to get the best of you in this life sometimes, son. Make you look foolish. Doesn't mean you're a loser."

"I never said I felt like a loser."

"Well, you shouldn't. Hell. People call me all kinds of things. I don't let it get me down. Fuck them, right?" He laughed. "Fuck them right in their pieholes."

A sickening feeling came over me: he was an old man holding a duck he'd stolen from a dumpster. He was giving me advice. Still, I refused to let myself get angry. Any day now I was going to leave Florida altogether and put the whole Dick Doyle mess behind me. I'd found a great new girlfriend, Joan; she was a young Chinese American, and soon enough I'd give Orlando notice, and she and I would head back north.

I tried to picture my real life then, the life waiting for me back home: I pictured the building I worked in, fifty-two stories tall, a glittering black tower rising above midtown Manhattan. I pictured my office, my desk, my leather chair, waiting empty. See? I thought. You have a good job out there. You own an apartment in Brooklyn. You are a real person.

"Who's saying I'm a loser?" I said.

"No one, buddy. I just meant that there's people on your side. That's all. Like Jerricho, my son. Who bought me this duck. The one I'm holding."

Just then Orlando's truck pulled into the lot. He must have seen what was going on, because instead of parking in his spot he skidded to a stop right in front of us. The old man jumped back to avoid the spray of gravel.

Orlando got out and took a bat from the cab. He was from Argentina, and though he was shorter than both of us, he was a thickly packed person.

"Get out of here!" he yelled at the old man, his accent rearing up. He pulled the bat back like he was about to swing at the old man's head. "Get off of my property!"

"Whoa, sir," the old man said. "I was just leaving."

"Oh, but you are not leaving with that." Orlando grabbed the duck and dropped it on the ground. Then he raised the bat over his head. "This item is being sold for ten dollars. You pay ten dollars to me and you can have it."

The old man studied the duck rocking on its side. "I'll give you two dollars," he said.

"Ten," said Orlando.

"Two twenty-five."

"Ten."

"It's got no beak. Two fifty."

Orlando waved the bat high in the air. "Ten."

The old man leaned over and spat on the duck. "Keep the change," he said. Then he turned and started walking away. "Oh, and Dick Doyle's a goddamned genius!" he yelled over his shoulder.

I took a step toward him, but Orlando grabbed my arm.

"What are you thinking of, talking to someone like that?" he said to me.

I watched the old troll vanish into the hedge. "I'm sorry. He started talking to me about Dick Doyle and—"

"Dick Doyle again," he said.

"I know."

"Get some sleep. Go home," Orlando said, and gently took the spear gun away from me.

It's difficult in this day and age to tell the difference between a real and an artificial plant. The technology has become so advanced. The age of rubberized stems and plastic leaves is long past. The synthetic plant of today is made from all kinds of designer materials—complicated organic compounds like fibercore and polywax and spongeform. For example, your typical synthetic palm tree, standing fifteen to twenty feet tall—the kind you find twisting up through every mall across America—its trunk is sculpted from a wood resin that sweats and breathes just like a real tree's. The leaves are spun from a special waxen silk; they have actual veins running through them. If I were to plant a synthetic palm tree next to a real one, and then bring you over and ask you to tell me which was which, you wouldn't be able to. Even if I let you use your hands. Probably the only way for you to discover the truth would be to gouge the trees open.

I'm not from Florida originally. Before relocating, I worked for a small marketing firm in Manhattan. My department was called Corporate Synergism, which, though it sounds exciting and dynamic, is really just a sexy way of saying "joint venturing." Basically, my colleagues and I helped companies market themselves to each other; we worked as corporate matchmakers. A client company would come to us hoping to form a relationship with some other company out in the world that it found very attractive. And we, in turn, would help that client company put together a proposal to offer its crush—a proposal that would explain, point by point, why together they had what's called applied synergistic potential.

The work was not the most exciting in the world, and the salary was modest, relatively speaking—only about seventy grand a year for starters—but I enjoyed my job well enough. It was a corporate life: I was invited to the restaurant openings and magazine launches. The gallery shows. I could get into the club with the movie-screen floor without having to wait in line. I'd received a key-card in the mail, inviting me to go to Locke, a new bar on the West Side. I was regularly sent free samples of products sold by companies we'd helped out: cases of Scottish vodka, a bedspread with a 700 thread count, a little robotic floor vacuum that zipped around and cleaned the apartment while I was out.

Ours was a young, competitive department. I was the new hire, but my colleagues, who for the most part were only a few years farther into their thirties than me, all made in the mid–six figures. My boss, Roddy, was only forty-two, and he had three homes already. He owned art he actually had to alarm.

I was on my way—that was how I felt. I was engaged to a woman named Pearl, just twenty-five, who was far and away the most beautiful girl I'd ever dated. She had the kind of face that moved through a crowd like a lantern. Huge blue eyes, a smile almost too big for her head. She was lean and graceful, with a dancer's body. In heels she was a good inch or two taller than me. She'd done some acting and now she was studying to be a playwright, taking graduate classes to get her master's, or whatever degree comes with playwriting.

I even owned my own apartment, a small duplex in a renovated factory building. Everything about the place was brand-new; the walls were moon white, the counters were made of brushed steel. The bedroom windows stood five feet tall—huge, industrial panels that afforded a perfect view of midtown Manhattan. In fact, if I slid our bookcase out and squeezed myself into the corner of the room, I could just make out my own office building.

Sometimes, if I couldn't sleep, I would climb out of bed and press myself into the corner and look out over the moonlit river until I found my building, then my office, and finally my window. There, I'd think. You fit there. And after a while a soothing fatigue would come over me, and I'd climb back into bed.

Then, one day in January, Pearl came into the den with a strange look on her face.

"What is it?" I said.

"You almost ready to go?"

"Ready to go where?"

"To see that guy I told you about? The one performing in the East Village," she said. "I've been going to see him sing every night this week. You promised you'd come tonight."

I looked down at the papers in front of me—part of a proposal by a company that manufactured high-end synthetic plants, everything from desk plants to full-size trees. Our client was hoping we might help it court a major home improvement retailer, one that had giant warehouse-like stores all across the country. This was the biggest deal I'd been handed so far. Our client had sent along an artificial fern as a sample of its work, along with a real fern. I had both pots next to each other on my desk.

"Here, try to tell the difference." I gestured for Pearl to touch the ferns.

"Max, I want you to come. It's important to me."

"Just feel."

She sighed and rubbed a leaf from each plant between her fingers. "Wow."

"Feels real, doesn't it?" I said. "They're a good company. Now smell."

She squinted at me as though I were suddenly very hard to see. "Max . . ."

"Fine. Okay." I closed my binder and got up. "Who is this guy again?"

"He's a country singer," said Pearl. "His name's Dick Doyle."

As soon as we entered the club, I could tell something strange was going on. Usually the artists Pearl got excited about—the musicians and painters and writers and such—were up-and-comers; they'd been written up in magazines and had some sort of buzz around them. And the people who went to see them perform were like us; they were in our crowd. But as we made our way toward the stage, I saw that Dick Doyle's audience wasn't our crowd at all. The people filing in were bikers and construction workers, security guards. Jeans and boots and even a little leather. It had been a long time since I'd felt overdressed in a button-down.

At ten o'clock sharp, an old cowgirl came out from behind the curtain to offer an introduction to Dick's show. She was dressed in cowboy boots and a denim shirt with fringe hanging off the sleeves. When she reached the center of the stage, she took off her hat and held it over her chest.

"Ladies and gentlemen," she began, "there is a story behind the man you are about to see here tonight. A story that has become an inspiration to many . . ."

I looked around at the crowd, expecting smirks and snickers, but everybody was just standing with their faces turned up toward the stage, listening. Even Pearl. I felt like checking outside just to make sure I was still in Manhattan.

"The story begins in Florida," the old woman continued, "with a man named Dick Doyle."

The audience erupted in cheers, clapping and stomping and whistling.

The old woman smiled and patted down the noise. "I know, I know," she said. "But back then, Dick Doyle wasn't anyone special, really," she said. "He was just your average country singer. Living and playing around town. Singing his songs at birthday parties and weddings. At the derby on Thursday nights . . ."

I wondered why she was talking about Dick Doyle as though the man were dead. Wasn't Dick backstage, waiting to come on? The band was already setting up.

"Oh, Dick was a real jokester, too," she said, smiling wistfully. "In between songs, he liked to poke fun at the audience, tease them a little, you know. Rib them."

The stage lights dimmed, but the spotlight on the old woman grew brighter.

"Except this one night, see," said the cowgirl, looking around at all of us, her face becoming grave. "Someone in the audience didn't take kindly to Dick's jokes. A man. He didn't like the way Dick was teasing him about his hair, which was long, you know, in a ponytail? And so, after the show was over, he waited for Dick outside the bar in his truck, and when Dick came out, this man . . . well, he ran Dick down."

He ran Dick down. I couldn't help a laugh from bubbling up. Pearl shot me a cold look.

The cowgirl went on to explain that Dick had spent two months recovering in the ICU at Orlando Memorial. He had some broken bones, a few busted ribs, a fractured wrist. But worst of all—and here she let out a long, sad sigh—the doctors discovered that Dick had brain damage.

"Hemorrhage-induced catatonia. That's what the docs called Dick's condition," she said. "The way I think of it, though, is like a trance that Dick's stuck in. The accident knocked Dick into a lifelong trance that he never wakes up from. Like one of those people that gets voodoo done on them."

"A zombie!" someone yelled from the audience.

"A zombie. Right," she said. "Except that in real life, zombies never wake up from their trances . . ." she said, putting her cowboy hat back on. "But . . . the amazing thing about Dick . . . is that on certain occasions, under very special circumstances, Dick can wake up from his trance.

"Circumstances, ladies and gentlemen, such as these here tonight. Because if there's one thing that Dick reacts to, one thing that can part those clouds sitting on his brain, it's the power of music . . ."

And here the woman took a deep bow, and then began backing away, off the stage. A moment later she returned with two men, both of them helping a fourth person onto the stage. This fourth person was a man about six feet tall, my height, average build, with a big trucker's mustache. He was wearing a string tie and a cowboy hat. His suit was bright purple, covered with musical notes made of glittering rhinestones. The crew stood Dick in the center of the stage and brushed him off.

I leaned over to Pearl. "That suit's giving me . . . *brain damage*," I said.

"Shh," she said.

The two assistants slung a guitar around Dick's neck and then adjusted the microphone so that it came right up to his mouth, which was hanging open slightly. His eyes stared out at nothing.

I glanced at my watch. It was already ten thirty. I felt a rumbling of agitation.

Country music started up from the back of the stage: a fiddle and a banjo, a slide guitar with that sad, watery echo.

"Look," said Pearl. "Look at Dick. Watch."

So I looked at him. He was just as I'd left him. Standing with his string tie too tight around his neck, gazing vacantly out into the darkness. But then, slowly, he began to show signs of life. His mustache twitched once, twice. He started blinking rapidly.

I would have laughed out loud, if I hadn't paid twenty dollars to see the show. To me, it all looked like bad acting. He scanned the crowd then, seemingly coming out of his daze. Where am I? Who are all these people? I couldn't help thinking of some of the student actors in Pearl's graduate program.

The crowd began clapping along to the music, cheering Dick on.

"Go, Dick, go!" they yelled. "Go, Dick, go!"

Dick's shaking hands slowly felt their way over the guitar, crawling over the body, the neck, eventually finding positions on the strings and frets. His playing was clumsy and lurching at first, but after a moment it smoothed out, became passable.

I glanced at Pearl; she was rapt, clapping and chanting, and I felt a creeping disdain for her. I spent the better part of my day assessing value—enumerating the attractive qualities of companies, making cases for or against them. I could not for the life of me see a case to be made for Dick Doyle. More than this, though, I couldn't see any benefit in a match between Dick Doyle's performance and my evening.

Pearl nudged me.

"Go, Dick," I said.

Dick leaned into the mic and started singing. His voice was nothing to crow about—nasal and whiny, typical country. The song sounded like a stock tearjerker to me, too; it was about a man who gets struck by a power line, finds himself a different person afterward, unable to fit his own life. Sniffle, sniffle.

I headed to the back to get a drink. The bartender was an older fellow. He looked reasonable enough.

"Can you believe this?" I said, when he brought me my beer.

He shook his head. It was hard to hear over the clapping.

I pointed a thumb over my shoulder at the stage. "That guy can't act for shit, huh?"

The bartender scowled, then took away my beer.

———

Late that night, I woke up to the sounds of Pearl crying. I got out of bed and found her dragging a suitcase down the spiral staircase.

"I'm leaving, Max," she said.

"Jesus. Wait a second," I said, trying to gauge the situation. "What's wrong?"

"Please don't try to stop me." She was already halfway down the stairs, so that only her shoulders and head were visible from my vantage point.

I rubbed the sleep from my eyes and checked my watch: two thirty in the morning. "Pearl. Come up here and talk to me."

She lugged the suitcase down another step. "No. We don't make each other happy. I'm not what you want."

"What are you talking about? Of course you're what I want. I want you all the time. More than I've ever wanted anyone. I'm all over you. Constantly."

She stopped to wipe her face. "I mean you don't want *me*, who I am. You don't have any interest in me as a person."

"I have a great interest in you. I'm marrying you, for Christ's sake," I said.

"But you don't have any interest in what I'm doing with my life. In what my goals are."

"Could you please just come up to the second floor, please?"

"You're always making fun of the theater, making fun of my friends. You don't take any of it seriously."

To be honest, I'm not a big fan of the theater. I have trouble losing myself in the action of a play. The actors always seem hysterical to me, scurrying around the bright box of the stage, screaming and crying and clawing at each other. Watching a play, I always feel like part of some team of psychiatrists that's been called in to observe a group of out-of-control mental patients.

"I come to the plays, don't I?" I said. "I hang out with you and your classmates."

"Name three of my friends from playwriting school. In fact, just name three of my friends."

"This is ridiculous. Of course I can—"

"Name two."

"Bonnie and Pat."

"Pat's my sister."

"The girl you went out with the other night. The flat-chested one. Her name starts with a *D*. Debbie?"

She proceeded to name all my friends from work, some I might have forgotten myself. Everyone in my department.

"What's the title of the play I'm working on right now?" she said.

It was on the tip of my tongue. It had "dirt" or "mud" in the title. Something mud.

She leaned her head against the iron banister and closed her eyes. A ribbon of hair fell across her cheek. The sight reminded me of how she looked in the mornings, just before waking up. Her expression so serious, brow furrowed in concentration as she swam up from that last dream.

"That singer tonight," she said, her eyes still closed. "Dick Doyle. All week I've been telling you about him, about how much I loved his songs. I must have spent twenty minutes just two days ago going on about how deeply his music spoke to me."

I tried to recall these conversations, but all I could hear of them were vague echoes. A few words here and there. *Trance. Stage. Dream.*

"I brought you tonight because I'd hoped that you might hear in those songs what I hear in them. I thought Dick's performance might affect you. But you didn't pay any attention."

"Do you have his CD? Give his record to me now. I'll listen to it. I promise."

She picked up her suitcase and continued down the steps. "I spoke to Belle, the woman who introduces Dick onstage. They're headed back to Florida in a couple of days. I want to go with them."

"Are you out of your mind?" I said, coming to the railing. "What are you, fucking brainwashed? We're getting married in six months. You're acting like a teenage groupie. You're twenty-five years old."

"If you need me I'll be at Pat's. I left my ring on the night table. I'm sorry, Max." Then she disappeared from view.

"Pearl . . . If you walk out that door, that's it. I'm locking you out! Pearl!"

The door shut.

I stood on the landing in my boxers, staring down into the vortex of our staircase. I was sure Pearl would come back.

"She's just going through something," I told my friends.

Two weeks later I was driving south on 95, toward Kwimper County, Florida.

Part Two: The Swampy Bottom

IT WAS EARLY MORNING BY THE TIME I REACHED MY MOTEL. I'D been up all night guarding the dumpster—awake for over twenty-four hours—but I wasn't tired in the least. In fact, climbing the steps to my room, I felt completely alert, almost hyper. The encounter with the old man had upset me more than I'd expected—all that talk of Dick Doyle. Still, I tried to get some rest. I took a sleeping pill. I shut the blinds against the morning and got into bed. After a full hour of lying there trying to sleep, I finally gave up and tossed off the sheets.

I still had a while before my girlfriend, Joan, showed up. Her family ran a bus service for old people called the Silver Coach. They had five vehicles in their fleet, which they drove around town along various routes, each route servicing a different set of assisted-living communities. The buses ran to all the places old people would want to go: the mall, the movies, the hospital, the library, the cemetery. On days I was off work, like today, Joan would come by the motel and pick me up and I'd ride with her while she drove her route.

I did what I could to pass the time. I watched a show on cable about black holes. I cleaned up the room, even though I knew the maid would come around that afternoon. I took a long shower, during which I tried and failed to jerk off. I shaved carefully. Then I got dressed and went out onto the balcony to have a smoke.

It was nearly nine by now and the roads were full of decent people heading off to work. I thought about checking in with Roddy, but I couldn't bring myself to call. When I first came to Florida, he'd been very supportive. He was always telling me to hang in there, to do what I had to do. He said he understood. But the last time I'd spoken with him, he'd sounded different.

"I have one question for you, Max. One," said Roddy. "Why is my phone telling me you're still in Florida?"

"I'm just tying things up," I said.

"You've been gone two months already. You know you're not getting paid this month."

"I understand. You've already been very generous, Rod."

"You're right. I have." He laughed, and then gave a deep sigh. "Please. Just tell me, Max. Is this really about Pearl, or are you having some sort of . . . I don't know . . . breakdown?"

I was lying in bed, watching a caterpillar descend from the air-conditioning vent above my bed. It was bright green, with hundreds of little legs, lowering itself on a silk thread. "I'm okay," I said. "Really."

"Because the longer you stay, the worse it looks. The worse *you* look, is what I mean."

"I'll be back before you know it," I said.

"Now," he said. "Come back now."

Before I knew it, three more weeks had passed. For some reason, though, I felt that there was still time. That doors were still open. After all, I had no intention of staying in Florida. *Florida?* Florida was the rank, swampy bottom of the country. The place people went to end things. Sticking out over the Gulf like a plank. I'd spent two years in business school and three summers interning ten hours a day just to get where I was—or where I'd been, before I left. If I'd been looking to relocate to Florida, I'd have taken a real job; I'd have gone hunting downtown, in the business district. But I wasn't looking. I wasn't starting over. I was with Roddy. The only reason I was working at all was to stave off some of the bills piling up back in the city. Things had been lean before I left, with all the new costs generated by the apartment. I needed some kind of income, even if only to live on while I was in Florida. I'd thought about waiting tables. I'd applied to drive a cab. I wanted something that paid cash. Something with no ties, that I could ditch at a moment's notice.

I'd been about to pawn Pearl's engagement ring when I'd noticed the HELP WANTED sign on Orlando's door. The job paid seventeen dollars an hour. More than I expected. Pawnshops got robbed a lot, Orlando explained, and, I admit, the danger factor held a certain appeal for me. I was in Florida because my fiancée had left me for a brain-damaged country singer: there were plenty of moments in each day that I wished someone would blow my fucking brains out.

More than that, though, the job at Orlando's was attractive because the work would be so different from what I was used to. No
pressure, no stress. I liked the idea of working somewhere I'd
never even visit in my real life. This was all just a detour. Plus the
shop was less than a mile from my motel.

I sat on the railing of the balcony, watching the traffic pass.
After a while the cars became blank panels of color sliding by below. A square of red. A square of gold. A rectangle of apple green.
Finally, around ten, the Silver Coach rolled into the motel parking
lot. I went down to meet it.

Joan pulled the lever that opened the door. "So, how'd the
dumpster treat you last night?" she said as I climbed in.

"Like a star . . . *Good morning!*" I said to the few old people already on the bus.

Joan watched me. "Are you okay? You look a little tense."

"I'm fine. Just tired," I said, and kissed her.

"Yum." She swung the door closed and pulled out of the lot.

Joan was twenty-one, ten years younger than me, a smart, beautiful girl. I'd met her at the supermarket near my motel. She was
waiting on line ahead of me and her cart was filled with hundreds
of mini juices—all for the coach, I eventually learned.

I'd taken a liking to her right away. She was responsible and
driven for her age, a go-getter, always helping out her family. And
yet there was still a touch of girlish rebellion to her—a wild streak—
which I found thrilling. Some nights, after we'd dropped all the
riders at their homes, Joan would park in a field near the bus lot
and we'd make love in the shuttle. The springs were especially loud,
creaking and groaning in a way that made even the gentlest sex feel
wild. Whenever I saw Joan's naked body, golden but for three small
kites of untanned flesh over her softest parts, I'd begin to ache like
I'd never ached for Pearl.

I always took a moment to appreciate this fact. I'd almost say it out loud: Pearl never compared to this. And then I'd give Joan a big kiss on her ass.

I watched her as she piloted the Coach out into traffic. She was wearing a tank top that exposed her shoulders and the top of her pale, freckled chest.

She caught me looking and winked. "Be good," she said. She wore her black hair in sharp bangs that came right down to her eyes, darkening them. I'd decided that she was the kind of girl I should have been with from the start.

Joan's was the longest of the five Silver Coach routes. It consisted of seventeen stops—six at actual communities, eleven at commercial and service sites—and it took a full hour to complete. Some of the old people had nurses who waited with them for the Coach to pull up. Others were still managing by themselves, which always impressed me. We'd drive up and find them waiting on the curb all alone, like packages for us to collect.

I'd ridden with Joan often enough that I knew some of them by now; I knew their stories. Most of the people on her route were still healthy, their minds sharp, their bodies working well. But, of course, there were a few who'd begun to deteriorate. Some were struggling with senility, others were just physically failing, their bodies slowly evicting them. One, a woman named Hattie, for example, had recently taken a bad fall and hit her head on the sink. Since the accident, she'd begun to forget words. It got worse every day.

"So, how are things with that thing of yours?" she said when we picked her up that morning. She sat right behind me with her nurse. Her gray hair was still short from her stitches. I could see the scar on the side of her head, pursed like a baby's frown just over her ear.

"You know, that thing," she said, looking at me, then at Joan, her eyes quizzical and terrified.

"My cold?" said Joan.

"That's right, your thing," said Hattie, though she seemed even more confused by this.

"It's almost all gone, Hattie. Thanks for asking."

"Oh, well, that's good," said Hattie. "Did you hear that, Charmagne?" she said to her nurse. "Her thing. That thing."

I tried to ignore Hattie's conversation with Charmagne as we continued along our route—first to the park, then the mall, then another mall—but the pathology of her injury was too fascinating: the way the rot was systematically moving through her vocabulary, infecting words, leaving them shapeless lumps. Her mother was a thing. The bus stop was a thing. The world was a thing. I was a thing.

I tried to picture Hattie's brain, to imagine what the deterioration process looked like, but all I could manage was a kind of gray coral reef couched inside her skull. I remembered what a diving instructor had once told me about coral. I was snorkeling with my family in the Bahamas and he'd warned me to make sure to watch out for coral reefs while swimming. Just touching a reef, he explained, even brushing it with your finger, could start a chain reaction that might bring down the whole organism.

Now, as we neared the second mall, I wondered if maybe this wasn't so different from how it was with the brain. Of course, a brain could heal from some kinds of trauma, it could rebuild connections, but once touched in certain ways, by certain hands, it was damaged goods.

"Thing thing on the phone," said Hattie. "Thing."

"Yes," said Charmagne, staring out the window at the passing palm trees.

I closed my eyes and tried to relax. Still, I couldn't help asking myself how different the beating Hattie's brain had taken was from the type Dick Doyle's had endured. Hattie certainly couldn't turn her shortcomings on and off. You could push Hattie onstage and shine a spotlight on her, but believe me, it wouldn't start her square dancing. *Stop,* I thought. *Cut it out.* But I could already feel the anger rising over how absurd Dick's story seemed. After all, what kind of phantasmagoric injury could be turned on and off with the flick of a stage light?

"What a phony that Dick is," I heard the old man from the dumpster say. "How do people fall for bullshit like that?" And I simply didn't know. I could not understand what sort of black magic Dick Doyle used to make himself so appealing. He didn't have brain damage. He wasn't an inspiration. There was no triumph of the human spirit going on at a Dick Doyle show. With his mustache and his fancy fucking cowboy boots.

An image of Dick flashed through my mind. I saw him at home, getting ready for his show that night. He had the mask down; he was completely alert and clear-eyed, singing into the bathroom mirror as he snapped up his cowboy shirt. He fastened his string tie and put on his hat, crooning away in that irritating voice of his. I could see dabs of shaving cream clinging to the bottom of his mustache.

He noticed my reflection in the mirror. "Oh, hey, Maxie," he said, which was what Pearl used to call me.

"Max? Hey," Joan said. "Are you all right?"

I opened my eyes and found that we were parked in front of the church. A couple of the old people were filing out, being helped down by attendants. I felt my face and discovered I was sweating.

"You were grinding your teeth really loud," Joan said. "What were you thinking about?"

"Nothing. I was thinking about how much fun it's going to be to get you out of here and up to New York. You're going to love it." I smiled at her.

"Don't think about that just yet, okay?" she said, and rubbed my thigh.

"Why?"

"Because I don't feel that we need to be thinking about that right now. Let's just enjoy it for a while, all right? Get to know each other. We have time."

"But we don't have time. I'm leaving soon. And I want you to come. Please come with me? Joan?"

Joan kissed me on the jaw. "You were clenching your teeth again," she said.

Orlando had recently seen Dick perform at the county fair. Penny for your thoughts, I said to him the next day.

"It's not my kind of music," he said. He'd just purchased a set of commemorative coins featuring the birds of the Southern marsh. He was cleaning them one by one with a cloth dipped in a mixture of vinegar and ammonia. The smell made my eyes water.

"But what did you think of Dick?" I said.

"I thought he was fucked up, man," Orlando said, blowing on a coin. "Before he started they had to wipe the drool from his face."

"You know, I don't believe people with trauma to the brain really act like that," I said, watching Orlando rub the coin dry with a piece of velvet. "They can't just snap out of it. They're not so aware of everything."

"I don't like these thoughts, my friend," Orlando said, and tossed the coin to me. On it was a picture of a woodpecker nesting in a tree. I slipped the coin into its case, which read: "An aggressive species, the pileated woodpecker is known to take over nests already inhabited by other, larger birds that it scares off by means of its hysterical laugh-like call."

"You were doing so well, too, Miller," said Orlando. "The last few weeks you didn't even mention the singer or her, the woman."

"Pearl."

"Where is this coming from all of a sudden? From that old man?"

"Nowhere. I'm fine. All I'm saying is that if Dick is faking, people have a right to know. You paid what, ten dollars to see him play dumb?"

"Do you remember," Orlando said, holding out the next coin, "how embarrassing it was for you the last time you acted on these thoughts, my friend? These same thoughts?"

I grabbed the coin from him. My first week in Florida had been very hard. The day I'd arrived I discovered that Pearl had moved in with Dick—that she was living with him in his family's farmhouse outside of town. On top of this, I learned from Pearl's sister, Pat, that she was likely seeing Dick, too—that she might actually be involved with him.

"She's got a new man in her life, is how she put it," said Pat. "Game over."

Even so, I made a big effort to win Pearl back during those first few days. I tried calling the farmhouse where Dick and Pearl were living. I even drove out to the property. No one would talk to me, though. Which was ridiculous. The least I deserved was some sort of apology. Because what Pearl had done wasn't fair. You don't just leave someone like that. No discussion, not even a warning shot. It wasn't right. But I was drinking a lot that week, too, so when the Doyle people called the police on me, I wasn't able to properly explain myself.

"Right," said Orlando, nodding. He stared me in the eye while he polished the next coin. "You remember. Your face in the gazette. Everyone making fun of you. Calling you a stalker. And so on."

He handed me the coin, which showed a picture of a golden warbler. "Let me tell you something, my friend," he said. "This man, Dick—he is not faking anything. You understand? He is a sick person. You are wrong in your thinking about this."

"You're entitled to your beliefs," I said.

"Well, I don't want violence near this store, understand? Not on my property. No way," he said. "If I get into trouble with the police because of you, Miller, then you will have something to worry about."

Orlando had lived in the States for only a couple of years and he retained a stark fear of run-ins with the police. He still had family in Argentina he hoped to bring over, a sister and her children. He'd told me about his situation one night a few weeks before when we'd gone drinking together and I'd confessed to having come to Florida to win back Pearl.

"My life," he'd said, tapping his wallet, "right here." Then he'd opened the wallet to let a chain of photos accordion out. He told me their names one by one: his sister, Lisette; her sons and daughters, William, Cee-Cee, Barbara, and Vaca. Each had his or her own photo and they were all posed in front of the same patchy dirt yard, so that when he dangled the pictures in one line, it gave the illusion that his relatives were dolls, figurines stacked one on top of the other, biggest to smallest, on a series of plain brown shelves.

"Orlando, I promise, I'm not going to do anything to Dick," I said. "I was just talking about him. I'm over it."

"Let me ask you one last thing, then, if you are so over it," he said. "Why haven't you gone to the fair down on Orange Blossom?"

"What does that have to do with anything?"

"Oh, it has to do with everything, my friend. Before the fair opened, again and again you said you wanted to take Joan there. But now the fair is about to close and you still have not gone. Why is that, Miller?"

"Maybe I don't feel like it. Maybe I've been busy here this week, with it being Dumpster Tuesday and everything."

"Maybe you haven't gone to the fair because this singer, this Dick is there, and you would not be able to control yourself when you saw him."

"I'll go this weekend. I'll take Joan on Saturday."

"No, see. I'm saying you should *not* go. I'm saying you should stay away. My point is that you yourself know you are not over Dick, as you say. You should listen to yourself more, Miller. Really listen."

"Orlando, look," I said, but Orlando made a hissing sound that meant shut up because we had a customer.

"We'll talk later," he said, waving me away.

I glanced up and saw a woman standing at the front door. Orlando inspected her through the gate. She wore a tracksuit and was carrying a small plastic bag full of gold chains. As soon as he buzzed her in she hurried over to the counter.

"Look what I got," she said, laying the bag on the glass. "Score." Dark sweat circles showed beneath her arms. Her fingers all had Band-Aids around the tips.

I got out the glass cleaner and went over to the jewelry case. I already knew how this would turn out, and I wasn't in the mood to watch. She would tell Orlando what her boyfriend or husband had told her the chains were worth when he gave them to her—back before he left her, which he would have just done, left her for someone else or simply disappeared—and Orlando would get out the nitric acid and the touchstone and test the chains; and of course they'd turn out to be worth hardly anything. They'd end up being gold-plated, not gold-filled, or 10 karat, or maybe not even gold at all.

I took my time cleaning the case, careful to stay at the far end, letting my eyes drift over the jewelry—the racks of gold chains, the tie clips and money clips, the watches. I glanced at the ring I'd given Pearl; it was resting near the back of the row, on a small black prop. I leaned in closer. Every movement I made ignited a wild circuitry of light in the stone. Pearl hadn't picked it out with me. There had been no deliberation. I'd bought the ring on impulse one day while I was on my lunch hour. I just went into the store and chose it—a standard, three-stone setting, platinum band—in less than half an hour. I had just felt like it was the right time. All my friends at work were married or getting married soon.

"Hey, Miller, look at this," said Orlando, at my side now. The woman was on her way to the door. Apparently her business with us was done. Orlando laid a nameplate pendant on the counter. *Angie.*

"It's funny," said Orlando. "That woman, Angie. She comes in here all the time. I bought this last nameplate for five dollars more than it's worth. I feel sorry for her, you know? Always making the same mistake?"

"I'm going to the fair and I'm bringing Joan," I said.

He shook his head, then took the box containing all the nameplates from beneath the jewelry case. "Do what you want, but like I said, I would stay away if I were you."

"No. I planned on going, and I'm going to go."

"Hey, it's your life," said Orlando, tossing *Angie* in with all the other names.

The Kwimper County Fair was not an impressive spectacle. This was clear from the moment Joan and I walked through the fairground's turnstile. The striped booths lining the thoroughfare were old and shabby—tented roofs sagging, duct tape patching holes in the walls. The rides were all falling apart too; the Ferris wheel creaked and groaned. The maze of mirrors was so smeared and dirty that finding your way out looked easier than getting lost. The only parts of the fair that appeared even the least bit impressive were the dance floor and the stage.

The dance floor was enormous and circular, painted a deep midnight blue, with a net of lanterns strung above it. The stage was simply a rectangular area level to the ground at the far end of the dance floor, but all around it rose a high scaffolding of lights and speakers. Stacks of hay bales stood at either end of the stage, and behind it loomed a tall, red stage-prop barn with a banner over its open doors that read BARN DANCE!!! in Western lettering. No one was performing yet—technicians were still climbing the scaffolding, testing the lights, the sound system—but people had already started to gather nearby for the first act. Just staring at the spot where Dick would soon be performing, I felt a prickle of agitation.

I looked away from the dance floor and out at the parking lot. Teenagers were sitting on top of their cars, drinking out of paper bags, smoking. Two were lying entwined on top of the Silver Coach. They were kissing with their mouths gaping open, like they were blowing life into each other.

I yelled at them to get down.

"Don't bother. They're just kids," said Joan. She took my hand and we meandered toward the rides. "You know, I recognized that name on the bill tonight," she said after a while. "I know that's the guy you had the whole fight with."

"I didn't fight with him. I—"

Joan squeezed my hand. "I just want you to know that you don't have to prove anything to me, that's all."

"I'm not. I'm fine," I said. We passed a giant canister that spun so fast the people inside stuck to its walls. Screams came whirling up from the bottom.

I kissed the top of Joan's head. "Why should I not get to take my girlfriend to the fair just because Dick Doyle is playing there? He's in the past."

Joan put her head on my shoulder. "I didn't mean to suggest anything," she said. "I just got nervous when I saw his name. I don't want you to have to deal with anything that's going to make you upset."

"Well, he isn't going to make me upset," I said. "I'm not going to think about him at all."

"Promise?" she said.

"Promise," I said.

Joan and I spent the rest of the day exploring the fair together. We rode the carousel. We went on the bumper cars, ramming into each other, teaming up against other drivers; the conductor rods at the back of our vehicles trailed sparks across the ceiling. For a snack we had steaming popcorn balls covered in caramel. And to my surprise, as we did these things, I felt my promise to Joan becoming true: I did start to forget about Dick. I forgot about Pearl, too.

I won a stuffed dog for Orlando, for him to send to his nieces and nephews. Joan popped a balloon with a dart and won a small mirror with gold stars painted around the border. We rode the Ferris wheel as the sun was sinking; the peak afforded a view of the whole landscape, the housing developments and citrus groves, the streetlights just starting to ignite.

Joan and I had dinner in the food tent, just to the side of the dance floor, so that we could listen to the bands as we ate. The first group was a Western swing ensemble, playing two-steps and country waltzes. Couples danced around the dark blue floor, spinning and dipping, sometimes stepping along side by side with their arms locked. Most of the dancers were old, and it made me feel good to be moving with them. They were still happy and in love after all these years, and even though Joan and I were two of the few young people on the floor, there was something oddly comforting about our synchronicity. The night air was cool, but the lanterns created little islands of heat to travel between. Joan felt perfect in my arms, and each time we navigated the shining blue floor I felt more sure that things would work out, not just between us, but in general. When the dance finally ended, I dipped Joan and gave her a long kiss.

"Excuse me," said a familiar voice.

I felt my stomach drop. I looked up and there she was, right in front of me.

"I thought that was you," said Pearl. The lantern light was in her eyes, making them sparkle blue. "I wasn't sure if I should come over. But, I don't know, I just wanted to say something to you—to you both, I guess. If that's okay."

I studied her face, the face I'd woken up beside for the past three years: the curve of her mouth, the faint mole beneath her eye. She was dressed in the style of that woman who introduced Dick onstage. She wore pink cowboy boots, a denim skirt with sleigh bells hanging off the hem. Her T-shirt had a picture of Dick on it— a scanned photograph of his face, wrung up into the pained approximation of a smile. It was then that I noticed Dick himself, standing right next to her.

He was gazing past me, at nothing in particular. His suit was bright red, with sequined playing cards on the lapels. His mouth hung slightly open; I could hear him breathing.

I looked away from him, back at Pearl. I was afraid that if I stayed focused on his face, even for one more moment, I'd lose it.

I tried to smile at Pearl. "You were saying?"

She tucked a strand of hair behind her ear. "I . . . I wanted to let you know how bad I felt about the police being called on you that time you came to the house. It wasn't Dick or me who did that. We weren't even there." She glanced at Joan, then back at me. "I just wanted you to know that."

Both women waited for me to say something. I felt as though I were balancing on a high post. I needed to stay very still. A breeze rolled over us, causing the lanterns above to creak and sway.

"That's fine," I said.

Pearl waited a moment. "I guess we should be getting back," she said. "We're on in a little while."

"Good luck up there," said Joan.

"Thanks," she said, and then turned to me. "It was good to see you." She smiled, but there was something very sad tucked into the corners of her mouth.

Hold on for a few more seconds, I thought. Both of them will be gone. Just be cool.

"It was nice meeting you," Pearl finally said to Joan.

"Nice meeting you too," said Joan. "And you," she said to Dick, whose hand suddenly shot out in front of Joan. The fingers were bulky and callused, with dark hair growing around the knuckles.

Dick's hand hung there between all of us, trembling.

"He wants to shake hands with you," said Pearl. "This is wonderful. He's hardly ever this aware offstage."

"I'm flattered," said Joan. She reached for his hand.

"No, no," said Pearl. "Please. Let him come to you. It's good for him."

Joan held her hand above Dick's.

All three of us stood there watching as Dick's twitching hand slowly rose, the thick fingers straining toward Joan's open palm. The hand seemed to take forever to ascend a few inches. When the fingers finally arrived, Joan gave them a gentle shake.

"Proud of you," said Pearl, rubbing Dick's arm.

After Joan broke from him, he let his hand fall back to his side. Then he took a few angling baby steps that left him pointed in my direction. I steeled myself. *Don't even think about it,* I thought. *Don't . . .* But his hand was already trembling at his waist.

"Do you want to shake hands with him, too, Dick? Is that what you want to do?" said Pearl.

She turned to me, excited. "Would that be okay? This is more than I've seen him try at once in I don't even know how long."

I studied Dick's eyes, searching for any glimmer of mischief. Nothing at all. Still, I decided that if this was a joke in any way, I'd strangle Dick to death.

I put out my hand.

Dick's hand began to rise again. The fingers shook violently, like the effort to lift them was too much for him. I kept my hand where it was, waiting. My heart was thudding in my chest.

"You can do it," said Pearl. "Shake his hand!"

Dick's hand hovered just beneath mine. I could feel the warmth from his fingers radiating up into my palm. I kept my eyes fixed on his, which, as always, peered out at nothing. It would be so easy to test him, to see if he was faking. All I'd have to do is take the hand in mine and squeeze.

"Come on, Dick," said Joan.

His spastic hand floated there, suspended. Our fingers were practically touching.

"You can, you can!" said Pearl.

"Do it, Dick," I said. "Go on."

Finally, the hand fell back to Dick's side.

Pearl sighed. "Ugh. I'm sorry. He was having such a good day."

"He did great, right?" Joan said to me.

"He did just fine," I said.

"Thanks. He's trying hard. It's a long road," Pearl said, slipping her arm around Dick's waist. "Well, take care. Both of you." Then she turned him around, and the two of them walked away.

I watched her go, the bells on her skirt faintly jangling.

"That was a nice surprise," said Joan.

I was suddenly aware of being alone on the dance floor with her. The stagehands were already setting up for the next band. I looked around to see if anyone was watching us.

"Hey, buster," Joan said. "I'm proud of you. You handled that very well. I thought we were going to have a problem, but you acted like a true gentleman."

I was still breathing hard. "I told you I'd be okay."

"Let's go home, Mr. Miller," said Joan, leading me off the dance floor.

"We can stay," I said, suddenly quite proud of myself. "We can dance to Dick's singing, if you want. It'd be nice to hear him."

"I think I've had enough of the fair for one night," she said.

As we made our way through the crowd to the parking lot, I felt better than I had in a long time; I felt as though a fog were lifting, a fog of rage and jealousy in which I'd been lost for weeks, maybe months. By the time we reached the Silver Coach I couldn't keep my hands off Joan. I was overwhelmed by a wild and joyous horniness.

"Down," Joan said, laughing as she unlocked the door.

But as soon as we were inside she was kissing me back, pulling my shirt off. I made for her belt, but she stopped.

"Wait. Let's not until we get home," she said.

I kissed her belly, unzipping the top of her jeans.

"There's too many people around," she said, but she was already unbuttoning her blouse. I looked out the windshield and saw no one close enough to worry about.

The coils were loud that night, groaning and crying beneath us. I held Joan's hips as we moved. She pressed back into me, her skin hot and soft against my own. I grabbed at her, wanting to envelop her, to be touching every part at once.

"That feels so good," she said, moving faster now.

I closed my eyes. I could feel the shuttle rocking on its wheels. The sounds the Coach made were exciting, the creaking and huffing, and yet beneath the racket I thought I heard something else, some other, deeper strain of noise. The sound was faint, but persistent. I listened harder, until I realized what I was hearing. The noise was a voice: Dick Doyle's voice.

I opened my eyes and saw something so shocking, I nearly froze: standing on the dashboard just behind the steering wheel, guitar in hand, was a miniature Dick Doyle. He couldn't have been more than six inches tall, a tiny doppelgänger, wearing a little red suit, a minuscule cowboy hat on his head. And he was singing to me; I could hear his voice beneath the squeaking of the seat, that high, whiny crooning of his.

But then I realized that, of course, this wasn't a miniature Dick Doyle at all; the figure was just a reflection. Joan had left the mirror she'd won on top of her bag, and it reflected the fair's stage. The gold stars around its border twinkled in the light. They hovered all around Dick, shimmering.

I turned away from the mirror and concentrated on Joan. I watched the shiny groove of her back, the bounce of her. I tried to listen to the sounds she made, to the rocking Coach. But beneath the noise, I could still hear Dick's nasal, grating voice. I craned my neck to get a look at the actual stage, but the Coach's windshield was angled toward the thoroughfare. All I could see of Dick Doyle was his reflection.

Hee-hee, went the springs beneath the seat. Hee-hee-hee. I thought back to how close Dick had let his hand get to mine a moment before, so close that I'd actually believed he was going to shake with me. I recalled that trick kids play on each other, putting a hand out, then yanking it back. Fooled you, shithead! Hee-hee-hee-hee. And there was little Dick, singing from the dashboard. The sequined playing cards flashed from his lapels.

I took off my watch and flung it at the mirror, but it missed and hit the windshield.

"What was that?" Joan said over her shoulder.

"Nothing," I said. "Don't stop."

"You threw something. I saw you. What's the matter?"

"Come on. Don't do this," I said, trying to get back into things.

But she was already looking out the windshield, at Dick onstage.

"Joan."

She pulled away. Then she started dressing.

"Joan, come on. I just got nervous that we were going to get caught."

"Don't lie," she said, pulling on her jeans.

"I'm not lying! I thought I saw someone peeking at us from over there. From behind that Plymouth."

"Stop already. I need to get some air." She pulled the lever and opened the door.

I grabbed her hand. "Joan, I'm crazy about you. I want you to come to New York with me. Joan!"

"Let me go!"

"Joan, please!"

She tried to pull away but I held on.

"Get off of me!" She yanked her hand free and got out of the shuttle.

"I'm sorry," I called after her, watching her vanish into the crowd. "I couldn't help it!"

A woman with a blanket under her arm walked by the Coach's open door and I suddenly became aware of my nakedness. I yanked the door shut and sat down in the driver's seat, which gave a loud, tired wheeze beneath my weight.

For a long moment I sat inside the empty Coach, the sweat on my body cooling. I stared out the window at Dick Doyle, trying to figure out how, exactly, he'd tricked me into becoming this—a man sitting naked and alone in a dusty parking lot. He'd led me away from my life, down, down all the way to central Florida. He'd turned me into someone I didn't recognize. A man I despised. I thought about returning to New York without anything to show for myself, returning with no one, to nothing.

I fished the keys from Joan's bag and started up the Coach. Then I slammed on the gas.

The chain strung across the front of the lot snapped with a twang as the Coach roared up out of the gravel lot and onto the stretch of grass leading to the stage. I turned on the high beams, which cut through the darkness like the white horns of a charging bull. I was vaguely aware of people on the dance floor screaming and scattering, but I had my sights fixed on the man onstage. He seemed unaware of the commotion; he just strummed his guitar and sang, the spotlight making the sequined designs sparkle across his suit.

Lanterns popped against the windshield, one after another, sending showers of sparks across the glass. The blue floor gleamed beneath the Coach's tires. Flecks of mica in the paint sparkled under the headlights, as though the floor were an immense body of water, an ocean I had to cross to get to Dick Doyle. Someone threw a soda against the driver's-side door, where it splattered all over my window; I plowed through a giant teddy-bear, which burst in an explosion of stuffing. All I saw was Dick Doyle, singing away at the end of that bright shaft of light, his hairy fingers moving over the guitar.

I pressed harder on the gas; the stage loomed closer and closer. I glared at Dick, waiting for him to look over, to see the Coach speeding toward him, but his gaze was vacant, aimed blindly at the dancing crowd. *Look over here!* I thought. *Call chicken!* Still, he kept on playing. I was so close now that I could smell the hay bales on-stage. I could hear his voice, not his amplified voice but the real thing. I could see the sweat stains on the brim of his white hat.

"Drop your mask!" I screamed. "Drop it!"

But Dick stayed where he was.

I stomped on the brakes, but the Coach was going too fast; the van hurtled toward Dick, screeching and fishtailing, smashing through hay bales. I pulled the emergency brake, and still the Coach skidded toward Dick, who was only now looking over, finally seeing what was about to happen. There was no fear in his face, though, only a lack of comprehension, bewilderment. He stopped playing. But that was all he had time to do before the Coach rammed into him. There was a horrible thud, and then the Coach slid to a stop.

"It's that stalker!" someone screamed.

"Call the cops!"

I glanced in the side-view mirror and saw Dick staggering to his feet behind one of the hay bales. His guitar still hung from his neck, but its front had come loose and was dangling by the instrument's strings over the empty wooden box of its body. Dick's hat had fallen off too. His hair stuck up in wild shocks. He looked over at me, dazed and blinking against the stage lights. The light had been in his eyes, I realized. That was why he hadn't seen me coming.

I put the Coach in reverse.

The tires squealed against the waxed surface of the stage. I watched in the side-view mirror as Dick wobbled on his feet, looking at me coming toward him with that same expression of confusion. *Who's the loser now?* I thought. *Who's the fucking fake!* Dick vanished behind the tail end of the Coach.

I was sure he'd dodge or dive to safety, but instead I heard a loud whump and a grunt and the crash of someone falling backward into stage equipment.

I jerked the Coach to a stop. The voices were closer now.

"Get him!"

"Grab his arm! Lord Christ, he's naked in there!"

I craned my head out the window. I saw Dick's leg hanging over a toppled speaker. The silver toe cap at the tip of his boot winked at me in the light. Beyond the boot Dick's face appeared with what looked like a smile on it.

I stepped on the gas again. The Coach lurched backward, but an amplifier was stuck beneath the tail. The tires spun and smoked. I rammed the lever into drive, but before I could hit the gas again a hand reached inside the window and had me by the face. Another one grabbed my hair. All the stage lights seemed to go out at once.

Part Three: Ballad with Thirty-six Wheels

SPENT THE WHOLE OF SUNDAY AT THE POLICE STATION, LOCKED in a common holding cell. The courts were closed for the weekend, so there would be no bail hearing until Monday morning.

All I did in the cell was lie on my cot. I hurt all over; I was covered in bruises from being dragged out of the Coach. One of my eyes was black and swollen and wouldn't stop tearing. The cell was nicer than I'd imagined it would be, clean and well lit, with six soft cots lining the wall. The toilet had a curtain that pulled closed around it for privacy. Only two other people shared the cell with me. Both were men sleeping off drunks. One lay on his back with an arm flung over his face. The other sat curled against the wall, his jacket around his shoulders like a cape. This man was older, and for a moment, when I was first led into the cell, I mistook him for the old man from the dumpster, but he was just a stranger.

On Monday morning the policeman gave me two calls. I called Roddy and I called Joan. But it was Orlando who came to get me late Monday afternoon. Driving back from the station, he hardly said a word. He looked haggard, and he kept his eyes on the road.

"I'm sorry if I embarrassed you," I said.

"I'm the one who's sorry, Miller. I should never have let you go see the singer. That was my mistake."

"No, I—"

Orlando hissed through his teeth. "Don't say anything," he said. "Just rest."

I leaned my head against the window, letting the glass cool the inflamed skin above my eye. The sun was just setting; all the day's color was draining into the sky, leaving the trees black. I thought of my apartment back in New York. I could see the same sunset pouring in through those huge bedroom windows, lighting up the floor like the deck of an ocean liner. I saw my little robotic vacuum, slowly dragging itself from room to room, its batteries nearly dead.

I closed my eyes. How had I let this all happen? How could I have been so stupid? An image of Dick's face came to me—his face the way it had looked in the Coach's windshield just before I knocked him down, confused and frightened and yet horribly blank. I felt a great shame welling up in me. Dick Doyle was not to blame. He wasn't a fake. He was just an unfortunate man, now made more so by my attack, left bruised and battered. I was lucky he'd survived at all.

By the time Orlando pulled into the pawnshop's lot, I felt ready to sleep for a thousand years. It took a great effort to get out of the car. Raoul, another clerk, was just locking up.

Orlando thanked him and sent him home. "Hey, Miller," he called to me then. "Come inside. Have a drink with me."

I looked at him through my good eye, then at my car, parked beside the dumpster. A drink sounded like heaven.

I followed Orlando inside the pawnshop, turning on all the lights.

"Back here," he said, heading to the supply closet. He unlocked the door and from a small box in the back he pulled a bottle of Gullick Single Malt.

"You've had that in the store the whole time I've worked here?" I said.

He shrugged and took out two plastic cups. "Sometimes, when I'm here at night, after you or Raoul or Sam leave, I call home." He poured Scotch into a cup and handed it to me.

It took me a moment to realize that by home he meant Argentina.

He took off his glasses and massaged the bridge of his nose. "I've been a fool plenty times over, Miller," he said. Then he took a sip of his drink. "Here. I want to show you something. Look at what came in the other day."

He opened the jewelry case and pulled out the box of nameplates. "I don't know why I keep any of these things," he said.

"None of them are worth much. And no one ever buys them from me." He sifted through the alphabetized bags of names until he found what he was looking for—a pendant reading *Orlando*.

"Look at that," he said, holding the nameplate up to the light. "My first Orlando. I think I must have every name in the box now. None worth anything."

I smiled, which hurt. "You got a Max?"

"Sure," he said, digging through the nameplates. "I think we got three or four." He pulled out a couple, then picked the nicer of the two and gave it to me.

I turned the pendant over. *Max*, in swooping gold letters. "What do you think it's worth?" I said.

He examined the pendant. "About . . . twenty-five cents."

We both laughed.

"Get the acid," I said.

He slapped me on the back, then took the nitric acid from the cupboard.

I put an empty bowl on the counter. Carefully, Orlando poured in the acid. Then he resealed the jug and locked it away.

"Cheers." I held up my cup of Scotch.

He nodded and tapped my cup with his and then we dropped the pendants in the acid.

"Hocus-pocus," he said.

"Exactly."

I watched as the letters began to fizz and break apart, turning the acid a rusty brown. An odor like vinegar emanated from the bowl. After a moment, the bubbles cleared and the reaction settled and all that was left of the pendants were a few metal rinds, floating and bobbing around in the acid.

"You go home now, Miller," said Orlando. "I'll take your shift with the dumpster tonight."

I shook my head, swallowing the last of my Scotch. "No way," I said. "I'm doing it."

"You've had a long day. You need to get some sleep."

"I want to stay."

He eyed me.

"I'll be fine," I said.

Orlando nodded, then went to get me the spear gun.

Spring nights in Central Florida are full of turbulence. Almost every cloud has a secret storm balled up inside it. They skid across the atmosphere, trailing strange, violent winds behind them, winds that sway the palm trees, blowing the mice that live in the leaves out into the sky.

I was enjoying my time outside, my last night guarding the dumpster. I lay on the hood of my car, watching the sky, which was clear and filled with stars and blinking satellites. The wind felt wonderful on my bare skin, warm and close and breathy. I felt far away from myself, completely alone in the world, but strangely calm, too.

The dumpster creaked on its base. I scanned the area, but saw no one. Just then I noticed the sound of an approaching car. I sat up and reached for the spear gun.

Headlights appeared from around the corner. They stopped at the end of the block. Someone exited the car, and though I squinted to make the person out, the headlights were pointed at me, and all I could see was a hazy red silhouette.

"Is that you, Joan?" I said. "Joan, I have some things to say."

"I'm not here to start trouble," said Dick Doyle.

The blood rushed out of my face. I shielded my eyes, but he was just a shadow and a voice.

Then the headlights went off and I could see him. He wore a
T-shirt and jeans, a trucker's cap on his head. One of his arms
hung in a sling. The fingers of his other hand were all splinted. His
expression was sharp and alert, though. Just the way I imagined he
lived in his private time.

"Well, well," I said.

"Look. It wasn't an act, at first," he said, walking toward me.
"After that asshole ran me down, I couldn't hardly do anything. It
was like someone padlocked my brain. But then things came back
to me. It was slow going." He stopped right in front of me. "It took
a long time to recover."

"So, who knows about this?" I said. "Who knows you're faking?"

He shrugged. "My family, my friends. I don't know. Whoever.
I'm not faking, though, because that's not what matters about the
act. That's not what it's about."

"Does Pearl know?" I said.

Dick sighed. He turned toward his car and gave a nod. A tiny
light went on inside and I saw Pearl sitting in the driver's seat. She
wore a kerchief over her hair, like an old woman. There were dark
circles beneath her eyes.

"I'm dropping the charges against you," said Dick.

"Why are you doing that?" I said.

"Because I want this to be over and done. I need it to be, man.
Look, if you want to go tell everyone I'm a fake, then go ahead. Be
my guest. Splash it all over the place. I don't care anymore. You
want to beat the shit out of me? You want to fire that spear through
my chest? I deserve it, right? I ruined your life or whatever you
want to think. Here. Go ahead. Shoot."

He flung open his good arm and waited.

"Really," he said. "Do it. Now's your chance. Fuck me up, man.
I stole your girlfriend, dragged you down here."

He lifted his shirt, revealing his belly. "Come on!" he said, angry now. "Do it. Here I am! Exposed!"

I kept waiting for the old anger to kick in, but it just wouldn't. None of my past with Dick Doyle seemed to matter anymore. I actually felt silly, standing there with my spear gun, facing off.

"Let's call it even," I said.

He squinted at me. "Hold up," he said. "You understand, right? This *has* to be the end?"

I glanced at Pearl sitting in the car, pale and exhausted.

"It is the end," I said.

Dick hesitated a moment, then let the hem of his shirt drop. He put out his splinted hand for me to shake. "Truce?"

I took his thumb in my hand and gently shook it. "Truce."

"Well, phew," he said. Then he looked around, as though just now noticing the store, the lot, the dumpster.

"Hey, I'm sorry about that handshaking thing at the fair. That was shitty of me. I was just feeling jealous. I mean, Pearl's a special lady, you know?"

"Yes," I said, though, much as I'd have liked to just then, I supposed I didn't know. I didn't know much about her at all.

"Bygones and buried hatchets, right?" Dick laughed, so cheerful all of a sudden. "So you have to stay out here all night, huh? Your boss told Pearl you'd be here till morning. That is one bad bitch."

I explained that it wasn't so bad.

"Still, that's a lot of downtime," he said. He reached into his back pocket and took out a CD. "This might be ridiculous, but I thought that maybe, if you've got nothing better to do, you could take a listen." He handed it to me.

On the cover was a picture of him with that same dazed expression on his face.

"Will do," I said.

Dick nodded. "Well . . . I'm going to get back," he said. "Listen, I'm glad we talked, brother."

He patted me on the shoulder with his better hand, and then turned and walked back to his car. As he got in, I cast a last look at Pearl, watching me from the driver's seat. I wanted to talk to her, to apologize, *something,* but she was already starting the engine. A moment later they disappeared down the street.

I walked back to my car. Inside, I took the CD from its case and slipped it into the player. The first song was about two truck drivers, a man and a woman, who meet over the CB radio. They start talking to each other one night, while driving their routes, just two lonely voices in the darkness.

It was a beautiful song and I hoped that I'd get the chance to listen to it with Joan the next day. I imagined myself lying on the couch with her, listening to the story together. The man and woman keep driving right past each other's trucks, barely missing each other without even knowing. In one verse the truckers come close to meeting: The woman eats at a truck stop, and the man comes in so soon after her that when he unknowingly sits down on her stool, her tip money is still on the counter. The change is still warm from her pocket.

The Star
Attraction
of 1919

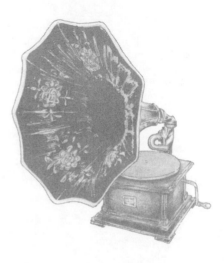

J OHN CIRCLED BACK OVER THE PUMPKIN PATCH, BRINGING THE plane lower this time, just to make sure his eyes weren't playing tricks on him. He'd been flying for over two hours straight; he felt dizzy from engine fumes and his goggles were smeared with gasoline. But as he brought the plane around, he spotted them again: forty, maybe even fifty people gathered among the pumpkins—a whole party waving at him, shouting and cheering, waiting for him to land. They were dressed formally, the men in sack suits and bright silk ties, the women in smart summer hats of pink or cream straw. They'd even laid out a runway, a long strip of white cloth that cut a clear, straight path through the pumpkin vines.

John wondered for a moment if he had the wrong town. He pulled his map from beneath the seat, unfolded it, and pinned it with his forearm against the leather rim of the cockpit. The map's edges whipped about as he did his calculations: he'd taken off from Poth, Missouri, at nine in the morning and followed the railroad tracks west across the grasslands until about eleven o'clock, when he'd landed to refuel. It was near two thirty in the afternoon by the time he'd lifted off again, and now it was just after five, which would put him at—John scanned the wrinkled expanse of eastern Kansas—yes, this had to be Bunting. It was the only town for a hundred miles in either direction, and when John looked up from the map he saw, as though to underscore the obviousness of his deduction, a water tower standing just to the south with BUNTING, KS painted across its tank.

He refolded his map and glanced again at the crowd assembled below, the tiny white blossoms of their faces. He slowed down to let them read the lettering painted on the bottom of his wings. On the left wing: JOHN BARRON. EXPERT PILOT. On the right: RIDES JUST $2!!! Then he leaned out of the cockpit to watch the reaction. Some of the men saluted and a few women waved as his shadow streaked over them.

John waved back, beaming. As he turned to the controls to ready his Curtis JN "Jenny" for landing, he felt an electric joy thrum through him: he had an actual welcome party. People had dressed up in fine clothes and hiked out to the middle of an empty pumpkin patch to welcome him to their town. He'd been barnstorming for three months now, since just after his twenty-first birthday, in February of 1919; so far he'd visited over thirty towns scattered throughout the Midwest, from Minnesota to Iowa to Nebraska and now down into Kansas, and never, not once, had there been a real welcome party waiting for him. Now and then he'd arrived in a new town to find some aviation enthusiasts standing out on the sidewalks, their Kodak Brownies aimed up at the sky. Sometimes a group of children, drawn outside by the Jenny's approaching whine, chased after him as he flew past. But most often, John flew into a new town to find no one waiting for him or cheering him on. Nobody even expecting him, save a telephone operator or two.

Now, as he started his descent—pushing on the Jenny's elevator, nosing her down toward the pumpkin patch—he tried to guess which of the women below was Marlene, the Bunting telephone operator he'd spoken with. Maybe the girl in the sleeveless dress at the back of the crowd? Waving a glove at him? John felt a small thrill at the thought of meeting her. He got along well with telephone operators. He made a habit to call ahead to every town he planned to visit and introduce himself to at least one telephone operator first. The women who worked the telephone lines in the kinds of towns John visited—country towns where a plane was still big news—usually spent their afternoons connecting the same people over and over again, knitting and reknitting familiar patterns: plugging Mr. Gray into Mrs. Beige. Wiring Mrs. Beige to Dr. Brown, and so on. A new voice on the line excited these girls. They joked and flirted with John. It was easy to get them on his side, to get them to help publicize his arrival. All it took was the promise of a free plane ride and they were swearing up and down that as soon as they hung up they were going to tell everyone they knew that an expert pilot was coming to town. And they were fun girls, too. Outgoing and social. The type to show him a good time, take him out to movie theaters and dance halls.

He'd called Marlene twice while he was still performing in the town of Poth, two hundred miles to the east.

"You owe me one," she'd said the last time they'd spoken. "I got the whole town waiting for you. You better be cute."

"I'll wipe off some of the grease. Just for you," said John.

"Well, try not to make me look bad. Everyone'll be out there when you fly in."

John had taken "everyone" to mean a couple of Marlene's friends standing outside the telephone offices, yelling hellos or whistling at him or maybe waving a scribbled paper sign. Nothing like this.

The women's lawn dresses shimmered in the sun, pale green and yellow and tangerine. At the back of the pumpkin patch stood a table lined with bottles of champagne. John tried to think up something extraordinary he could do for Marlene to thank her for preparing all this for him. He could make a banner for her: MARLENE, MARLENE, BUNTING QUEEN. Something like that, and fly it over town. Or he could buzz her house at sunset, shower her yard with flowers.

John took the plane low as he crossed the edge of the pumpkin patch. Green, unripe pumpkins rushed by beneath his wheels. He tilted the tail down, dragging in wind to slow the plane. The levers trembled in his hands. Through the blur of the propeller he could see the men and women part, moving away from the makeshift runway to give him room.

The Jenny hit hard, knocking John against the controls, but then it bounced, rising and leaping forward. John shoved on the elevator and brought the plane back down. Pumpkins burst against the wheels with dull, sickening thuds. The sour odor burned his nose as bits of pumpkin meat splattered across his face, getting in his mouth, slapping across his goggles. The pulp fouled up the wheels too. The plane skidded and spun, tossing John around the cockpit, the world a cyclone of shouts and colors, until finally the Jenny whipped to a jarring halt.

John tried to catch his breath, but his chest hurt where the lever had punched into him.

"Hello?" said a woman's voice. "Are you all right in there?"

John winced and pulled off his goggles. "Just part of the act," he said, wiping the pumpkin from his face.

He ran a hand through the sticky tangle of his hair and looked around. What a dream-like vision, all of these men and women dressed in fancy clothes, gathered around him in the middle of a pumpkin patch. Each woman carried a single pink rose. A large house stood off in the distance, just beyond the edge of the field. The sight sent a pang of excitement through John; he might actually get to sleep in a bed that night.

This, he thought as he took it all in—the party, the pumpkin patch, the warm afternoon sunlight—this was what he loved best about barnstorming. Between the last five towns combined he'd made seventy-two dollars profit, but this morning he'd landed to a champagne toast and a warm bed. You never knew when your luck would turn. You just cranked the propeller, lifted off, and followed the silver thread of the railroad tracks.

John climbed out of the cockpit and stood on the plane's wing. Everyone, the men, the women, seemed stunned to silence by his arrival. Probably none of these people had ever seen a plane before, John thought. And even if they had seen a plane, they'd never had one roar to a stop right in front of their faces. He scanned the crowd for Marlene.

"Ladies and gentlemen of Bunting," he said, unzipping his leather aviator jacket. "I can't thank you enough for this warm welcome. When I saw all of you gathered here, I almost cried tears of joy."

A young man approached John with a bottle of champagne. "Now you're really trying to make me cry," John said, taking the bottle. He popped the cork and let the fizz run down his glove before taking a long sip.

The man's fist hit John on the side of the head. It flew up out of nowhere and knocked him backward against the fuselage. Champagne splashed across John's face and chest. Through the ringing in his ears, he heard people shouting, rushing around. The man who'd hit him climbed up on the wing and stood over him now, a huge silhouette blocking out the sun.

John braced himself for another blow, but before his attacker could swing again, an arm slid around the man's waist and yanked him down off the wing.

A hot throbbing started in John's temple. When he touched the side of his head, his fingers came back wet with blood. Two men were struggling beside the wing of his plane. The man being restrained was young, about John's own age, with a thick black mustache. The man holding him was older, his beard streaked with gray.

"This boy is probably a present from someone, Charley," said the older man. "I'm sure he's here as a gift to you."

"Who sent him, then?" said Charley, writhing.

"Why don't you stop thrashing about and ask him?"

Charley glared at John. A vein shaped like a tiny lightning bolt pulsed at the center of his forehead. "Well?" he said. "Are you a gift?"

"I'm here to offer you the gift of flight, if that's what you mean," John said. He scanned the crowd, waiting for a reaction, but they seemed frightened and confused. Some of the women looked like they were about to cry. John felt a cold, sinking sensation in his stomach.

"This party is for me, right?" he said. "John Barron? The pilot?" He gestured to his plane. Strings of pumpkin seeds dangled from the lower wings. "Is there a Marlene here?"

"For you?" the older man said. "Son, this is a wedding. You've crashed into my daughter's wedding." He pointed to the aisle runner—the long strip of white cloth John had mistaken for a runway—lying rumpled and torn beneath the wheels of the plane.

"I'm the groom," said Charley, pointing a thumb at himself. "And that was my champagne, asshole."

John felt very weak all of a sudden. It was then that he noticed, standing at the far end of the field, behind the crowd, a young girl in a white dress. She stared blankly at John, her dark red hair pinned above her face. She had one hand on the fence railing; the other hung limp at her side. Her dress was decorated with intricate beadwork that sparkled in the late sunlight. A bouquet of pink roses lay at her feet.

Then, all at once she turned and ran toward the house, her dress dragging behind her in the grass. Charley ran after her.

John felt a growing, painful pressure on the side of his head.

"Come down from there. You're bleeding," said the father of the bride. "Let's get you some medical attention." He put out his hand.

John reached for it but grabbed only air. A wave of panic hit him. He felt an overwhelming need to escape from there, to climb back into his plane and lose himself in the cold, oceanic emptiness of the sky. But he was so dizzy.

He turned to the crowd. The men and women were blurs to him now, watery shapes smearing into one another. "Sorry about the misunderstanding, everyone," he said, blinking hard. "If one of you would just point me to the nearest petrol station, I'll be on my way."

Then he stepped down from his plane and passed out in the grass.

John woke with a start. The skin around his temple felt hot and swollen, and when he touched it, he found that someone had taped a small gauzy bandage over his cut. He knew he should lie back down and ice his head, but all he could think about was getting back to his plane. He threw off his blankets and sat up. How long had he slept? Slipping on his aviator jacket, he opened the door to his room and peered out. The hallway was dark and empty.

John snuck past the other bedrooms and headed downstairs. When he reached the foyer, he stopped and wrote a note on a pad by the telephone.

Dear Sir,

*I apologize for destroying your daughter's wedding. All moneys
I have at present have been laid beside this note to pay for
damages.*

Sincerely,

John M. Barron (Pilot)

John placed a stack of dollar bills beside the note—practically everything he had. The bills were wrinkled and dirty and the pile sponged to one side. John frowned and picked up the pen.

I will send more once I make some.

He read over his work one more time and, satisfied, opened the front door and slipped outside into the foggy morning.

The light was still poor. It had to be at least an hour before sunrise—not a good time to fly, but John didn't care. He looked around until he spotted the silhouette of his Jenny, still parked in the pumpkin patch, ready to lift off again. He hurried over.

As he approached the plane, though, he noticed a figure sitting on the lower port wing. Lord God, he thought. Charley. Waiting to pound him. John struggled to come up with some way of avoiding a fight, something he could say, but when he neared the plane he saw that the figure wasn't Charley at all, but a girl. The bride.

She was still wearing her wedding dress. On her feet were a pair of scuffed black boots. Her hair hung down the front of her shoulder in a long red braid. To John she looked like a discarded fairy-tale character, a princess plucked from a storybook and dropped onto the wing of his plane in a heap of twinkling fabric.

"I left a note," John said to her. "I'm not trying to sneak off."

The girl nodded at a valise sitting beside the plane's wheel. "I am," she said.

It took John a moment to understand her.

"You're joking," he said.

"I don't weigh a pound more than a hundred and ten," she said. "And I'm good with maps."

John ran a hand over the back of his neck. What was it about pilots? he wondered. What made the lonely girls fall so hard for them? Maybe it was the outfit?—The cap and gloves, the scarf snapping in the wind.

"Don't flatter yourself," said the girl, as though she'd sensed what he was thinking. "I'm about to leave a man behind. I'm not looking for a new one."

John climbed aboard. "Sorry," he said. "I don't need a copilot."

"I won't get in your way."

"You're in my way now," he said, brushing past her. He opened the supply box and removed the doping tape. "I need you to move off the wing. I have to check for tears in the linen."

But the girl didn't move.

When he tried to crawl over her, she grabbed his wrist. The force of her grip startled him, and he looked at her, truly taking her in for the first time. She was prettier than he'd thought. Her face was soft featured and pale, almost translucently white, but her eyes were a warm, clay brown. They stared back at him in a way that was neither desperate nor pleading. Just determined.

"You owe me this," she said. "You ruined my wedding."

John jerked his hand back, but she held on to him.

"I'll yell," she said.

"Miss," John said, "why are you doing this?"

"That's my business," she said.

John sighed. "Look, even if I agreed to take you, I don't have enough petrol to get us both to the next town. We're too heavy together."

She nodded at the garage to the east of the house. Stacks of green-and-white petrol cans stood in rows behind the cars.

The girl let go of John's wrist but kept her eyes trained on him.

"Have at it," she said.

John rubbed his wrist. A nice fix he'd landed in this time. He glanced at the house; a lamp was already lit in one of the windows. He knew taking the girl was a bad idea, but he felt too weak to argue. He was hungry; his head hurt. His body felt like an empty pouch.

"I'll take you to the next town," he said. "Then you're on your own."

The sky was clear and calm, totally windless, perfect for flying. But the whole way to Gunnison, John couldn't relax. He hated that the girl was suddenly there, in his cockpit, uninvited; he kept his eyes fixed on the back of her head, watching for any signs of trouble.

He never knew how a passenger would react once the plane took off, and he had a bad feeling about her. She was wearing a wedding dress, for fuck's sake. Plenty of perfectly normal-seeming customers went to pieces in the air. Out of nowhere. Regular men and women cringing and shaking, huddling inside the cockpit. Some got sick. Some fainted. A few even seemed to go completely crazy. An old man in Minnesota, for example, had pulled a .32 on him two hundred feet above the earth. The man had threatened to shoot if John didn't land the plane immediately. Another woman had stood up in the cockpit and undressed mid-flight. She was a large person, and John could still see the pale flag of her body rippling in the wind.

And all this had happened on $2 rides, rides that lasted five minutes and never rose more than a few hundred feet off the ground. Now, with this girl as his passenger, he flew at a steady altitude of nine hundred feet, high above the thinning clouds. The cold blasted them, but the girl seemed so calm, sitting primly in the front cockpit, staring out at the empty sky through her oversize goggles. Too calm, to John's mind. It was unsettling; she never pointed or turned to him to ask a question. Never leaned out of the cockpit to swim a hand through the wind. She acted as relaxed as someone riding on a bus. Probably she was holding it all in, he thought. Any moment now she'd burst into hysterics. And why not? Why not one more disaster? Lately John's luck had only been getting worse. He'd made some good money back in Michigan, some in Iowa too, but that was weeks ago. Soon it'd be the heat of summer, blazing sun, the engine overheating. Barnstorming three months and already he was getting tired.

Just look at yourself, he thought: broke, injured, exhausted, responsible for the total ruination of a wedding. And now saddled with a weird, runaway girl. All at once, the old worries came rushing back. Maybe he was wrong to have bought the plane. Maybe being a pilot was a ridiculous idea. Maybe he should give up now, before something truly awful happened. He could sell the Jenny for parts, go back to New York. He still had a job waiting for him at Sweet Fizz, the soda bottling plant where he'd worked with his father, Rollie Barron, before enlisting. Rollie had told him so just a few days ago.

"Dale keeps asking me when you're coming back," Rollie had said. "I told him I don't know, but he keeps on about it. Says he'll hold you a place as long as he can."

"Good to know," John had said.

"You've got his telephone number, John? The number to his

office?" Rollie had a slow, sleepy way of speaking. John could picture him in their small apartment in Williamsburg, sitting on the stool by the telephone. He could see his father's face as they talked, round and pink and dimpled, a boyish face despite the gray hair. But a sad face, also. With a weariness hanging about the eyes.

"I don't need Dale's number," John said.

"It's no trouble to find," Rollie said. "I wrote it down somewhere around here."

John heard his father rummaging around the desk. "Thanks anyway, Rol."

"Here it is."

"I'm fine."

"Just take it. In case."

"No pen."

John was calling from a farmhouse where he would spend the night. The owner had seen John land in a nearby field and invited him in for dinner. As John spoke, the man and his wife washed dishes together over the sink basin. They stood with their hips touching. Every now and then the man would say something to make the woman laugh and she'd smack him with a dish towel. Watching the two of them irritated John. His father was an old man alone in a dingy apartment.

"I have to go," John said into the phone. "I'm sending you some money."

"No, no. Don't be silly. I'm fine."

"Guess," John said.

"Oklahoma?"

"North."

"Kansas?"

"East."

"Missouri?"

"Bingo."

"Missouri. I'm looking forward to seeing the postcard."

Along with money, John sent his father postcards from every state he visited. "Maybe I'll fly you here after I get back."

John's father laughed. "I'm fine where I am."

"I'm going to kidnap you. You're not going to have a choice."

"Talk to you soon, John."

"Okay." John waited for a moment, listening as the line went dead.

The train tracks below the plane began to edge west, and John pushed on the rudder, following the curve. He wondered if he should call Rollie from Gunnison, get Dale Morton's number. There was no harm in giving Mr. Morton a ring after all, just to check in. But as soon as John began to imagine his conversation with Mr. Morton, he could hear, in the background, the sounds of the plant: the hiss of the soda water tanks, the tamping down of crown cork caps. The clink and rattle of bottles moving down the line. Worst of all, he could hear the floors, the terrible peeling noise they made whenever anyone lifted a boot. Sweet Fizz specialized in fruit-flavored sodas, and the plant's floors were always sticky with dried syrup— cherry, grape, lemon. No matter how many times custodial hosed them down, the floors stayed gluey. They gummed onto John's boots, sucking at the heels, the toes, making every step a tiny act of violence, a ripping back of himself. And the residue remained on his boot soles long after he clocked out. Walking home from the plant, alley cats would often slink out from the shadows to follow him and lick at his footprints.

John pushed the memory from his mind. He didn't want to think about Sweet Fizz or Rollie or any of it. He took out the map and opened it against the cockpit's rim. Look at that, he thought to himself, staring at the grand sweep of the country. Forty-eight whole states to explore. He could visit any place he wanted to. All he had to do was call ahead, get some telephone operators on his side, and that would be that.

He glanced at the girl sitting in the front cockpit, loose strands of hair flying around her head. He'd be glad to be rid of her.

They reached Gunnison at around nine in the morning. It was much smaller than John had expected, like a sketch of a town: a train station, a church. Hardly anybody was out on the sidewalks.

John circled the surrounding farmland until he found a property he thought would make a good operating station. It lay just on the outskirts of town, a modest estate, less than twenty acres. John brought the plane down right in front of the farmhouse.

A family stood waiting on the front porch, apparently led outside by the sound of the approaching plane. A farmer in denim coveralls, his wife, and three blond children hiding behind their legs.

John hopped down from the cockpit. "Hello, there!" he said to the children. "Are you three the owners of this beautiful farm?"

The children clung tighter to their parents. A piano of pale, unfinished wood stood on the porch.

"Go on and look at this, now," the farmer said. He was entirely bald, built with big plates of muscle across his shoulders and chest. He wore tiny gold-rimmed spectacles that flashed in the sun. "Husband and wife flyers. That's a development."

John laughed. "She isn't my wife," he said, helping the girl down from the cockpit. Strangely, her wedding dress seemed even brighter than it had that morning. The beadwork glittered. Maybe the wind had polished it up, John thought.

"Well, whose wife is she, then?" said the farmer's wife.

"Exactly," said the farmer.

John froze, suddenly realizing the scope of his mistake. Tales about the kidnapping and seduction of young women had become wildly popular in the last year. One appeared in the papers practically every week: a story about a pretty fiancée or new bride followed home from the dance hall or nickel dump by a man looking to sell her into white slavery. The man would wait for her to turn a corner and then jump out at her from the shadows, blowing powder into her face—shimmering, soporific powder that caused her vision to swirl and darken and close in on her like a gloved fist. And then, once she passed out, the man would roll her up in a carpet and carry her off.

Both the farmer and his wife were staring at John, waiting for an explanation. He could see their suspicions hardening. The girl would tell them he'd kidnapped her. She was taking revenge on him for destroying her wedding. How had he been so stupid? He could already see himself being shoved into a police wagon, see his Jenny being impounded.

"I didn't mean that, sir," John said to the farmer, who stood staring at him from the porch.

"Oh?" said the farmer.

"He meant he likes 'blushing bride,' instead of wife," said the girl. She slid an arm around John's waist. "Wife sounds so chilly, don't you think?"

The farmer's wife laughed. "I have thought that, in fact."

Not knowing what else to do, John put his arm around the girl's shoulders and gave her a squeeze. The pebbled fabric felt scratchy against his skin. He smiled at the farmer and his family.

"My blushing bride," he said.

The farmer nodded. "Del Bradison," he said, putting out his hand.

John went to shake, but the girl beat him to it.

"Mrs. Helen Barron," she said, smiling in her wedding dress and boots. "Pilot."

The crowds in Gunnison turned out to be better than John had expected. More than forty people showed up at the farm to ride on his Jenny that first afternoon. He was busy from morning to sunset. The farmer, Mr. Bradison, helped him set up a small table in the grazing field where Helen could sit and collect money from the waiting passengers.

At first, John didn't like the idea of trusting Helen with the money, trusting her to sit there with all his bills in a pot. But what could he say in front of Bradison and his family? No matter, though; he knew there was no way for Helen to steal without him finding out. He could count the passengers himself. He knew his math.

It was an easy format. For $2 a customer got a quick tour of the town's landmarks—the church, the school, the mill, and then back. For $3, John flew a stunt with them, a barrel roll or free fall, maybe even a death spiral, if the customer was feeling particularly adventurous. For $5 he'd take a photograph with them in front of the plane. When he needed fuel, he paid one of Bradison's daughters a nickel to a make petrol run for him. Which she did by hauling cans back and forth from the garage in a toy wagon. To his surprise, John went through three cans in the first afternoon alone.

Bradison let them a room in the attic, at the back of a storage space. It was hot and cramped inside, and John slept poorly the first night. He spent a good deal of time staring at the lump beneath the covers that was Helen, wondering how long he'd be stuck with her.

The second day in Gunnison was even better than the first, financially speaking. John could hardly believe his luck. At least two-thirds of the people who'd rode with him the day before were back to go again. Some went three, even four times. And lots of them wanted extras this time around. They wanted the tricks—the rolls and spins during their flights. Afterward they paid for photos with John and Helen beside the Jenny, the wooden propeller gleaming behind them.

It wasn't until late in the afternoon, the line to ride still snaking toward Bradison's barn, that John realized Helen was at least partly responsible for his new popularity. He was coming in for a landing with a passenger, a young boy who'd brought his basset hound up with him, when he noticed a knot in the line of people waiting to ride. The knot was at the front of the line, up near Helen's table. As he touched down, he saw that Helen was talking to them, the whole group. She was saying something funny, gesturing with her hands, and the crowd was chuckling—really laughing now, some of the women covering their mouths or stomachs, slapping their knees, convulsing with laughter.

"Watch out, mister," said the boy, looking back at John from the front cockpit, the goggles too big for his head.

John turned and saw a cow standing in the Jenny's path. He yanked the elevator and wrenched the plane upward, just missing the animal. The boy held tight to the dog on his lap. Its long ears flapped in the wind.

Again that evening, John couldn't sleep. The attic room felt even hotter than the night before. The dust stuck to his skin, creating an itchy film. But deep down he knew that there was more to his sleeplessness than just the heat. The day had been one of the best of his career. He'd made forty-three dollars, which was practically unheard of for him, especially on his second day in one town. He squinted across the mattress at the buttoned back of Helen's nightgown.

"How'd you do that today?" John said.

"How did I do what?" she said after a long moment.

"This." John reached beneath the edge of the mattress and pulled out the envelope of bills. "What did you say to those people to get them to keep coming back?"

Helen glanced at him over her shoulder. "I didn't *say* anything. I was just talking to them."

"Talking to them about what?"

"I don't know. I made up some stories about places we'd flown. Our travels. Don't you ever talk to them while you're up there?"

"I'm usually a little busy," John said. "Flying the plane?"

Helen turned toward him, propping herself on an elbow. Again John was struck by how pretty she looked. Her hair was down, softening her face.

"Well, you should try catering to your customers," she said. "It's just good showmanship."

"I cater to them," he said.

"Maybe to the girls . . ." She smiled at him.

John couldn't help smiling himself.

"That's right," she said, about to laugh. "I see right through you. Expert pilot."

"So, what about it?" he said. "I don't have time to make friends."

"Right," she said. "A night of fun. Then on to the next town."

"Exactly," said John.

"So where, oh where, great pilot, are you off to next?"

"I don't know." John glanced up at the small, dirty window near the room's peak. "I thought I'd head south before it gets too hot.

Fly through Oklahoma, Texas, west toward California. Or maybe I'll go north, up to Montana."

"I heard Montana's nice," Helen said. "Lots of moose." She lay down again, her hair pooling around her head.

"What about you?" he said. "Where are you headed?"

"I don't know," said Helen. "I'll figure it out. Trains run in all directions, right?"

"I could take you someplace myself," said John. "I mean, if you want a lift."

"That's all right," said Helen, yawning.

"Well then I'll give you money for a ticket. You earned some of that pot today."

"I'll be okay," she said.

John watched her as she adjusted her sheet, getting comfortable.

"I'd take you with me, you know," he said, "but I don't work that way. It's just impossible."

"No one's asking," said Helen.

"I'm just saying," said John. "I'm a solo act. No partners."

"A one-man show."

"That's right. So you get some dough from today, but that's it."

"Fine," said Helen.

But the next morning, no mention of the train was made. Instead, the two of them left Gunnison together, flying south in John's Curtis Jenny.

It took them two days to cross into Oklahoma. They moved in little hops, traveling forty, fifty miles a flight. The engine was too loud for them to communicate without yelling, so for the most part, they flew in silence. Helen kept the map up front with her, and she spent long stretches of time studying the names of cities and rivers. The strangest ones she yelled out to John.

"Kangaroo, New Mexico!" she called over her shoulder.

"I passed through Dirty Hand, Minnesota, a couple of weeks ago!" John called back.

The weather was perfect spring on the first day, and the prairie was in full bloom, bright with paintbrush and bluebonnets, pink clusters of catchfly. The fields shimmered; every few moments the wind skated a secret pattern through the grass. Ponds and lakes mirrored the sky. For a while John and Helen followed the train tracks, dipping down whenever a train passed, waving at the faces pressed to the windows.

They made camp less than a hundred miles from the Oklahoma border, on the open grassland. While Helen unpacked the blankets, John went to wash their goggles in a nearby stream. By the time he came back to camp, Helen had a small fire going.

"Make yourself useful, why don't you?" John said.

Helen stirred the fire with a stick, sending a swarm of sparks into the sky. "How far do you think we came today?"

"I don't know." John opened a can of noodle soup and poured the broth into his pot. "A couple hundred miles. Those lights up there, that's likely Barley." He sat down beside Helen and held the pot over the flames.

"I think that's Yupa," said Helen.

"Can't be. We didn't come far enough."

"Look for yourself," she said, spreading the map on the ground. He noticed that she was no longer wearing her engagement ring. Instead, she wore a simple gold band that appeared too big for her hand. Likely, John realized, this was the ring she was supposed to give to Charley during the wedding ceremony. It slid and jiggled on her finger as she traced their path across the map, reminding John of costume jewelry, of children playing dress-up.

"See?" she said. "Yupa."

"Beginner's luck," John said, handing her the soup pot to hold. He unlaced his boots and lay back on his elbows.

By now the sun had sunk beneath the horizon and the sky was dark. Fireflies emerged from the grass and flitted about the plane—landing on the wings, the fuselage, the propeller—turning the Jenny into a blinking outline.

Helen warmed the soup over the fire. Back in Gunnison, she'd bought some pairs of men's long johns to use as camping pajamas, and she was wearing one set now. The knuckles of her spine were visible through the waffled fabric and John felt a sudden urge to trace them with his finger, the way she'd drawn the plane's path on the map.

She looked at him out of the corner of her eye. "So, what's the story, Mr. Barron?"

"What do you mean?"

"I mean," she said, "when did you first realize you were in love with me? What was the moment?"

John felt his stomach tense up. He stared at her.

She laughed, causing the soup to slosh around in the pot. "Relax. What I'm saying is, if we're going to be a flying couple, we need a story to tell the customers.... So?"

John considered the question, but nothing came to mind. "I don't know," he said. "When was it you realized I was the guy for you?"

"Hmm." Helen dipped a finger in the soup and tasted it. "It'd have to be," she said, "the night you first took me flying."

John waited for her to go on.

She raised her eyebrows at him. "What?" she said. "You don't remember? It was only six months ago. You were just back from the war—"

"I never made it overseas," John said. "I wanted to, but the army kept me stationed in Texas. Place called Platter. I did get to learn to fly, though."

"Like I said, you were just home from your time in Texas. I was still living in our hometown of Layman, Missouri. With my parents." She held the pot low over the flame, moving it in a slow circle. "I hadn't seen you in two whole years," she said. "I was so lonely. You didn't write much—you couldn't—so I had no idea whether or not you were coming back. I used to sit alone in my room at night and just cry. My folks bought me a phonograph to cheer me up. But the records always made me sadder. I used to listen to them and feel sorry for myself. Everything I heard was about something I'd never get to do, someplace I'd never see with you."

She put the pot on the ground to cool. "The night you came back, I remember, I had on that record 'My Dark Star.' About the guy and girl who're separated. And they wish on the same star? It's such a sappy one, but it really got to me. I kept listening to it over and over. And then, out of nowhere, I heard a knock on my window. I didn't even know you were back yet.

"You had this airplane with you, too. It was parked right out in my parents' yard. I could see it from my window, gleaming in the moonlight. . . . I almost screamed, I was so happy. But you didn't say anything to me. Didn't even say hello. You put your finger to your lips, to tell me to keep quiet? And then you took my hand and we went out the bedroom window and climbed down the rain gutter together. You flew me all around town. Past the water tower. Down over the rooftops. I still remember the weather vanes spinning behind us, because you flew so low."

Helen fell silent.

"Wow," John said. "I'm a romantic guy."

"You can be. When you try."

John took two spoons from his pocket and handed one to her. "Oh, I'm always trying."

"That's the problem, actually," Helen said, taking a spoon from him. "Lately you've been a little too romantic."

"Do tell."

"Oh, I don't know," Helen said, spooning soup into her mouth. "It's just that, these last few weeks, it's been a bit much. With all the lovey-dovey stuff, I mean. The kisses and the hugs and the constant *I love you*s."

John took a swallow of soup. "You're saying I'm smothering you."

"A little. It's like every second: 'Oh, Helen, I just love you so much. I mean, you're so beautiful and smart and funny and—' "

"I'll try to rein it in."

"That's all I ask," Helen said, tipping the pot for him so he could get at the heavier noodles. "Too much romance just scares a girl off sometimes."

"You know," said John, "you're a pretty good actress, Helen."

Her face broke into a wide grin. "You think so?"

Though it was hard to tell in the dim firelight, John thought he saw a blush rise on her cheeks. My blushing bride, he thought.

"I half believed you myself," he said.

"I used to take lessons, when I was a girl," she said.

He offered her the last of the soup, but she shook her head.

"I wouldn't have thought they had acting classes in a cow town like Bunting," he said.

"Where?"

He finished drinking the final bit of soup. "Back in Bunting, Kansas," he said.

"I'm sorry," Helen said, grabbing the pot from him. "I've never been to Kansas. I'm from Layman, Missouri. Born and raised." Then she headed down to the river to clean up for bed.

The next morning they woke to find that the weather had turned on them. The winds had picked up; dark storm clouds crowded the sky. They tried to fly farther south, but the going was difficult. One rattling jump after another. John would take the plane up through the cloud cover to see if the air above was calm, find out the atmosphere was all roiling turbulence, and have to come back down. He'd land in a field, wet and chilled, wait a while, and then try again. It wasn't fun, but through the whole ordeal Helen never questioned him, never complained. She never got scared either—never seemed to, at least. Even when the plane hit wind swells that nearly tipped them out into the sky, she just put her hand on the rim of the cockpit to steady herself and waited, trusting that soon enough, John would set things right again.

She was a strange bird, he thought, studying the back of her head. The interlacing weave of her braid. The small white cups of her ears. He liked her, though. He could tell already. She was intelligent and funny, with opinions on everything under the sun. Whenever they landed to gas up, she started in: Charlie Chaplin was the best actor in Hollywood; didn't John think so? Prohibition was one of the stupidest ideas in history. In a hundred years, the country would have at least eighty states to it. Maybe even a hundred.

Around one in the afternoon, the weather finally cleared, and they made a hurried push south. Helen used the map to help guide them, and John quickly discovered that she had a keen eye for navigation; she often spotted subtle natural markers in the landscape before he did. A dried riverbed. An overgrown cattle path. A road sign, bleached white by the sun.

By three o'clock they were into Oklahoma. By four they were less than a hundred miles from the town of Mooney, their destination. The only trouble they had came when the plane's radiator cap snapped off at six hundred feet up. Exposed to the open air, John knew, the radiator fluid wouldn't be able to cool the engine, and the plane would be in danger of overheating and stalling out. There was no way to reach the cap from the cockpit, though. To reseal it, he'd have to climb out on the wing—a maneuver he'd managed in the past, but hated to perform. The wing doping was slippery, and the slipstream was tricky; the current could shift violently behind the propeller.

Helen's face went pale when he told her what he was about to do. "What are you talking about?" she screamed. "Who's going to fly the plane?"

"Just hold the controls as tight as you can!" he yelled, already standing up in the back cockpit. "This'll take less than thirty seconds!"

The stunt went smoothly; Helen held the levers dead-steady while John slipped out onto the wing and screwed the cap onto the radiator nozzle. As he was climbing back into the cockpit, he gave Helen the thumbs-up, but she stayed frozen in position, gripping the controls, apparently afraid to let go. Her brown eyes looked huge to him, magnified behind her goggles.

They reached Mooney around seven o'clock, too late in the day to start barnstorming. John landed the plane in a scrub field just outside town. He figured they could relax that night, then go charging into Mooney early in the morning. Get in a full day of showboating. Besides, it was a Friday night. No better time to barnstorm than a bright weekend morning.

They set up camp beside a small pond, cooking a can of tomato soup for dinner. By the time they were done eating, the sky was dark.

"What did it feel like out there today?" Helen said as she laid her blanket beneath the starboard wing.

"What did what feel like?" John asked. He was already wrapped in his blanket on the port side of the plane.

"What does it feel like to be out on the wing like that?"

John laced his fingers behind his head. The night sky was clear, the stars brilliant. The full moon sat low on the horizon, like a dime balanced on its edge. "It was cold," he said. "The wind's strong out there."

"But what did it feel like?" Helen said, lying down. "Out there all alone? So high up?"

"I don't know, Helen. It felt like being out on the wing."

"Would you teach me how to do it?"

John glanced over to see if Helen was kidding, but she was just a shape in the darkness.

"What's to teach?" he said. "You just climb out. There's nothing special about it."

"So can I try tomorrow?"

John laughed. "No."

"Why not, if there's nothing special about it?"

"Because," he said. "There's no reason for you to go out there. The cap is fixed. Plus, it's dangerous. You could get blown off. I had trouble holding on myself today."

"Just for a minute. I won't even let go of the cockpit rim."

"Forget it."

Helen sighed and lay back down. "What a mean husband I've got."

"I thought that was how you liked them."

"I said I didn't like it when my man gets too romantic on me. I didn't say I wanted him mean."

"Go to sleep."

"Do you think we'll get a crowd tomorrow? The town seemed pretty big on the map."

"Go to sleep."

"I could see the cemetery from the air, too, right before we landed. And it looked huge."

"Go to sleep."

"The stars are too bright. I can't."

Less than a minute later, though, Helen was asleep.

John lay awake beneath his wing for a long time. He stared up at the night sky, trying to let its twinkling clockwork lull him to sleep. But Helen's mention of the Mooney cemetery had reminded him that tomorrow was Saturday; in the morning, Rollie would visit the Williamsburg Cemetery, where John's mother was buried. He made the excursion every week of the year, no matter the weather. He always went early, just after dawn, when the grounds were still empty and glistening wet, crows roosting on the gravestones. John had accompanied him on many occasions, but June, John's mother, had died giving birth to him; he had not known her, and standing with his father before the small bronze plate in the grass, he always ended up feeling strangely excluded, his presence an intrusion.

John pulled the blanket around his shoulders. Down in the pond the fish were busy feeding, leaping from the water, snapping caddis and mayflies from the air. He closed his eyes and listened to them as they broke the surface, gasping, then splashed back down. As a young boy he'd often fantasized about a world in which death affected people the way it did fish: where, instead of dropping to the ground, a dying person would suddenly begin to float, lifting from the earth, drifting higher and higher. He had not thought about the notion in years, but it came back to him now as he lay beneath the wing of his plane, and he fell asleep picturing a sky full of floating bodies, men and women rising toward the clouds.

———

John woke the next morning to find Helen standing over him in a blue satin dress.

"Well," she said. "What do you think?"

"What time is it?" he said, rubbing his eyes.

"It's six. The sun's just coming up. So? What do you think?" She planted her hands on her hips and turned a full circle.

He yawned. "Ballroom open early today?"

Helen dropped her arms to her sides. "It's called showman-ship, thanks."

"Where'd you get it?"

"You don't think this makes for a good costume? Sort of a 'lovely lady of the skies' thing?"

John sat up. The dress was sky blue with a white silk flower pinned to the belt, and Helen looked very beautiful in it.

"It's nice," he said.

"Nice?"

"Pretty."

Helen curtsied. "Why, thank you kindly, Mr. Barron. I bought it back in Gunnison, with some of the money I got for my bridely duds."

John stood up and stretched, his muscles sore from lack of sleep. "You sold your wedding dress?"

"Sure. It hurt like hell to wear. Charley's mother was the one who picked it out, not me. Made me bleed beneath the arms. Will you fasten this for me?" She turned around and held up her hair, revealing the smooth plane of her back, crossed at the center by the lace webbing of her brassiere. The sight sent a slight tingle through John, and as he began fastening the dress's hooks, he realized that this was likely the first time he'd ever seen a girl's full back exposed to daylight. All of his romantic experiences had taken place at night, under the added darkness of secrecy. Hurried trysts in closets and barns and the back of cars. All whispers and fumbling.

"You have a mole on your lower back," John said, working his way up the hooks, "that's shaped like a peanut."

"I suppose that's good to know."

"I thought so."

A loose strand of hair dropped through Helen's fingers, falling to the nape of her neck.

"I haven't thanked you yet," she said. "Have I?"

John paused. "Thanked me?"

"For taking me with you." She turned her head slightly, eyeing him over her shoulder.

He went back to fastening the dress. "I didn't have a choice, remember?"

"You did, though," she said. "You could have just taken off yourself."

"All done," John said, clasping the final hook.

She turned to face him, releasing her hair, allowing it to fall down her back. The first sunlight was in her eyes, making them sparkle. "You could have left me in Kansas. With Charley," she said. "But you didn't."

John stepped away. "Who's this Charley you keep talking about?" he said, pulling his pants up over his long johns. "I don't know any Charleys. Never have." He stepped into his boots. "Now come on, before some other husband-and-wife flying team beats us to Mooney."

Helen leaned in and gave him a kiss on the cheek. "Yes, dear."

They made a strong buzz over Mooney. John took the plane all the way up to eight hundred feet before dropping into a steep dive. By the time they leveled out over the town's eastern edge, they were traveling at nearly eighty miles an hour, so fast the Jenny's bracing wires began to vibrate and hum.

John gave the tail some drag as they came shrieking past the town limits. Clapboard shacks gave way to neat rows of plain brick homes and then to storefronts, early sunlight flashing across their display windows, and then the town began to thin out again, to recede, the buildings shrinking, walls changing back to wood and then to tin and soon John and Helen were crossing out of Mooney altogether.

"What do you think?" yelled Helen.

"Can't tell yet! See on the second go-round!"

John waited until he and Helen were a few miles out of town, flying over the neighboring farmland, before bringing the plane back around. As they neared Mooney again, John let up on the gas, dropping the plane to forty miles an hour. The purpose of a first buzz was to draw people outside, but the point of the second was to reel them in: give them time to gawk and point and read the lettering on the wings. Slow and low to get the dough, he thought, and already he could see the residents of Mooney pouring into the streets, shouting and waving at the Jenny.

"Got a full house today!" Helen shouted from the front cockpit.

John motioned to his chin. "Your strap's undone!"

Helen felt around beneath her jaw until she found the dangling ends. "Thanks!" she said, retying her leather helmet. "Well! I guess this is my stop!"

Then, before John could say anything, she took hold of the bracing wires and hoisted herself out of the cockpit.

John gripped the levers. "What are you doing?" he screamed. "Get back in here! Helen!"

But she was already maneuvering her legs over the cockpit's rim.

John grabbed for her arm, but there was no way to reach without letting go of the controls. Furious, he sat back down and watched, helplessly, as she lowered herself onto the wing. Once she'd found her footing, she crouched down beside the fuselage and braced against the wind.

"Here! Hold on to the mooring!" John yelled, pointing to a small loop of rope at the wing's base.

Helen crawled toward him, the wind blowing her dress around her head. As she grabbed hold of the mooring, John seized her shoulder strap.

"Get into the cockpit!" He tried to pull her up, but her hold on the mooring was too strong. He could feel the satin about to rip in his fist.

"Just fly the plane!" she said, trying to shake him off. "I'm fine!"

"The slipstream's too strong! You'll fall!" John yelled. He thought about grabbing her by the hair, dragging her up into the cockpit with him.

"You've got bigger problems!" she said, gesturing forward with her chin.

John glanced up: the town's telephone cables loomed dead ahead. He let go of Helen for only a second, to give a quick pull on the elevator, jerking the plane into an incline, but by the time he turned back to her, she was already halfway to the wing's tip. The wind tore at her dress and her hair, but she moved quickly, sliding her boots across the inward struts, working hand over hand along the bracing wires. Soon enough she was at the very end of the wing, wrapping her arms around the outer posts to secure herself.

John checked the crowd. Main Street was filled with spectators; men and women were already rushing down the sidewalks in the direction of the Jenny, stumbling, tripping over one another, everyone screaming and pointing at Helen.

John saw that she was arranging herself in some sort of theatrical pose now: extending her arms, leaning all the way back over the wing's edge. She closed her eyes.

"Hang on!" he yelled. "I'm going to slow us up!"

Helen nodded, but stayed frozen in position.

John decelerated to thirty-five miles an hour, minimum flight speed. As the plane passed over the bulk of the crowd, Helen tossed her head back, letting her hair stream out from beneath her pilot's helmet. Even through the engine noise, John could hear the cheers. Faces, frightened and amazed, rushed by in a blur. Hands whizzed past, straining open, reaching for her. John tried to imagine the scene from the ground, tried to picture himself suddenly looking up and seeing a pretty girl soar past on the wing of a plane. He'd admit it: she did make a sight out there. Posing like a woman standing on a cresting swing. Her hair billowing out, the satin dress trembling against her body. He put pressure on the rudder, dipping to starboard slightly so that the last of the audience might get a better view of Helen.

The entire population of Mooney appeared to be rushing after the plane as it crossed out of town—a crowd of at least four hundred people. John could see an actual dust cloud rising behind the throng.

"I want to live my whole life out here!" Helen yelled from the wing's tip. She had one arm wrapped around the post; the other she held out in the open air.

"Well, you can't!" John said. "I'm landing. Get in!"

Reluctantly, Helen began making her way back toward the cockpit, slipping between the bracing wires, hopping from strut to strut. Again John was impressed with how smoothly she moved. When she reached the fuselage, she grabbed hold of the rim and pulled herself up.

"Hey! Look at the crowd!" she said, pausing with one leg in the cockpit.

John banked hard, spilling Helen into her seat.

Mr. and Mrs. John Barron were Mooney's guests of honor that night. The mayor treated them to a private dinner at Bungay's, the town's nicest steakhouse. Then they were handed free passes to the new movie theater, where, along with a packed audience, they watched the new Fatty Arbuckle tickler. Afterward, the crowd led them to a pub off Main Street, a warm, charming establishment with cherry-wood floors and a long zinc bar. The pub's owner sat John and Helen at his best booth, located beneath a small stained glass window depicting his family's coat of arms. He was a gregarious man, and as the three of them drank, he peppered John and Helen with questions about their travels. How many states had they visited so far? Had they ever crashed?

Helen glowed in his company: every answer she gave became a story; every story a performance. Again and again she tried to involve John in the conversation, deferring to him, asking him to confirm details, but John couldn't muster the energy. He knew he should be enjoying himself—here he was, the toast of the town—but instead he found the whole scene strangely irritating. Everything Helen said made the pub owner double over with laughter, slapping the table, wiping his eyes. The conversation kept lurching forward without John noticing. Whenever he looked down, a new round of drinks sat foaming on the table.

"I think it's because I studied dance for so long," Helen was saying. "I was part of a troupe back in Missouri."

"A ballet troupe?" the pub owner said.

"No. Modern style. We went around teaching people how to do

all the newest fads. The turkey trot, the grizzly bear. The Charleston. At first we just performed in Missouri, but soon people started hearing about us and we ended up going all over the country. There were twelve of us. We drove around in a bus. Once we even made it to New York. We got to perform in front of the Statue of Liberty. This wasn't just us, though. It was a big showcase. There were troupes of girls everywhere from all over."

"Let me guess," the pub owner said. "That's how you met John? Dancing?"

Helen laughed. "Us? No." She turned to John. "Do you want to tell him? How we met?"

John took a sip of his beer. "I crashed into her wedding," he said. "She was about to marry another man."

"You what?" said the pub owner, waiting to burst into hysterics.

Helen opened her mouth, but said nothing.

"I'm just kidding," John said. "We grew up together. We've known each other forever."

A small jug band set up beside the bar began to play a rendition of J.P. Brakeman's "Hillbilly Delight."

"These guys are magical," the owner said, excusing himself to dance with his wife. "Please. Enjoy. I'll be back."

Once he was gone, John and Helen fell silent. For a long time they sat watching couples dance. The music was lively, and the wood floor shook with the stomp and tap of boots.

"So, Mr. Barron," Helen said, "will you at least treat me to a dance?"

"Too tired." He took a sip from his glass. "Go ahead. There are ladies dancing together in the back."

Helen put her hand over his. "John, I didn't mean to upset—"

"I don't want to talk about it," he said.

Helen waited for him to say more.

"I'm fine, Helen. Really. Go dance." He moved her hand off his. She sighed and got up from the booth.

The day had been busy; all morning and afternoon John had given rides and taken photographs beside the plane. He'd had no chance to speak to Helen privately about what had happened in the air that morning. By now, though, he was sick to death of thinking about it. He'd replayed the incident in his mind hundreds of times already, in the plane, at dinner, during the movie; he couldn't help conjuring it up: even now he could see the scene, see Helen pulling herself up out of the front cockpit, arms shaking, see himself reaching for her, grabbing nothing. He finished the last of his beer. The notion of discussing things at this point only made him angry.

Besides, he thought, there was nothing to discuss. She'd gone out on the wing. The crowd had loved it. Story over. Yes, he wished that she'd talked the idea over with him beforehand; because no, he didn't like surprises thrown at him in the middle of a performance—who would? But what purpose would squabbling with Helen serve? Why should he care that she'd gone for a stroll on the wing? What did it matter to him? In the end, Helen's wing-walking had given him the best day in his barnstorming career. They'd made over sixty dollars together. In less than seven hours. Enough money to take a whole week off, fly around the South, do some sight-seeing. In fact, he realized, he should be thanking Helen. He should be marching up to her and scooping her off the dance floor.

And yet he didn't feel like thanking Helen at all. Watching her dance, twirling from hand to hand at the other end of the room, he felt like ditching her for good.

He laid a quarter on the table for the beer and got up. As he crossed the room, he realized that he wasn't entirely sober, and he ran a hand along the wall to steady himself.

At the door, the barmaid approached him. "Your money, Mr. Barron," she said, handing him back his quarter.

The night was cool for summer, and the breeze felt good on John's skin as he made his way through the dirt streets. The house he and Helen had been invited to stay at for the night was located on a farm at Mooney's western edge. The owners were two identical brothers, pecan farmers and amateur aviation enthusiasts who'd each taken three rides with John that afternoon. As he neared the end of Main Street, John spotted the property; the brothers had left a lantern hanging above the door of their barn so that he and Helen might find the house in the thick darkness beyond the town's commercial district.

John unlatched the wooden fence and crossed into the brothers' orchard. The pecan trees stood in tight rows; the tips of their branches crossed in places, knitting together a loose maze of archways and tunnels that stretched toward the house. Stumbling, John made his way across the orchard. The ground was soft and damp and fallen pods lay scattered in clumps. He fell twice before reaching the house, dirtying the knees of his pants.

Inside, John headed to the kitchen to wash up. On the counter he found a freshly baked pecan pie with a note beside it. He picked up the paper, squinting through the darkness.

For Mr. and Mrs. Barron. A token of thanks.

John opened a drawer and removed a fork. He scooped a ragged chunk from the pie and stuffed it into his mouth. The texture was perfect, crunchy and thick with maple butter, but the taste was too sweet. John could barely get the bite down without feeling sick. When he went to the sink for water, he noticed a phone standing on a table by the window. He headed over and picked up.

A girl's voice came on the line. "Operator."

"Which operator?"

The girl paused. "Fourteen?" she said.

"No. What's your name?"

"Why do you want to know?"

"I was just trying to be friendly. I thought you might be tired of being treated like a nobody all day. Operator this, operator that, connect me to wherever. Forget it, though."

The line was silent.

"My name's Patricia," said the girl.

"Patricia. That's beautiful. See? Now I'm picturing a beautiful girl, sitting at a switchboard somewhere, pretty brown hair—"

"Blond."

"Pretty blond hair. Big green eyes."

"You sure lay it on thick."

"Is it working?"

"Keep going a minute and I'll tell you."

But then there was a rustling on the line. John heard a man talking in the background, and when Patricia came back on, her voice was flat.

"Connection?" she said.

John gave her the number.

The phone rang eight times before Rollie picked up.

"Hello?" he said, sounding hoarse and sleepy.

"Guess," said John.

"Who is this?"

"It's John. Your son."

"John? What time is it?"

"It's only eleven o'clock. Snap out of it and guess."

Rollie coughed. "I don't know. Missouri."

"South."

"Kansas."

"Kansas is west. I'm in Oklahoma. It's beautiful. I'm calling to tell you to tell Dale Morton to go fuck himself."

"Tell who what?"

"Tell Dale Morton not to keep a job for me at Sweet Fizz. I'm not coming back."

"I'll tell him, if you want, John. But let's talk about this some other time, okay? It's too late for me right now."

"Too late," John said. "Right."

"Be careful," said Rollie. Then the line rattled and went dead.

John replaced the receiver. He considered heading to bed, but decided instead to go out to the barn and check on the plane.

Most farmers didn't like John parking the Jenny inside their barns; the engine dripped oil, the tires left tracks. At best they allowed him to station the Jenny beside or behind their barns, to afford at least a bit of shelter from the elements. But the Calbraith brothers had insisted John use their barn to house the plane. They'd even cleared out some of the pecan barrels to make extra room.

John took the lantern down and slid open the barn door. As he stepped inside, the odor of the plane hit him: a rich mixture of petrol, doping varnish, and old leather. The scent warmed him, and he felt a sudden, deep affection for his Jenny. How beautiful she looked too, standing beneath the rafters at the back of the barn, her linen wings shining pale gold in the lantern light. John thought back to the very first time she'd taken him up, during his orientation at Fort Hawley: how frightened he'd been, clutching the cockpit rim, teeth clenched, as his flight instructor lifted off. He'd experienced a kind of primal, childlike terror, watching the Texas grassland fall away beneath the wheels. But then a transformation had occurred, and his terror had changed to pounding exhilaration, and, finally, delight. Because now, for the first time in his life, he felt entirely apart. He could see the horizon in all directions: see it as it was, a brilliant white ring encircling the world. A string had been broken—that was the sensation—and John could feel himself drifting higher, released.

"You cutting out on me?" said Helen.

John turned to find her standing in the doorway. "No," he said. "Just partied out."

Helen slid the barn door closed. "And here I thought you were Mr. Party," she said. "There were at least a couple of telephone ladies at the pub, you know."

"Ha-ha."

She walked over to him, kicking a stray pecan ahead of her. "Someone's in a bad mood."

"I'm not in a bad mood. I just don't like surprises. That's all."

"So," Helen said, resting a hand on the propeller blade, "what was the surprise?"

John squinted at her, confused.

"Was it all the money we made?" she said. "The people taking us out afterward? What?"

"The wing-walking, Helen. You shouldn't have gone out on the wing without talking to me about it first."

"The wing-walking," she said, nodding. "You're right. That wasn't polite of me."

"Polite? You could have fallen off and gotten killed."

"True," she said. "But that'd be my problem, wouldn't it? I mean, you could just go on barnstorming. Get yourself a new girl. A new Mrs. Barron."

John pushed past her, heading for the door. "We're a team. You should have talked to me. That's why I'm angry."

"Wait," Helen said.

John yanked the door back.

"John!"

He stopped, the door open before him. "What?"

"No more surprises after today," Helen said. "I promise. I'll ask you first about everything."

"Fine. Done. I'm going to bed."

"Not yet," Helen said.

"Helen . . ."

"I want to ask you something."

John sighed and leaned against the door frame.

"Do you think I'm a coward?" Helen spun the propeller blade.

"What are you talking about?"

"A coward," she said. "Do you think I'm a coward?"

"Of course I don't."

"Well," Helen said, spinning the blade again, harder this time, "I am."

John walked over to her. "You're not a coward, Helen."

Helen nodded and continued smacking the propeller through its rotation. With each slap the blade twirled faster, until John caught it.

"You walked out on the wing of a plane today. I think that qualifies as brave."

"No, it doesn't."

"Yes. It does." He bent his knees, trying to look her in the eye, but she wouldn't let him. "Helen, you're the bravest person I know."

"Don't say that!" Her voice echoed through the dark barn. She tried to push him away, but he caught her wrists. "Listen to me. I'm telling you," she said, struggling against him. "I'm telling you . . ."

John pulled her to him and kissed her. He could taste salt on her lips, and beneath that, the warm sweetness of her mouth.

She broke from him. "Stop!"

"I was so scared today, Helen," he said. "I was terrified."

"Don't, John," she said.

He kissed her again. She struggled against him, trying to tear free, but he held on to her, and then, suddenly, she was kissing him back, her body pressing into his, her hands fastening behind his neck. He wanted her so badly; he couldn't touch enough of her at once. He moved her back toward the plane, then got his blanket from storage and laid it beneath the wing. Her eyes wet, she took his hand and pulled him down with her.

Afterward, they lay curled together beneath the starboard wing. John lit the lantern, and the two of them watched it burn, the flame sending a thin stream of vapor up toward the rafters.

Helen stuck one foot out from under the blanket and warmed her toes by the lantern glass. "So, where are we off to next?"

"Wherever we want." He kissed the top of her head. "We could head west. Take a vacation together."

"Could we go to California?" Helen said, yawning.

A bat darted down from the loft, then disappeared again.

"Why not? We could both use tans," John said.

Helen pulled his arms tighter around her. "You know, I've never seen an ocean," she said. "Not in my whole life."

Moments later she was asleep. John felt her ribs slowly expanding and contracting beneath his hands, and the sensation warmed him. He decided that early in the morning, before Helen woke, he'd sneak out to the main house and borrow some paint from the brothers. Then he'd creep back into the barn and—with Helen still asleep—he'd lie down beneath the port wing and paint her name across the linen surface. He imagined the lettering, bold but elegant, black against the cream-white wing: HELEN BARRON! THE FLYING BRIDE!!! He pictured himself a bystander to his own show, a man on the ground, shading his eyes, watching the approach of the Jenny. He felt the thrill of first reading those words printed on the bottom of the wing, then of seeing Helen standing above them, the main attraction, a pretty girl in a blue dress, head thrown back, the wind in her hair as she passed overhead.

In the morning, though, she was gone, along with her valise and John's map of the 1919 United States. He searched the house, questioning the Calbraith brothers; he combed the town of Mooney, the stores and restaurants, the hotels. She was really gone. But that night, he could pull Helen close to him, cupping his body to hers. She let out a little moan, and he kissed her bare shoulder.

ACKNOWLEDGMENTS

There are many people who helped in the creation of *Voodoo Heart*. A first and special thanks has to go out to Scott Tuft, Owen King, and Eric Ozawa, who've helped these stories along from their most nascent and terrifying forms. Also, for their friendship, heartfelt thanks to Dante Williams, Karl Haendel, Craig Teicher, Brenda Shaughnessy, Matthew Gilgoff, Doris Cooper, and Kevin Newman.

I've been very lucky with teachers over the years, but I owe a singular debt of gratitude to Binnie Kirshenbaum for her wisdom, encouragement, and friendship. Thanks, too, to Alan Ziegler and the great faculty of the Columbia University Graduate Writing Department; Leslie Woodard for giving me the chance to teach writing; Dorla MacIntosh for taking me under her wing; and to my students, for the constant inspiration and ridicule.

To the editors who've helped make the stories what they are: Michael Ray of *Zoetrope*, Michael Koch and Heidi Marschner of *Epoch*, Hannah Tinti and Maribeth Batcha of *One-Story*, and Rob Spillman, Holly MacArthur, and Ben George of *Tin House*.

In appreciation of my champions: Jennifer Lyons, my wonderful and tireless agent; Susan Kamil, my brilliant editor, whose dedication to the craft of writing is continually humbling; and Noah Eaker, the best editorial assistant this side of the Mississippi.

A special thank you to my family: my folks, Jon and Wendy Snyder, for being almost embarrassingly supportive; to my sister and best friend, Susie Snyder; to Dana, Ed and Jessica Luck; and to my grandparents, Claire and Milton Zaret for first sparking my imagination.

My deepest love and gratitude to my wife, Jeanie Ripton, who has always believed in these stories, even when I've had trouble. And who makes it all worth it.

And a final thanks for guidance and inspiration to the wily spirit of Mr. Elvis Presley.